DISCARD

HAWAIʻI SEA TURTLE RESCUE

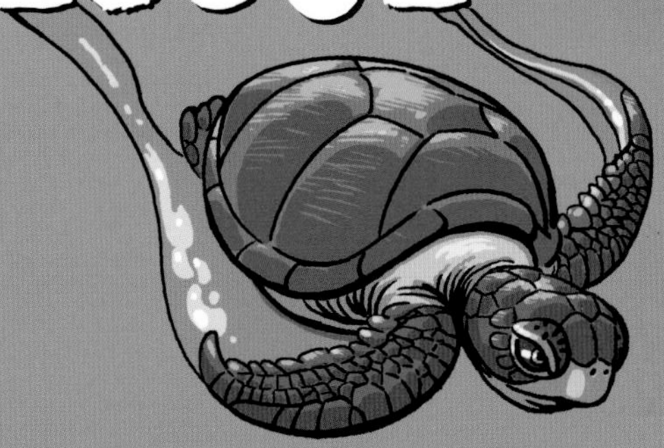

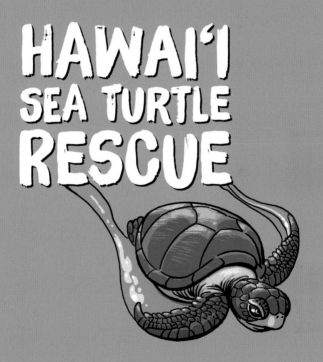

Also in the
Fabien Cousteau Expeditions

GREAT WHITE SHARK ADVENTURE

JOURNEY UNDER THE ARCTIC

DEEP INTO THE AMAZON JUNGLE

HAWAI'I
SEA TURTLE
RESCUE

WRITTEN BY

JAMES O. FRAIOLI

ILLUSTRATED BY

JOE ST.PIERRE

MARGARET K. McELDERRY BOOKS

NEW YORK   LONDON   TORONTO   SYDNEY   NEW DELHI

AUTHORS' NOTE

Hawai'i Sea Turtle Rescue is a work of fiction based on actual expeditions and accepted ideas about the ocean and its inhabitants.

MARGARET K. McELDERRY BOOKS
An imprint of Simon & Schuster Children's Publishing Division
This book is a work of fiction. Any references to historical events, real people, or real places are used fictitiously. Other names, characters, places, and events are products of the author's imagination, and any resemblance to actual events or places or persons, living or dead, is entirely coincidental.
1230 Avenue of the Americas, New York, New York 10020

For information about special discounts for bulk purchases, please contact Simon & Schuster Special Sales at 1-866-506-1949 or business@simonandschuster.com.
The Simon & Schuster Speakers Bureau can bring authors to your live event. For more information or to book an event, contact the Simon & Schuster Speakers Bureau at 1-866-248-3049 or visit our website at www.simonspeakers.com.
Interior design by Tom Daly
The text for this book was set in Chaparral Pro.
The illustrations for this book were rendered digitally.
Manufactured in China
1221 SCP
First Edition
10 9 8 7 6 5 4 3 2 1
Library of Congress Cataloging-in-Publication Data
Names: Fraioli, James O., 1968- author. | St. Pierre, Joe, illustrator. Title: Hawai'i sea turtle rescue / written by James O. Fraioli ; illustrated by Joe St.Pierre. Description: New York : Margaret K. McElderry Books, [2022] | Series: Fabien Cousteau expeditions | Audience: Ages 8-12 | Audience: Grades 4-6 | Summary: Junior explorers Bianca and Baylor join Fabien Cousteau and local conservationists in Hawaii on their mission to rescue endangered sea turtles, while also encountering a variety of wildlife among the coral reefs of Molokini.
Identifiers: LCCN 2021020741 (print) | LCCN 2021020742 (ebook) | ISBN 9781534420977 (hardcover) | ISBN 9781534420960 (paper-over-board) | ISBN 9781534420984 (ebook)
Subjects: CYAC: Graphic novels. | Sea turtles—Fiction. | Turtles—Fiction. Rare animals—Fiction. | Scientists—Fiction. | Hawaii—Fiction. | LCGFT: Graphic novels. Classification: LCC PZ7.7.F72 Haw 2022 (print) | LCC PZ7.7.F72 (ebook) | DDC 741.5/973—dc23
LC record available at https://lccn.loc.gov/2021020741
LC ebook record available at https://lccn.loc.gov/2021020742

TO THE EFFORTS AND INDIVIDUALS WHO ARE DEDICATED TO THE EDUCATION AND PRESERVATION OF SEA TURTLES. AND TO THOSE ORGANIZATIONS AND VOLUNTEERS WHO ARE COMMITTED TO CREATING A HEALTHIER OCEAN ENVIRONMENT BY REMOVING GHOST NETS AND OTHER MARINE DEBRIS, WHICH ARE AMONG THE GREATEST DANGERS TO MARINE LIFE.

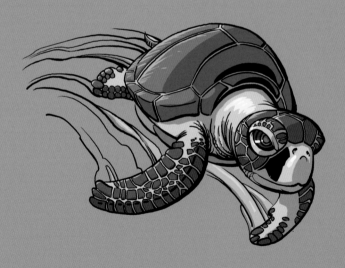

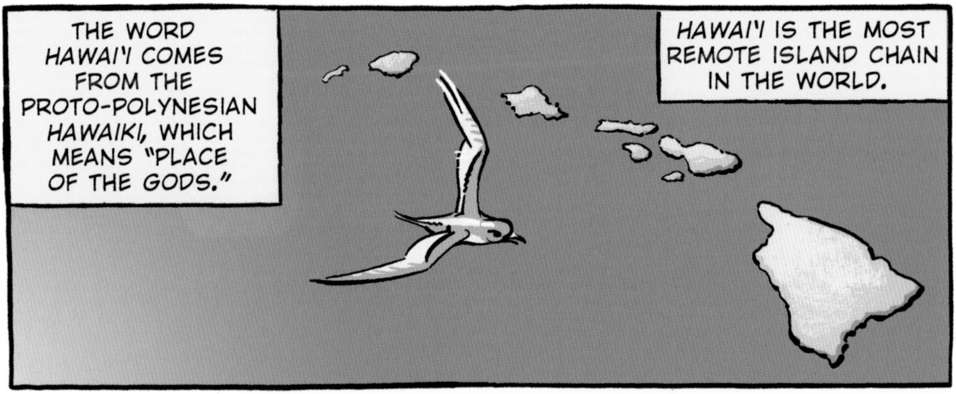
THE WORD *HAWAI'I* COMES FROM THE PROTO-POLYNESIAN *HAWAIKI*, WHICH MEANS "PLACE OF THE GODS."
HAWAI'I IS THE MOST REMOTE ISLAND CHAIN IN THE WORLD.

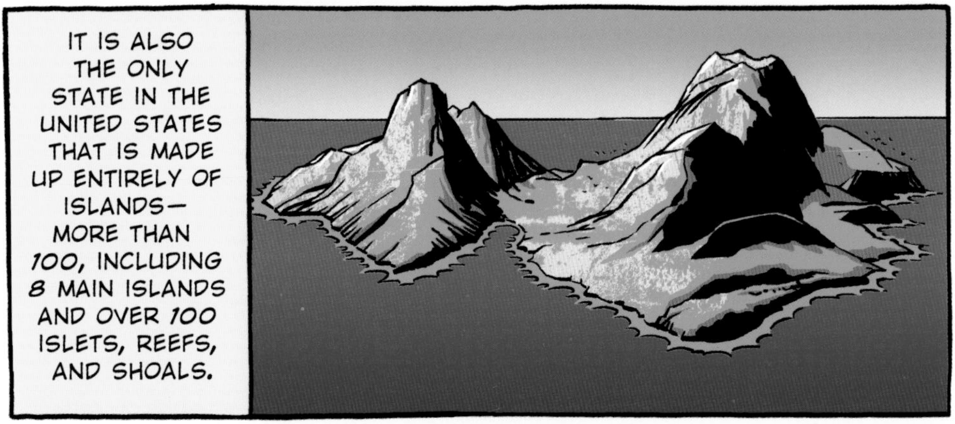
IT IS ALSO THE ONLY STATE IN THE UNITED STATES THAT IS MADE UP ENTIRELY OF ISLANDS—MORE THAN *100*, INCLUDING *8* MAIN ISLANDS AND OVER *100* ISLETS, REEFS, AND SHOALS.

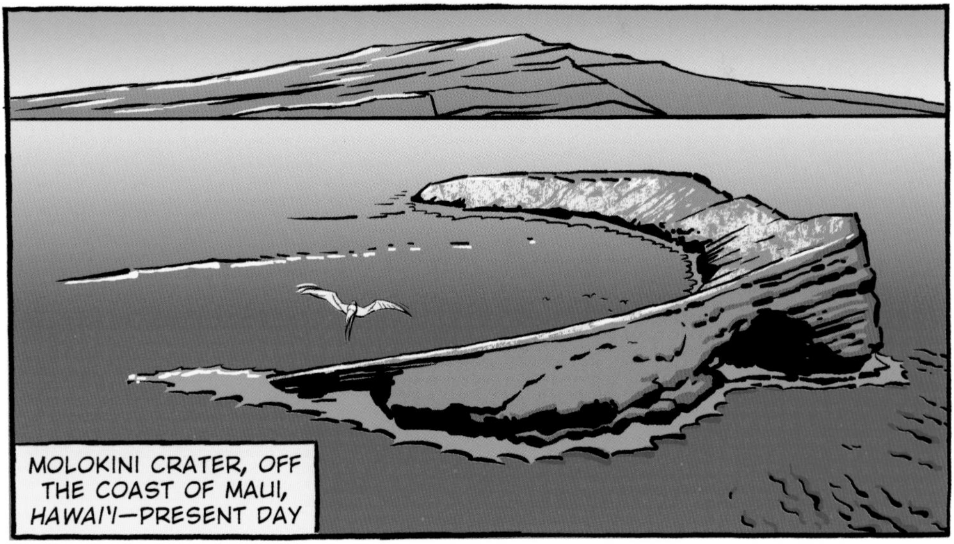
MOLOKINI CRATER, OFF THE COAST OF MAUI, *HAWAI'I*—PRESENT DAY

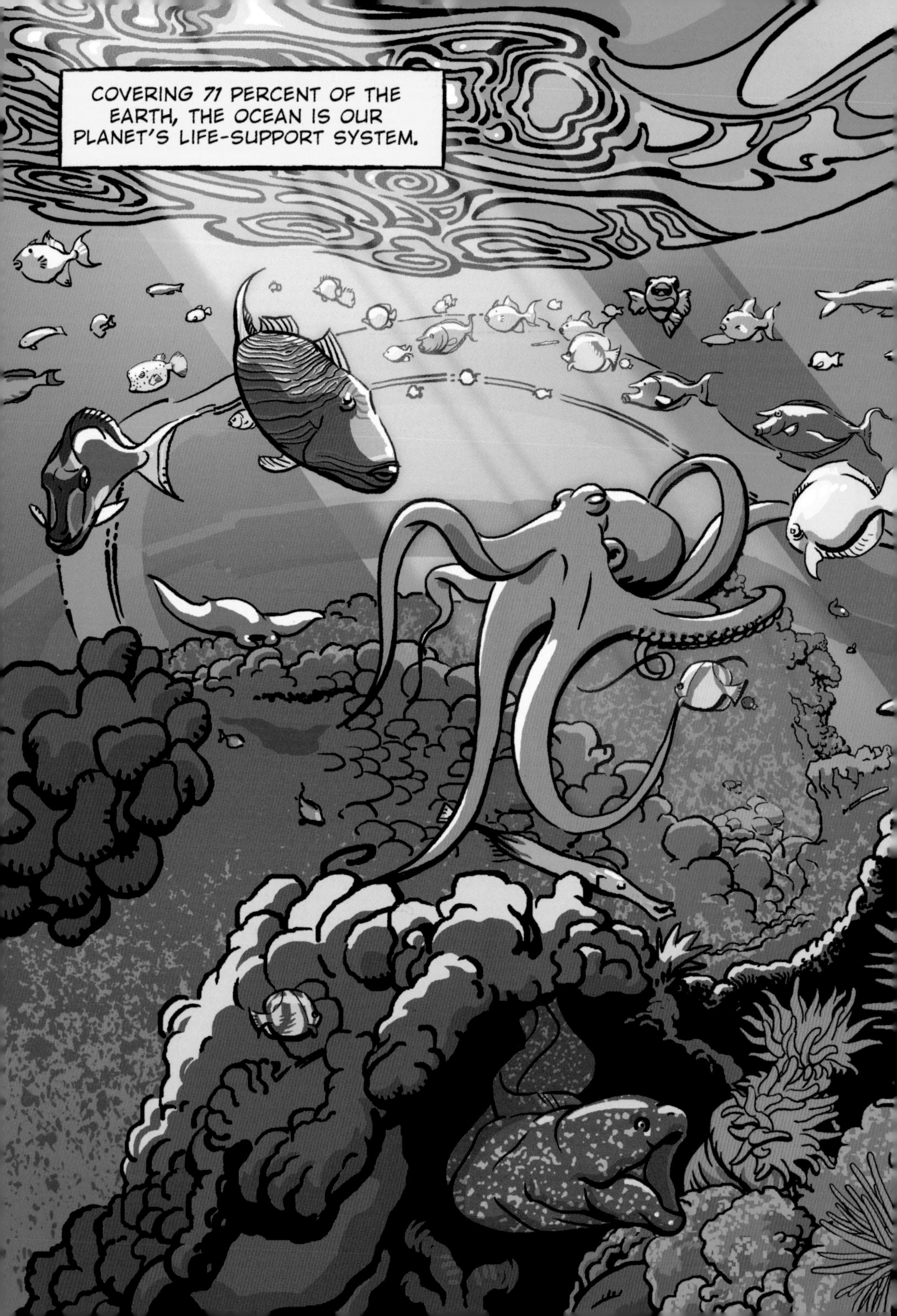
COVERING 71 PERCENT OF THE EARTH, THE OCEAN IS OUR PLANET'S LIFE-SUPPORT SYSTEM.

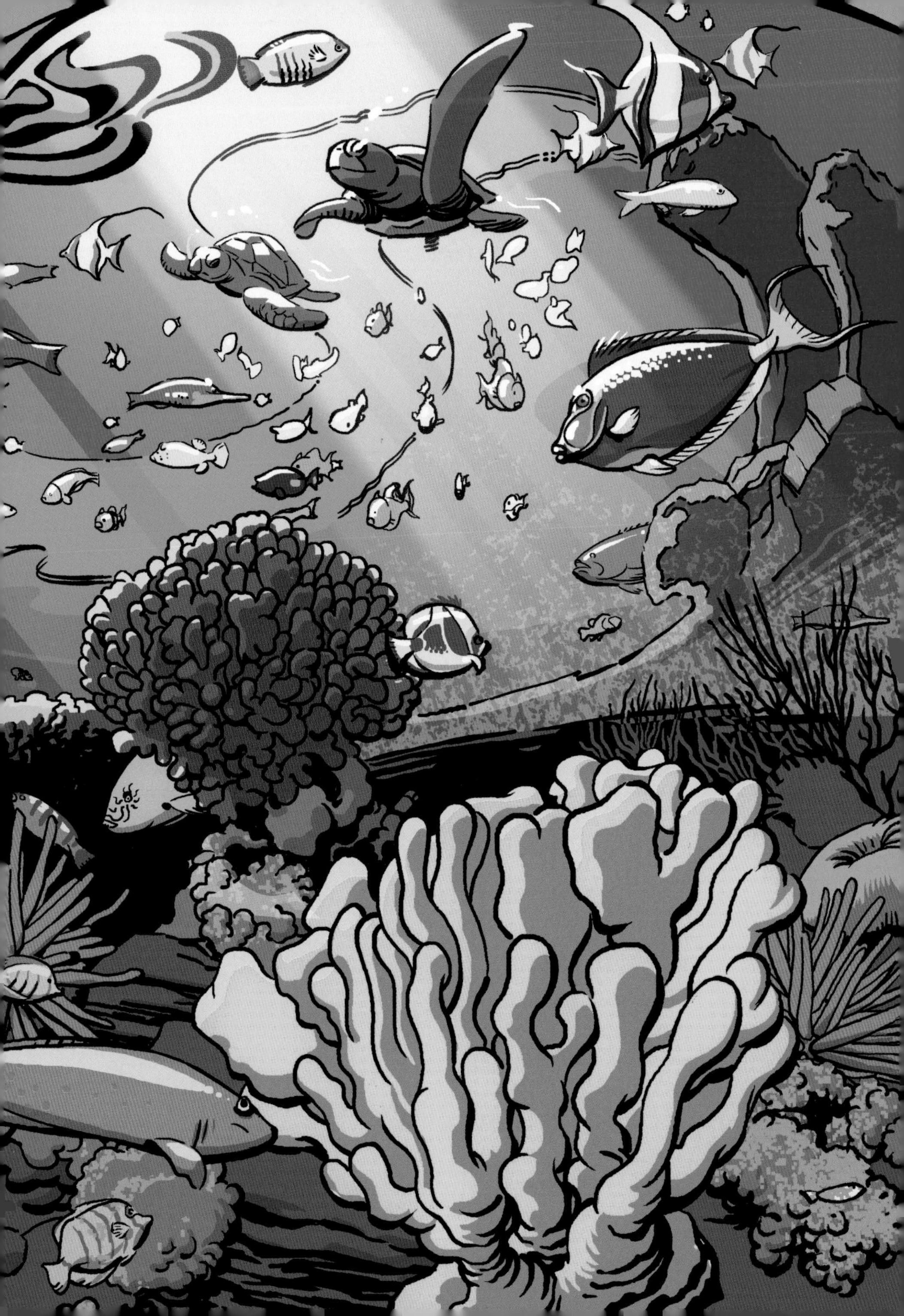

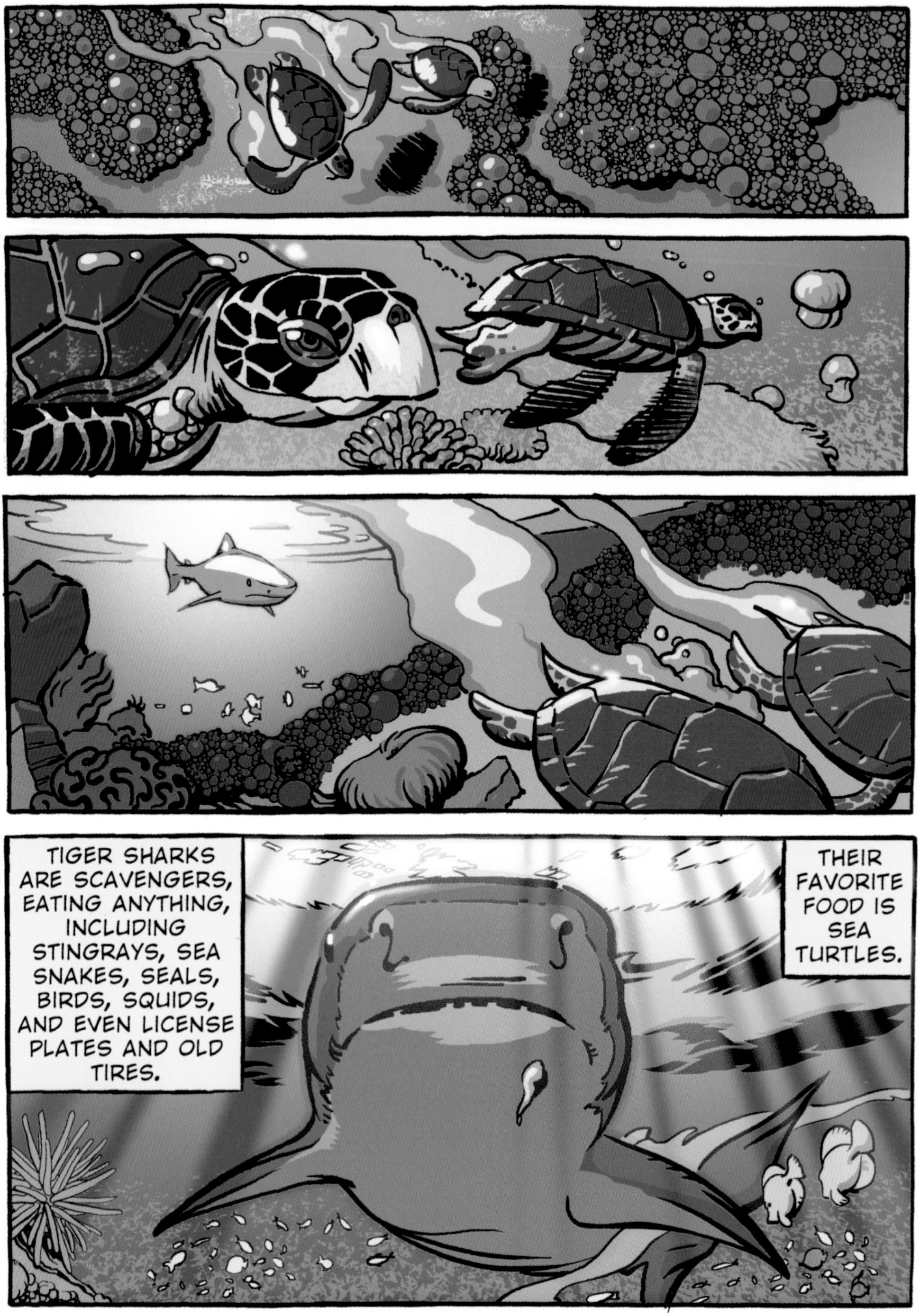
TIGER SHARKS ARE SCAVENGERS, EATING ANYTHING, INCLUDING STINGRAYS, SEA SNAKES, SEALS, BIRDS, SQUIDS, AND EVEN LICENSE PLATES AND OLD TIRES.
THEIR FAVORITE FOOD IS SEA TURTLES.

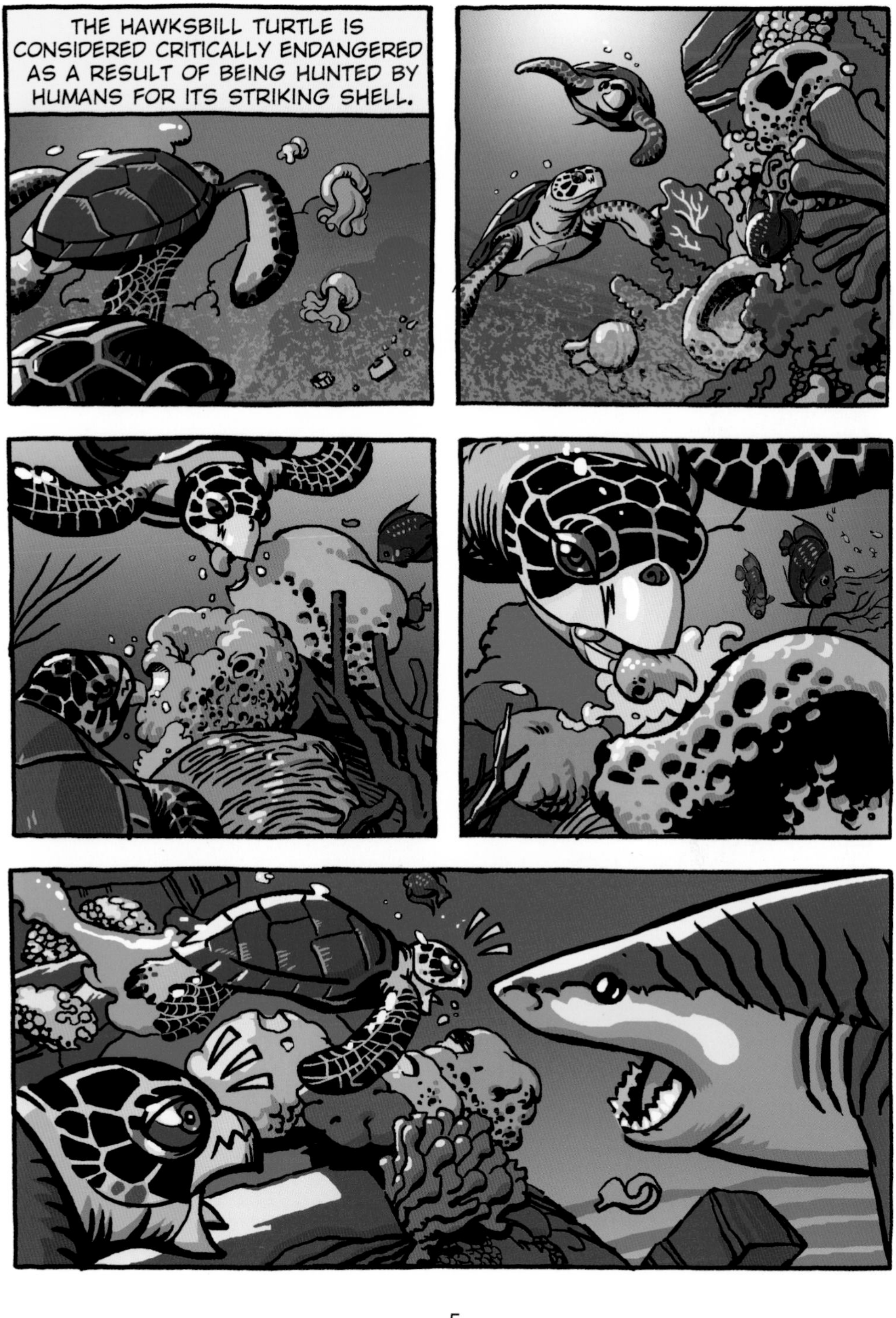
THE HAWKSBILL TURTLE IS CONSIDERED CRITICALLY ENDANGERED AS A RESULT OF BEING HUNTED BY HUMANS FOR ITS STRIKING SHELL.

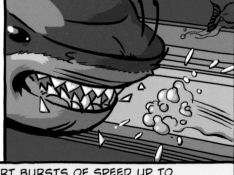

SEA TURTLES CAN REACH SHORT BURSTS OF SPEED UP TO
30 MILES PER HOUR.

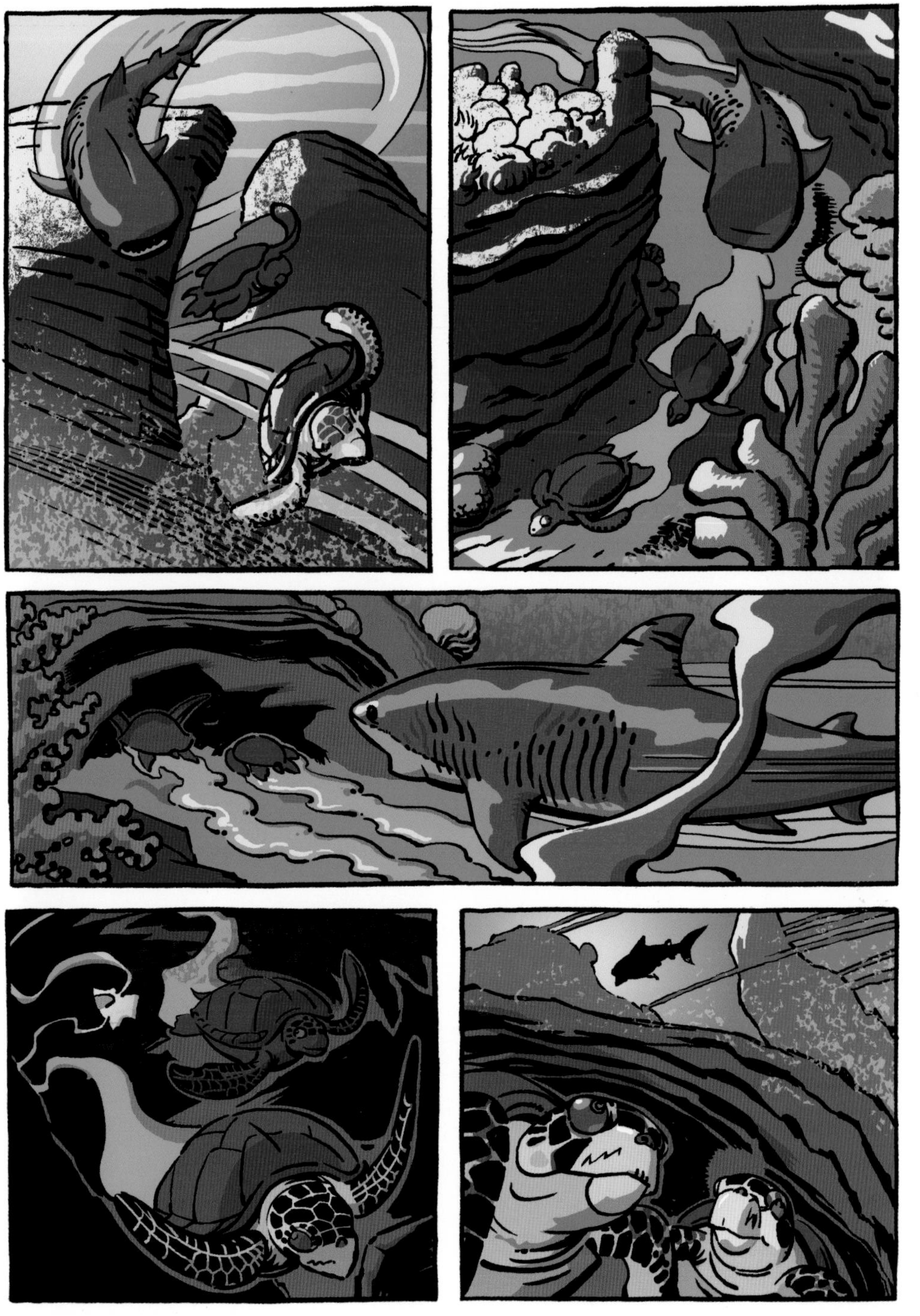

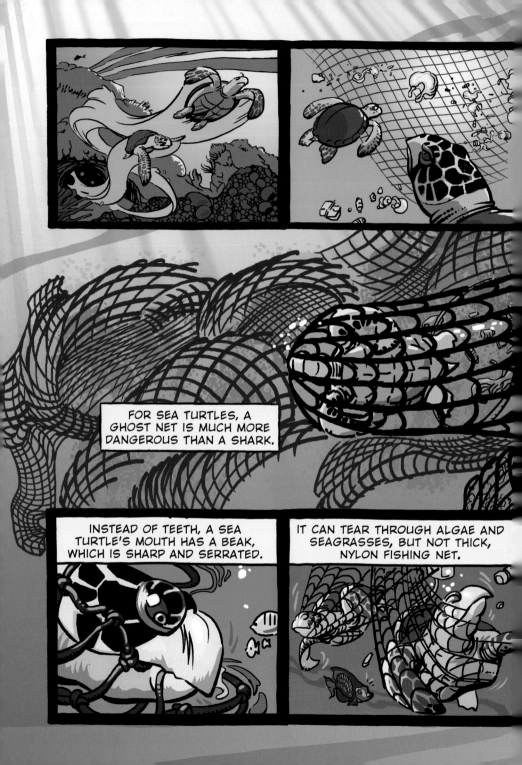

FOR SEA TURTLES, A GHOST NET IS MUCH MORE DANGEROUS THAN A SHARK.

INSTEAD OF TEETH, A SEA TURTLE'S MOUTH HAS A BEAK, WHICH IS SHARP AND SERRATED.

IT CAN TEAR THROUGH ALGAE AND SEAGRASSES, BUT NOT THICK, NYLON FISHING NET.

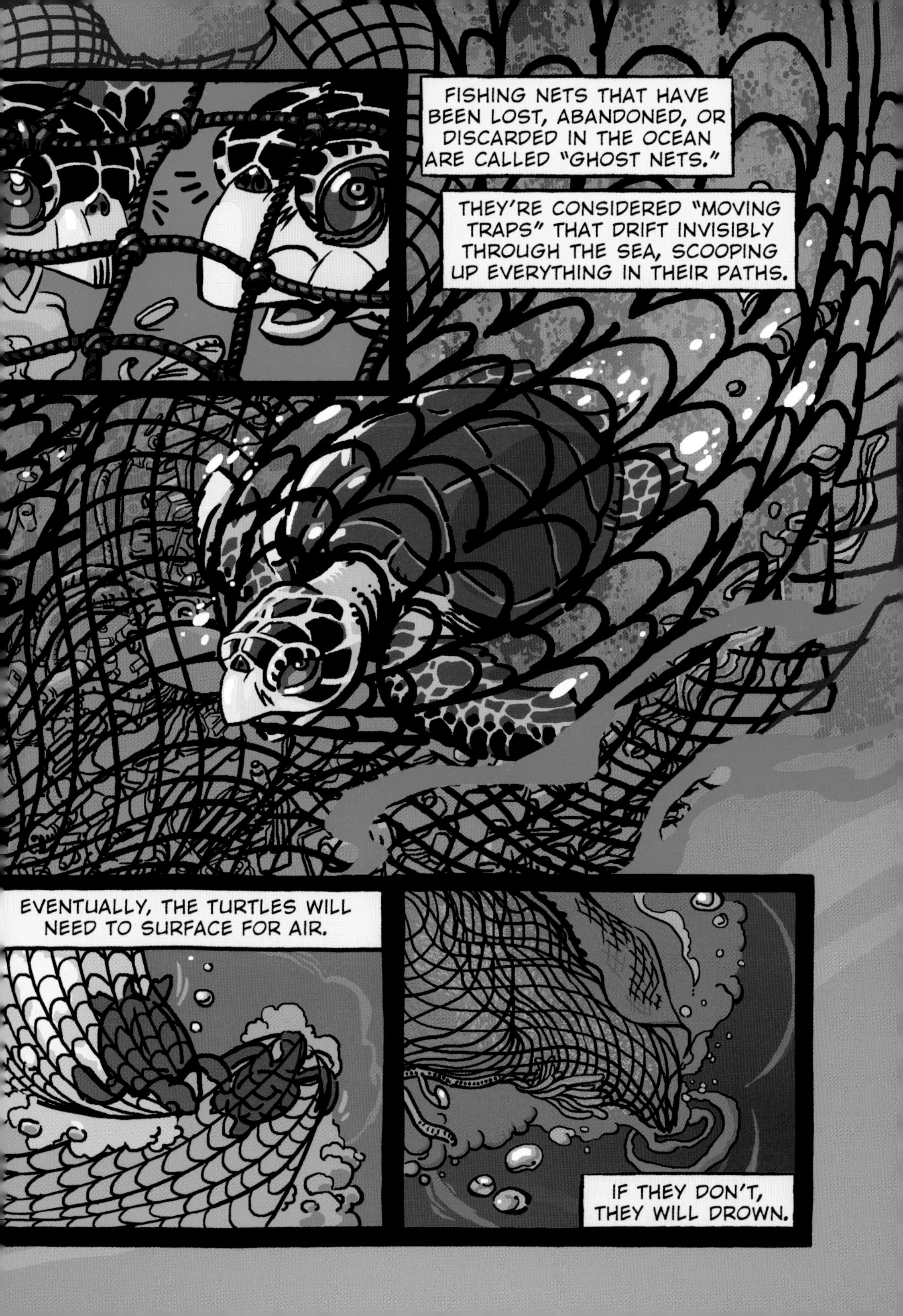
FISHING NETS THAT HAVE BEEN LOST, ABANDONED, OR DISCARDED IN THE OCEAN ARE CALLED "GHOST NETS."
THEY'RE CONSIDERED "MOVING TRAPS" THAT DRIFT INVISIBLY THROUGH THE SEA, SCOOPING UP EVERYTHING IN THEIR PATHS.
EVENTUALLY, THE TURTLES WILL NEED TO SURFACE FOR AIR.
IF THEY DON'T, THEY WILL DROWN.

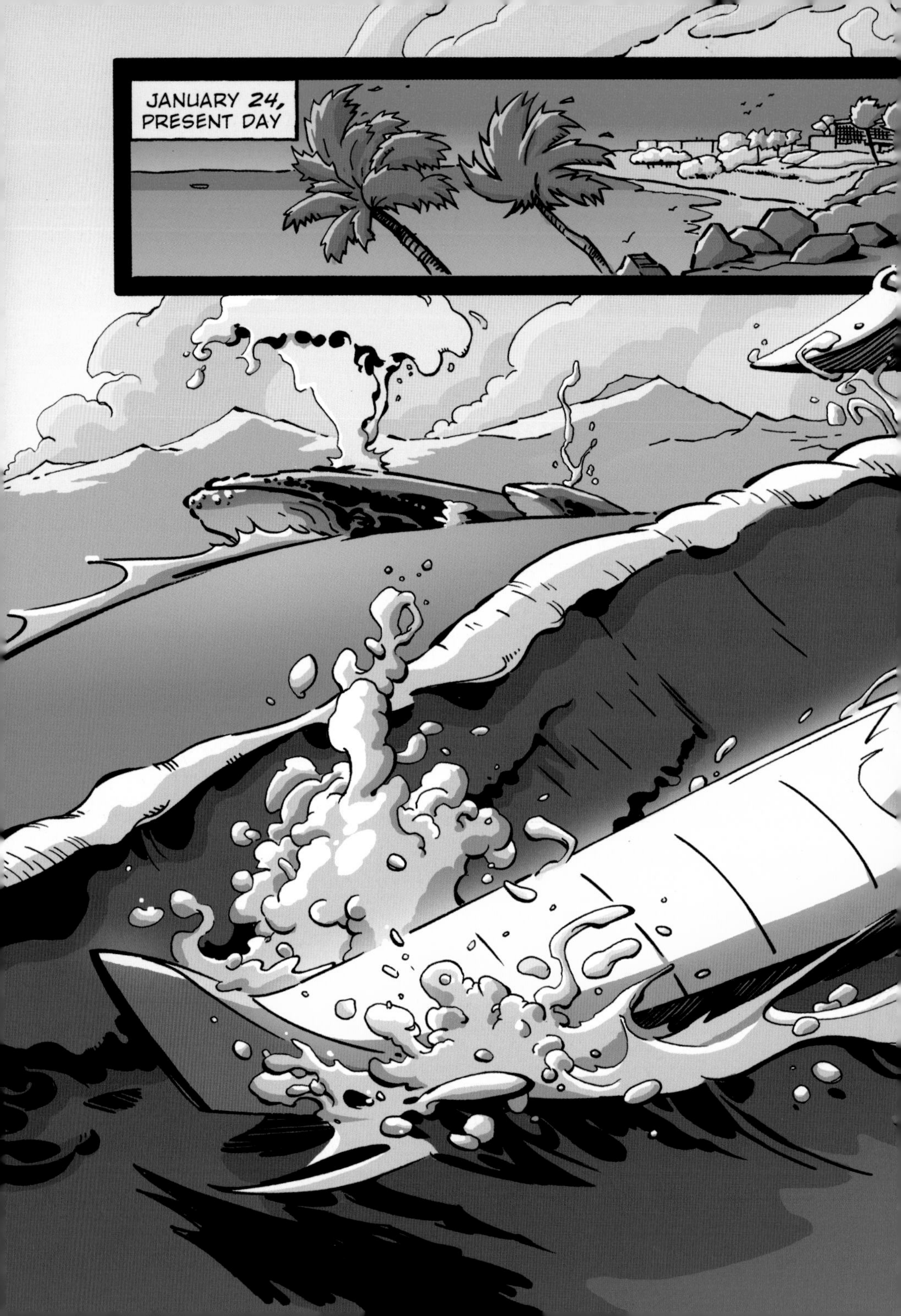
JANUARY 24,
PRESENT DAY

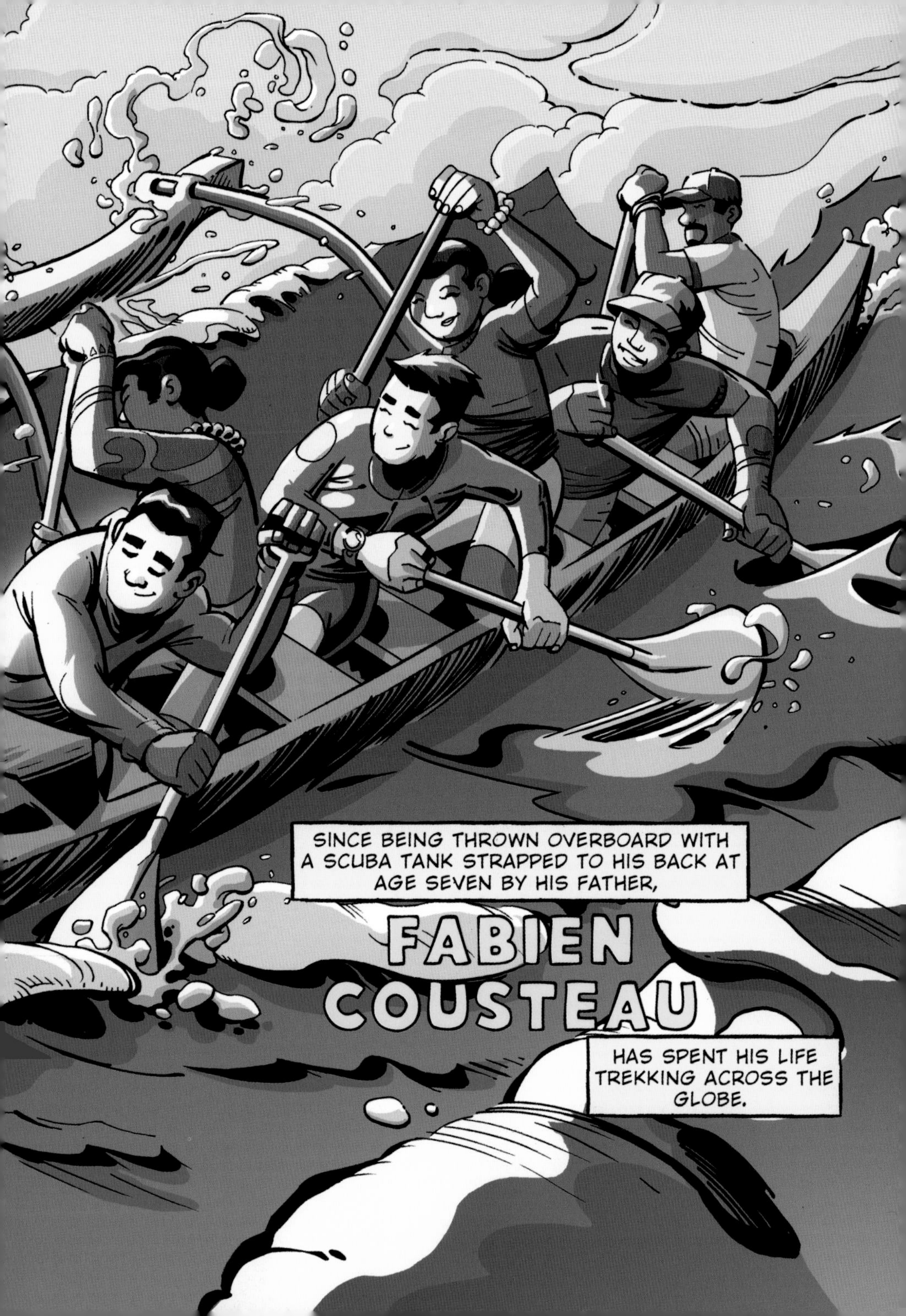
SINCE BEING THROWN OVERBOARD WITH A SCUBA TANK STRAPPED TO HIS BACK AT AGE SEVEN BY HIS FATHER,
FABIEN COUSTEAU
HAS SPENT HIS LIFE TREKKING ACROSS THE GLOBE.

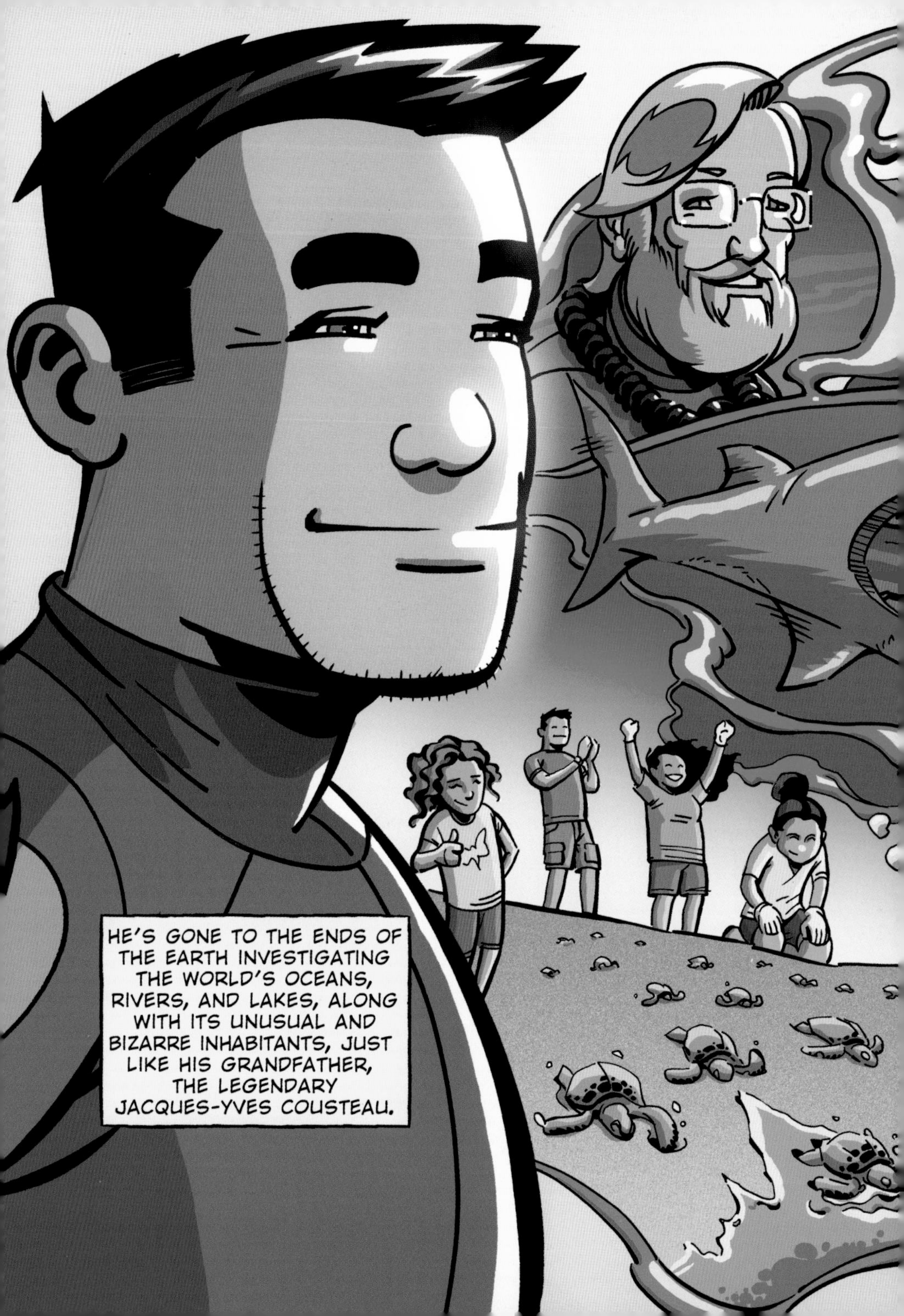
HE'S GONE TO THE ENDS OF THE EARTH INVESTIGATING THE WORLD'S OCEANS, RIVERS, AND LAKES, ALONG WITH ITS UNUSUAL AND BIZARRE INHABITANTS, JUST LIKE HIS GRANDFATHER, THE LEGENDARY JACQUES-YVES COUSTEAU.

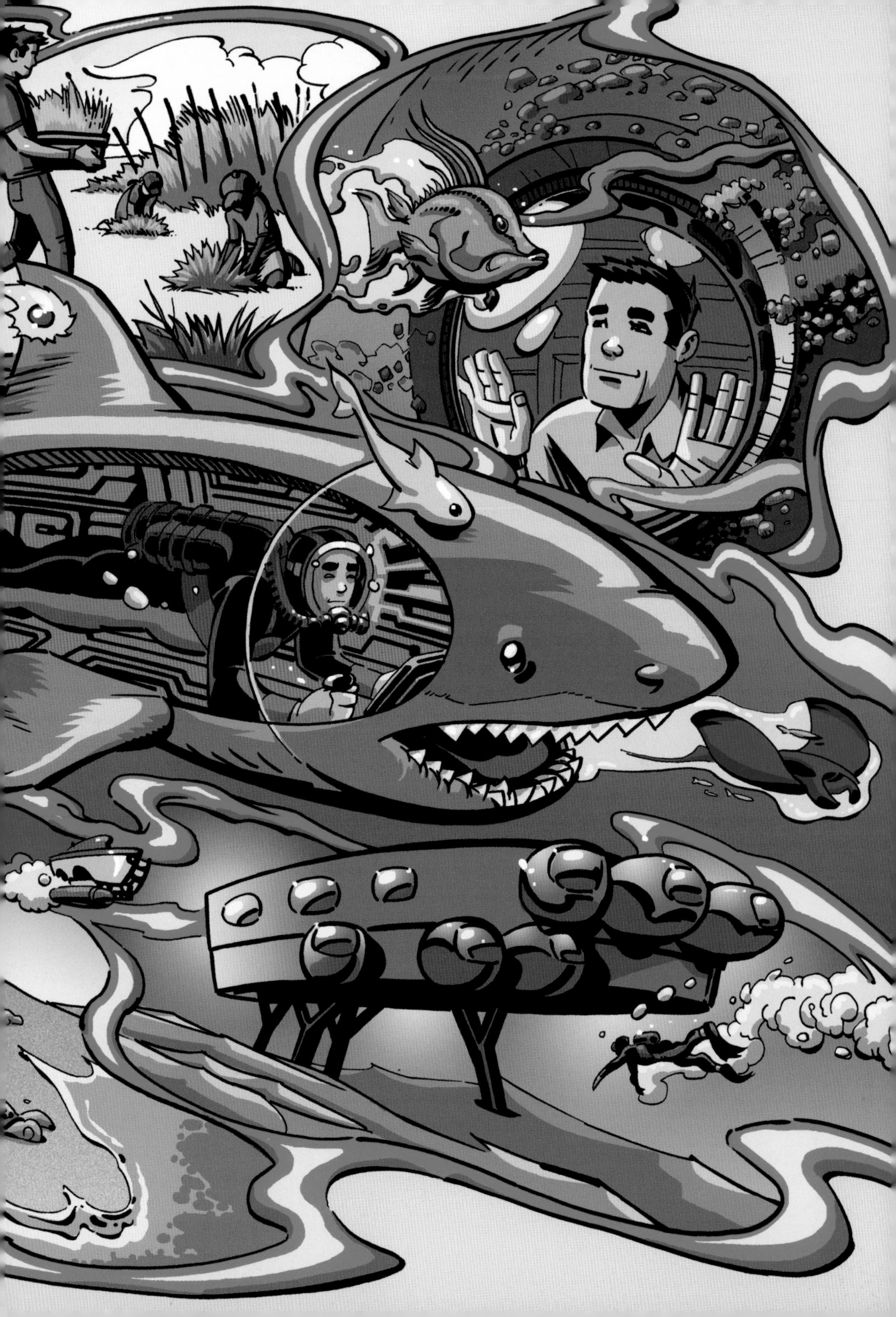

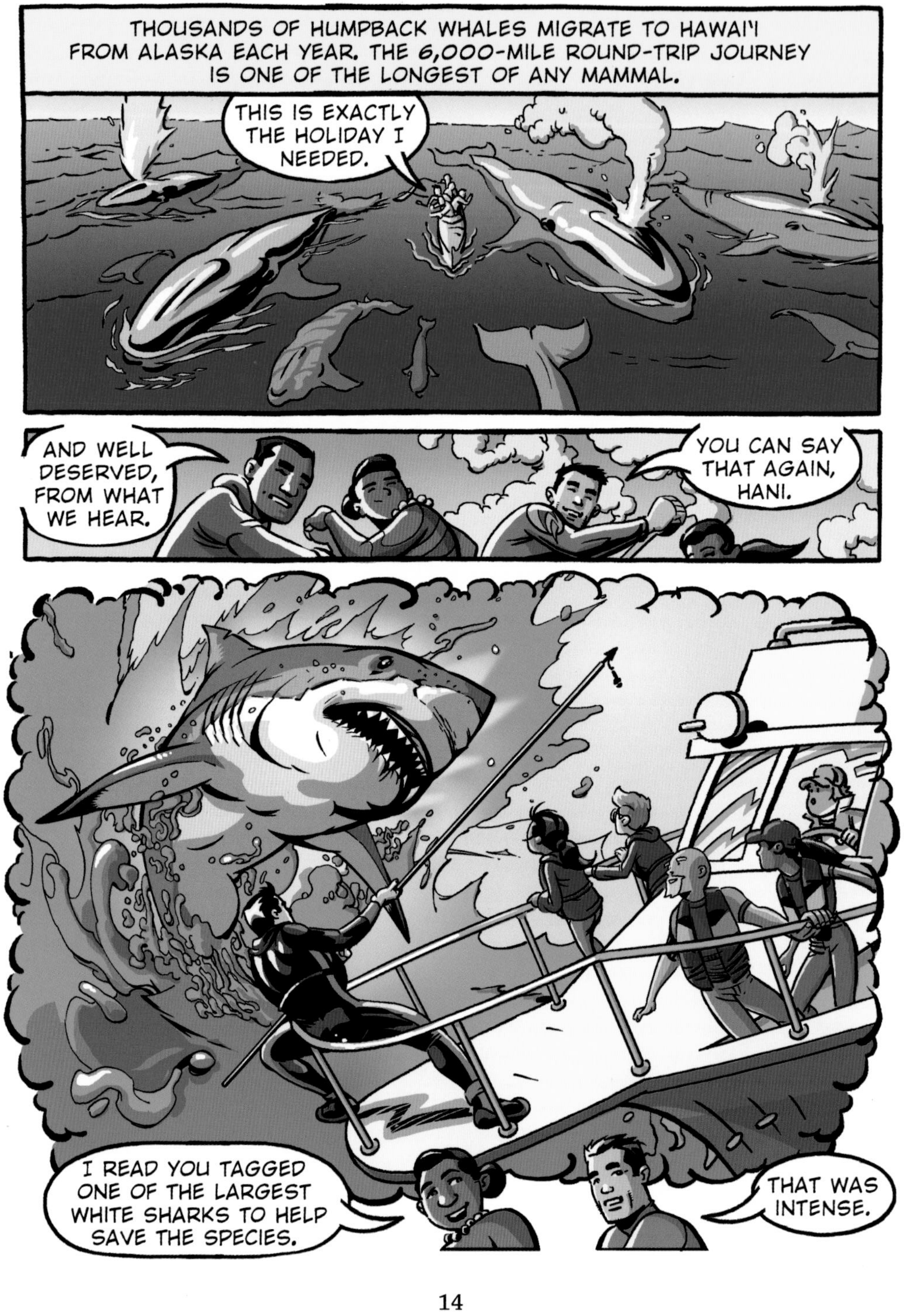
THOUSANDS OF HUMPBACK WHALES MIGRATE TO HAWAI'I FROM ALASKA EACH YEAR. THE 6,000-MILE ROUND-TRIP JOURNEY IS ONE OF THE LONGEST OF ANY MAMMAL.
THIS IS EXACTLY THE HOLIDAY I NEEDED.
AND WELL DESERVED, FROM WHAT WE HEAR.
YOU CAN SAY THAT AGAIN, HANI.
I READ YOU TAGGED ONE OF THE LARGEST WHITE SHARKS TO HELP SAVE THE SPECIES.
THAT WAS INTENSE.

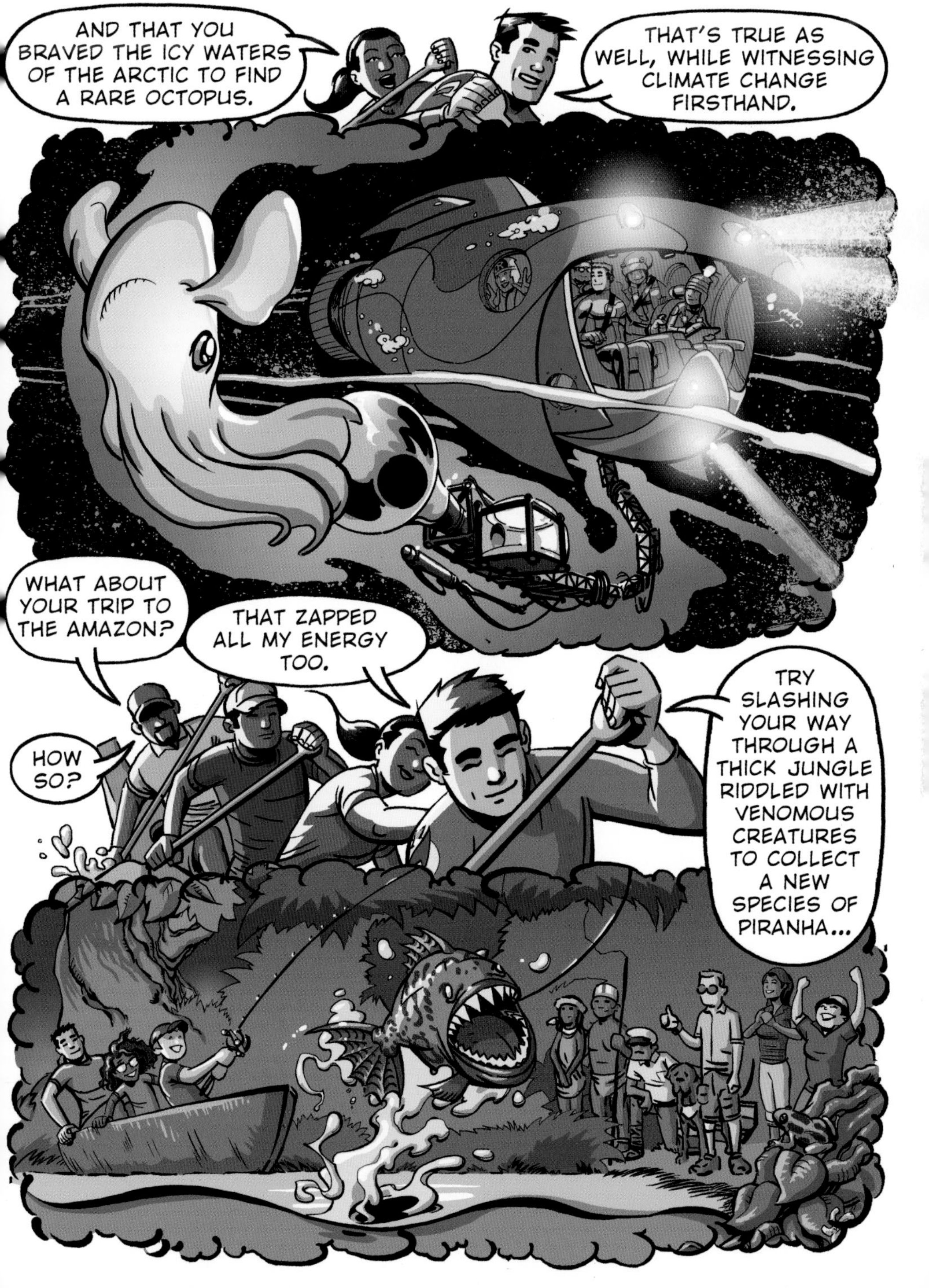
AND THAT YOU BRAVED THE ICY WATERS OF THE ARCTIC TO FIND A RARE OCTOPUS.
THAT'S TRUE AS WELL, WHILE WITNESSING CLIMATE CHANGE FIRSTHAND.
WHAT ABOUT YOUR TRIP TO THE AMAZON?
THAT ZAPPED ALL MY ENERGY TOO.
HOW SO?
TRY SLASHING YOUR WAY THROUGH A THICK JUNGLE RIDDLED WITH VENOMOUS CREATURES TO COLLECT A NEW SPECIES OF PIRANHA...

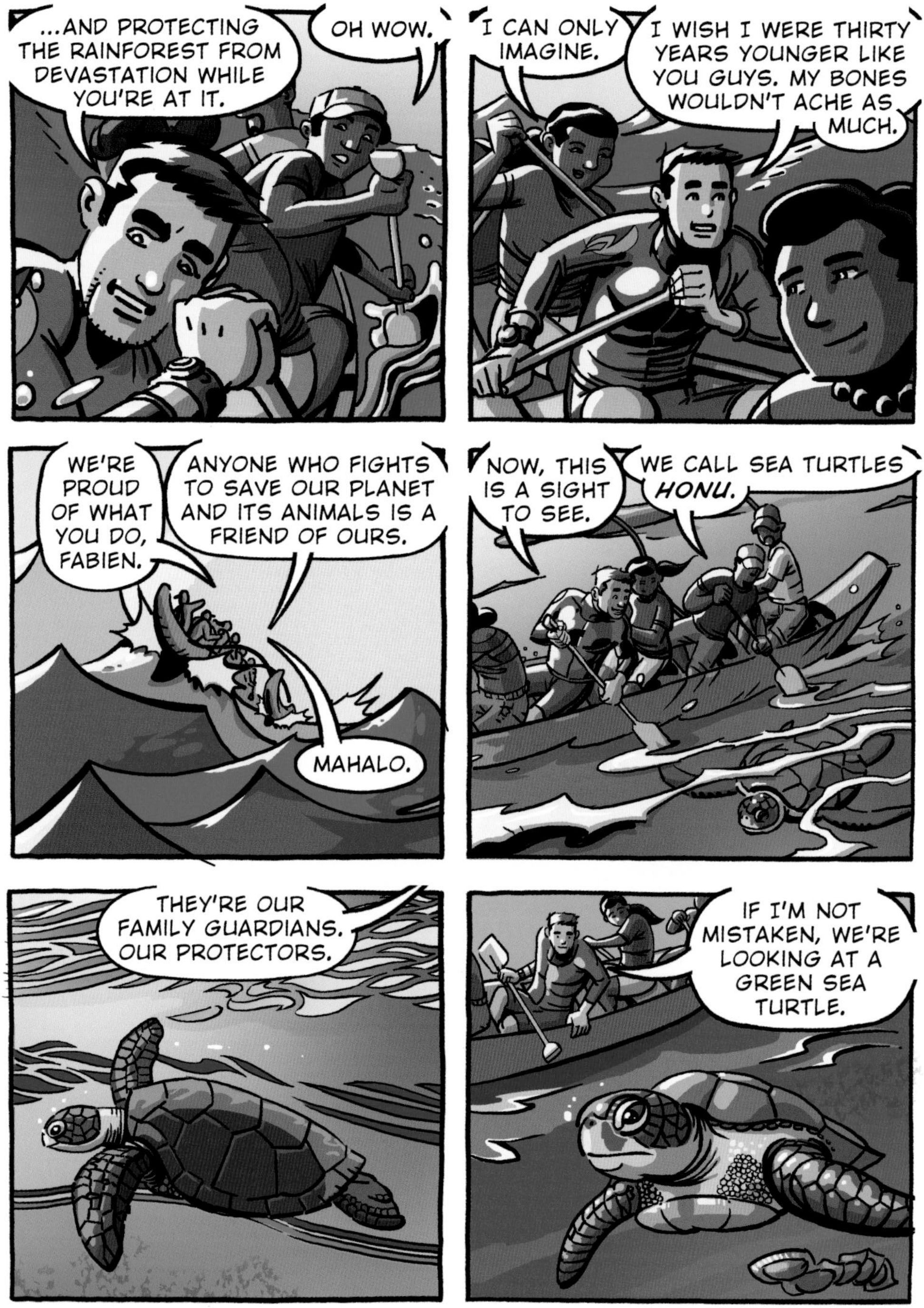
...AND PROTECTING THE RAINFOREST FROM DEVASTATION WHILE YOU'RE AT IT.
OH WOW.
I CAN ONLY IMAGINE.
I WISH I WERE THIRTY YEARS YOUNGER LIKE YOU GUYS. MY BONES WOULDN'T ACHE AS MUCH.
WE'RE PROUD OF WHAT YOU DO, FABIEN.
ANYONE WHO FIGHTS TO SAVE OUR PLANET AND ITS ANIMALS IS A FRIEND OF OURS.
MAHALO.
NOW, THIS IS A SIGHT TO SEE.
WE CALL SEA TURTLES *HONU*.
THEY'RE OUR FAMILY GUARDIANS. OUR PROTECTORS.
IF I'M NOT MISTAKEN, WE'RE LOOKING AT A GREEN SEA TURTLE.

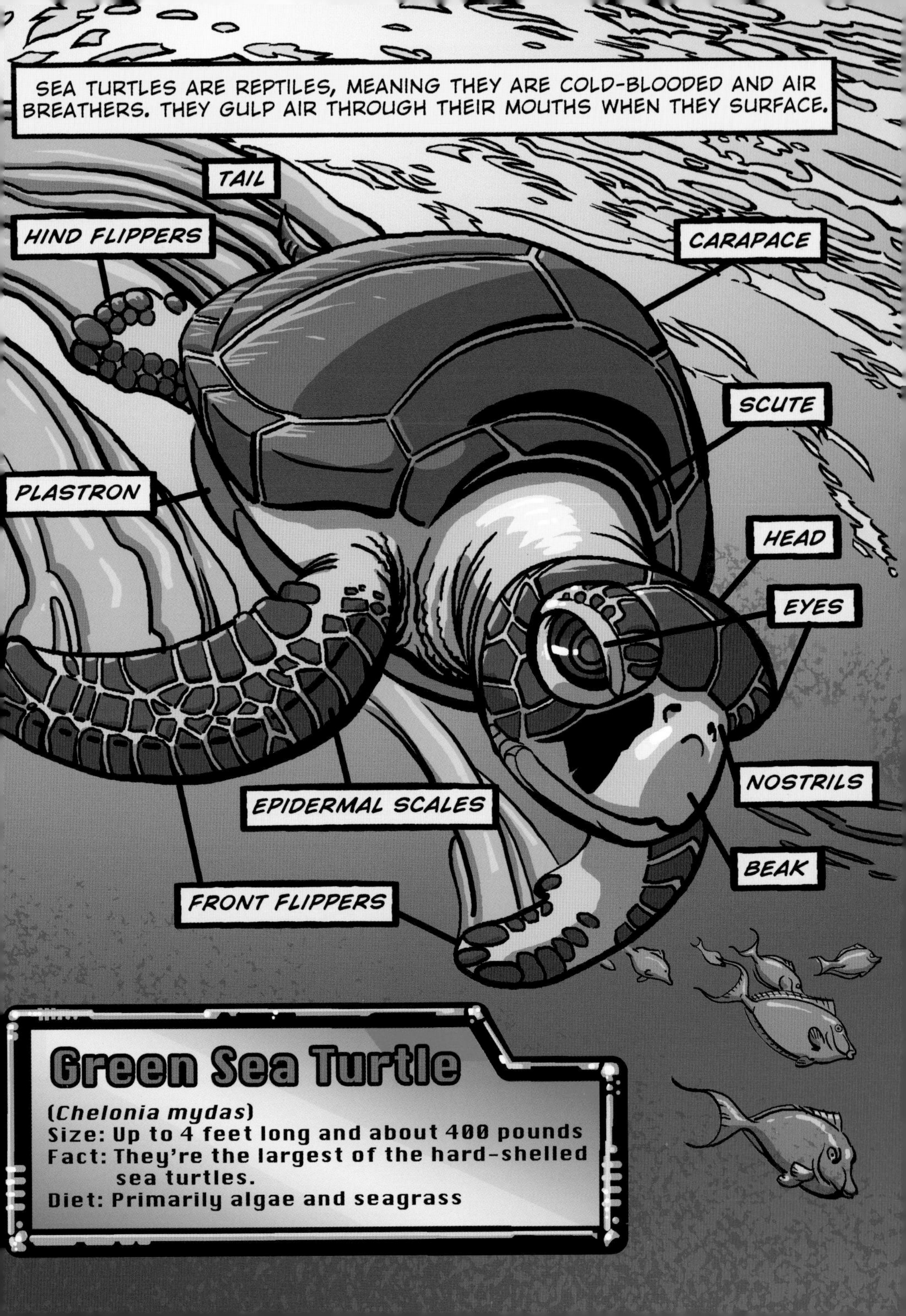
SEA TURTLES ARE REPTILES, MEANING THEY ARE COLD-BLOODED AND AIR BREATHERS. THEY GULP AIR THROUGH THEIR MOUTHS WHEN THEY SURFACE.
TAIL
HIND FLIPPERS
CARAPACE
SCUTE
PLASTRON
HEAD
EYES
NOSTRILS
EPIDERMAL SCALES
BEAK
FRONT FLIPPERS
Green Sea Turtle
(*Chelonia mydas*)
Size: Up to 4 feet long and about 400 pounds
Fact: They're the largest of the hard-shelled sea turtles.
Diet: Primarily algae and seagrass

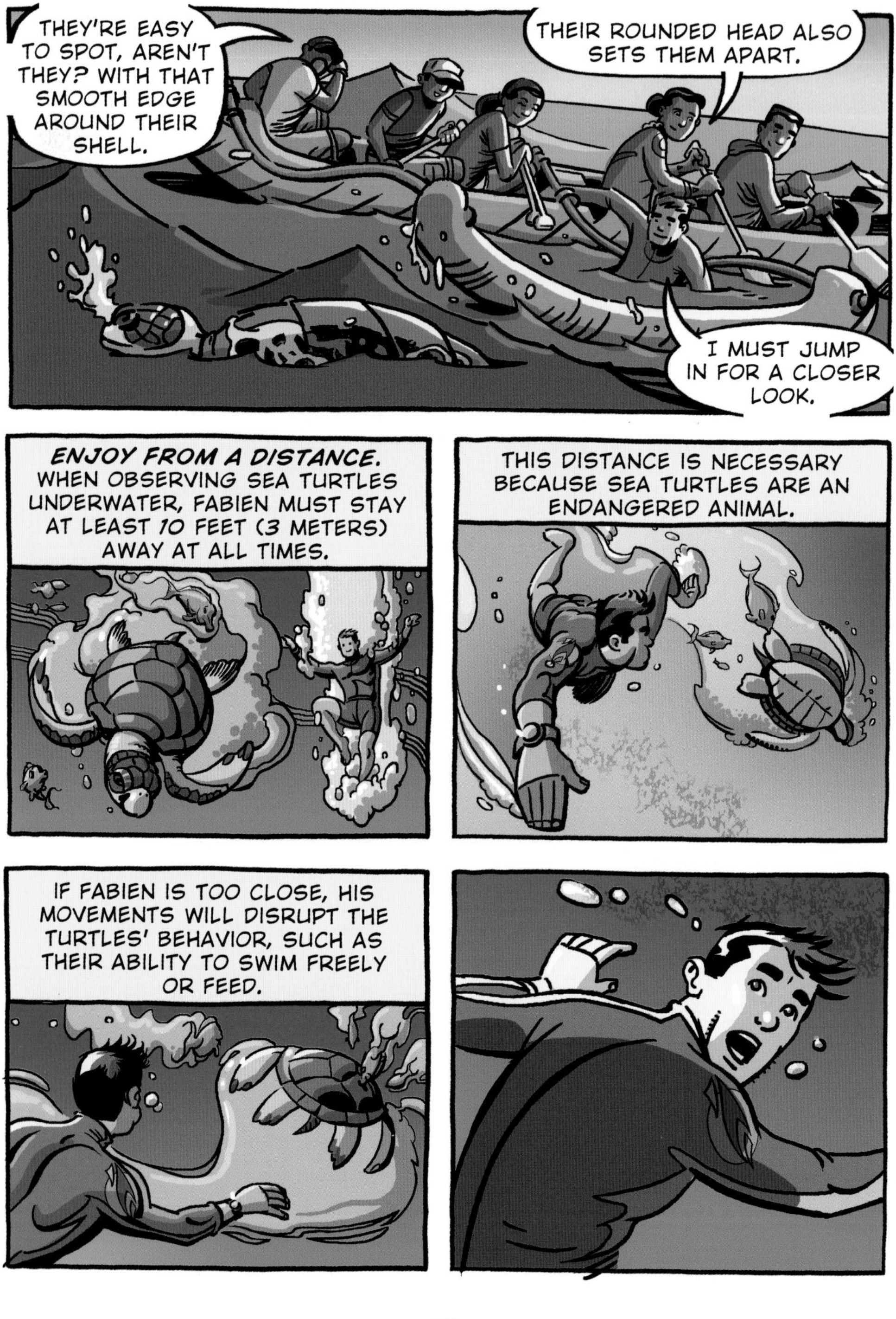
THEY'RE EASY TO SPOT, AREN'T THEY? WITH THAT SMOOTH EDGE AROUND THEIR SHELL.
THEIR ROUNDED HEAD ALSO SETS THEM APART.
I MUST JUMP IN FOR A CLOSER LOOK.
ENJOY FROM A DISTANCE. WHEN OBSERVING SEA TURTLES UNDERWATER, FABIEN MUST STAY AT LEAST 10 FEET (3 METERS) AWAY AT ALL TIMES.
THIS DISTANCE IS NECESSARY BECAUSE SEA TURTLES ARE AN ENDANGERED ANIMAL.
IF FABIEN IS TOO CLOSE, HIS MOVEMENTS WILL DISRUPT THE TURTLES' BEHAVIOR, SUCH AS THEIR ABILITY TO SWIM FREELY OR FEED.

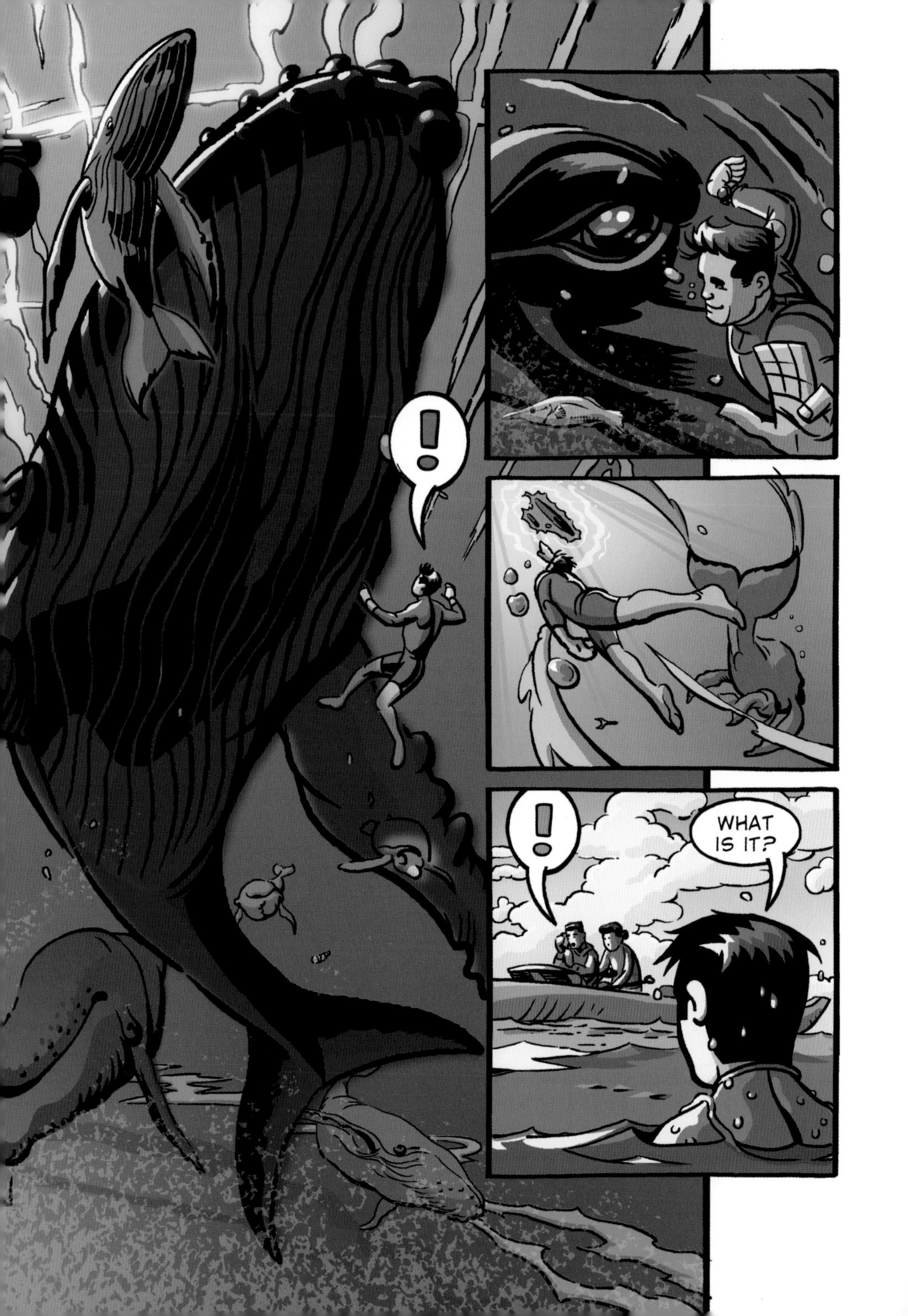
!
!
WHAT IS IT?

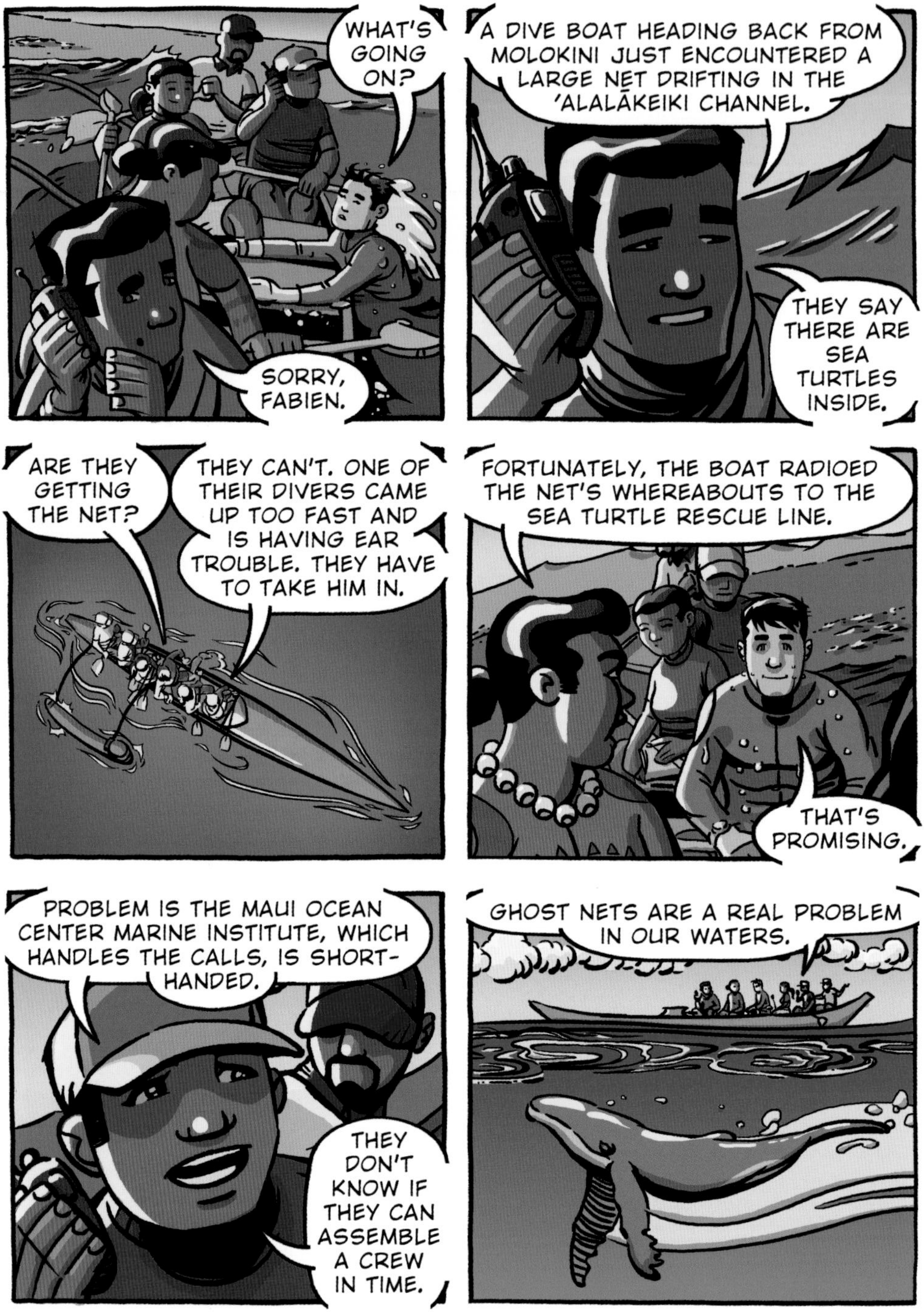
WHAT'S GOING ON?
SORRY, FABIEN.
A DIVE BOAT HEADING BACK FROM MOLOKINI JUST ENCOUNTERED A LARGE NET DRIFTING IN THE 'ALALĀKEIKI CHANNEL.
THEY SAY THERE ARE SEA TURTLES INSIDE.
ARE THEY GETTING THE NET?
THEY CAN'T. ONE OF THEIR DIVERS CAME UP TOO FAST AND IS HAVING EAR TROUBLE. THEY HAVE TO TAKE HIM IN.
FORTUNATELY, THE BOAT RADIOED THE NET'S WHEREABOUTS TO THE SEA TURTLE RESCUE LINE.
THAT'S PROMISING.
PROBLEM IS THE MAUI OCEAN CENTER MARINE INSTITUTE, WHICH HANDLES THE CALLS, IS SHORT-HANDED.
THEY DON'T KNOW IF THEY CAN ASSEMBLE A CREW IN TIME.
GHOST NETS ARE A REAL PROBLEM IN OUR WATERS.

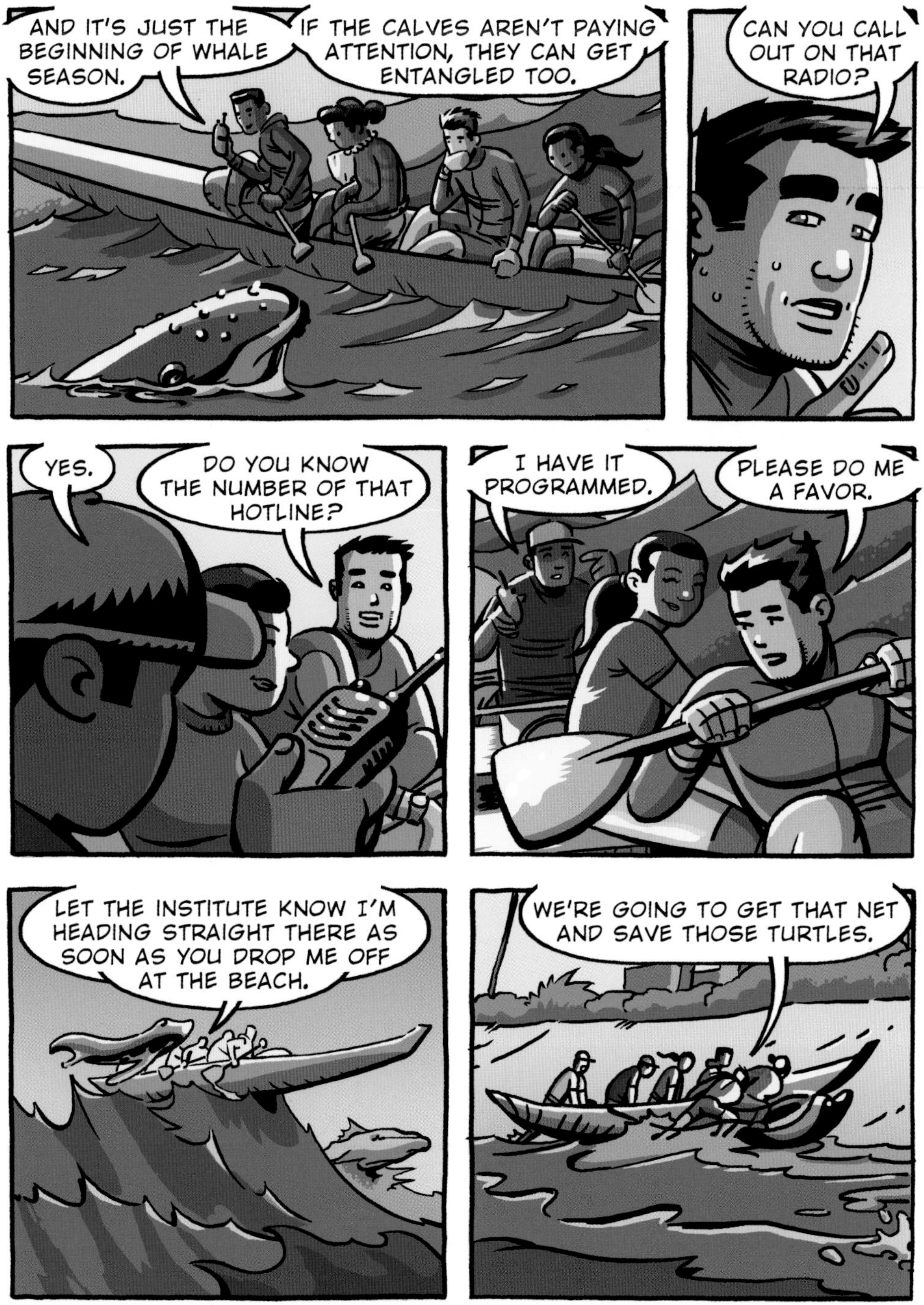
AND IT'S JUST THE BEGINNING OF WHALE SEASON.
IF THE CALVES AREN'T PAYING ATTENTION, THEY CAN GET ENTANGLED TOO.
CAN YOU CALL OUT ON THAT RADIO?
YES.
DO YOU KNOW THE NUMBER OF THAT HOTLINE?
I HAVE IT PROGRAMMED.
PLEASE DO ME A FAVOR.
LET THE INSTITUTE KNOW I'M HEADING STRAIGHT THERE AS SOON AS YOU DROP ME OFF AT THE BEACH.
WE'RE GOING TO GET THAT NET AND SAVE THOSE TURTLES.

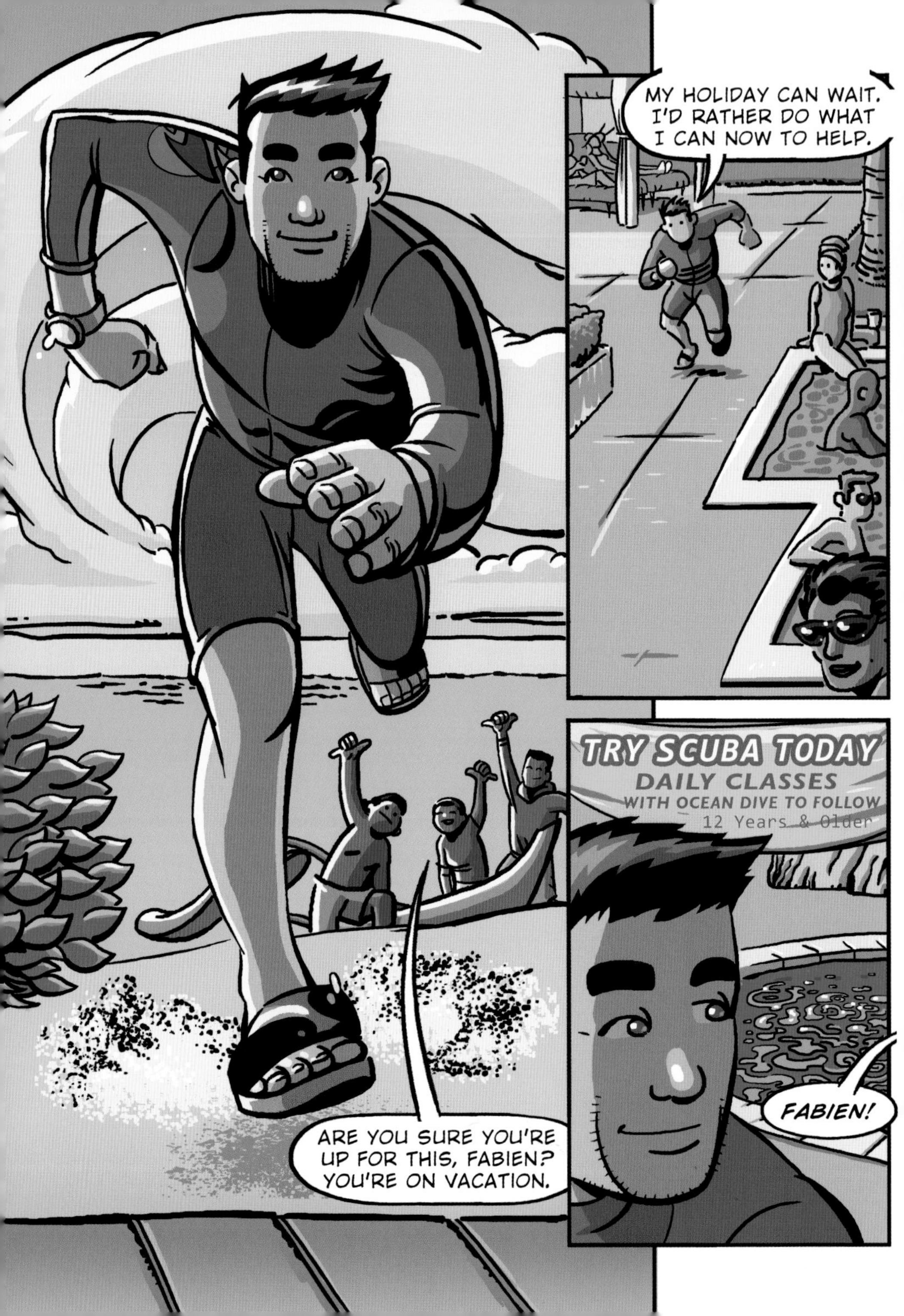
ARE YOU SURE YOU'RE UP FOR THIS, FABIEN? YOU'RE ON VACATION.
MY HOLIDAY CAN WAIT. I'D RATHER DO WHAT I CAN NOW TO HELP.
TRY SCUBA TODAY
DAILY CLASSES
WITH OCEAN DIVE TO FOLLOW
12 Years & Older
FABIEN!

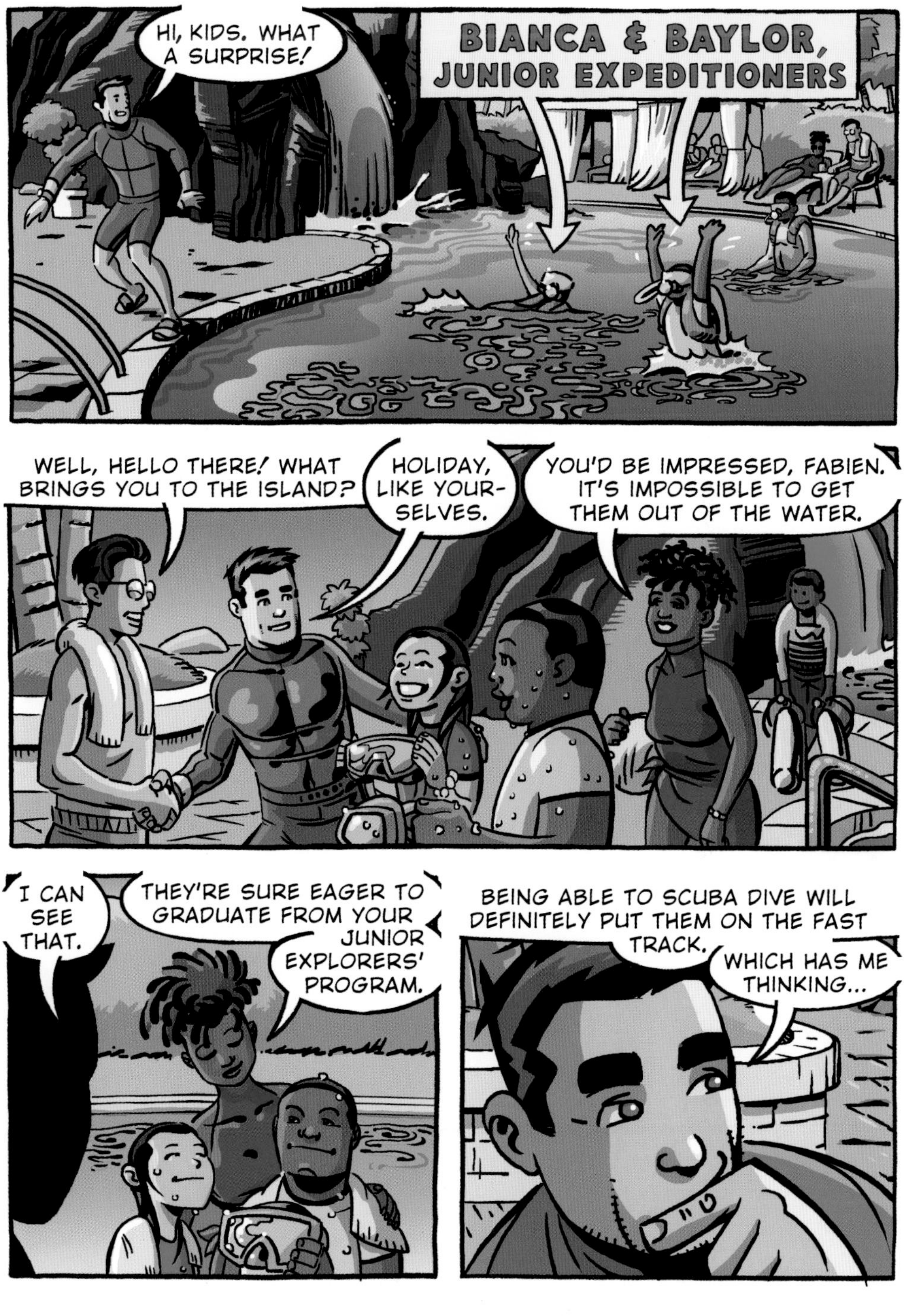
HI, KIDS. WHAT A SURPRISE!
BIANCA & BAYLOR, JUNIOR EXPEDITIONERS
WELL, HELLO THERE! WHAT BRINGS YOU TO THE ISLAND?
HOLIDAY, LIKE YOURSELVES.
YOU'D BE IMPRESSED, FABIEN. IT'S IMPOSSIBLE TO GET THEM OUT OF THE WATER.
I CAN SEE THAT.
THEY'RE SURE EAGER TO GRADUATE FROM YOUR JUNIOR EXPLORERS' PROGRAM.
BEING ABLE TO SCUBA DIVE WILL DEFINITELY PUT THEM ON THE FAST TRACK.
WHICH HAS ME THINKING...

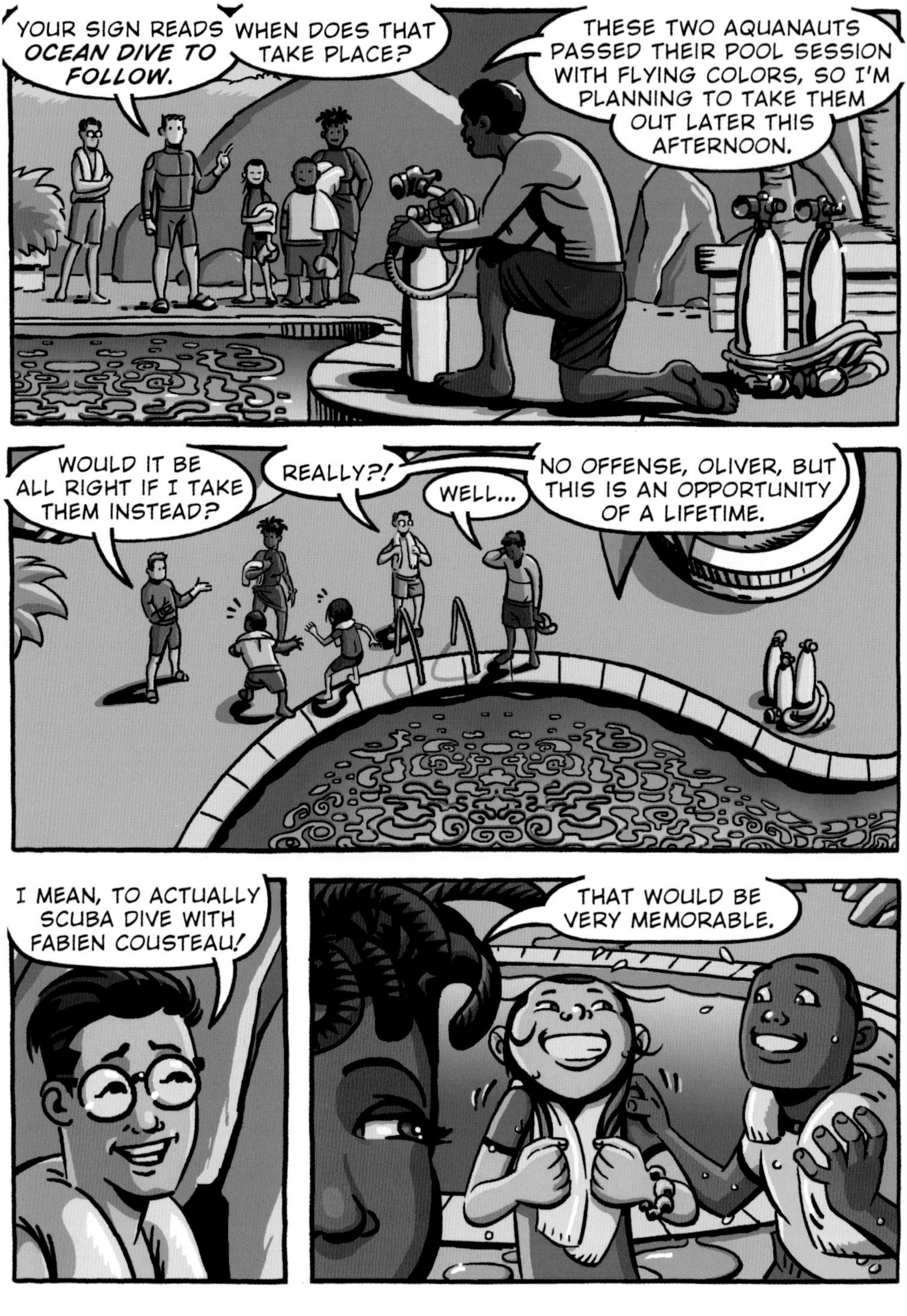
YOUR SIGN READS *OCEAN DIVE TO FOLLOW.*
WHEN DOES THAT TAKE PLACE?
THESE TWO AQUANAUTS PASSED THEIR POOL SESSION WITH FLYING COLORS, SO I'M PLANNING TO TAKE THEM OUT LATER THIS AFTERNOON.
WOULD IT BE ALL RIGHT IF I TAKE THEM INSTEAD?
REALLY?!
WELL...
NO OFFENSE, OLIVER, BUT THIS IS AN OPPORTUNITY OF A LIFETIME.
I MEAN, TO ACTUALLY SCUBA DIVE WITH FABIEN COUSTEAU!
THAT WOULD BE VERY MEMORABLE.

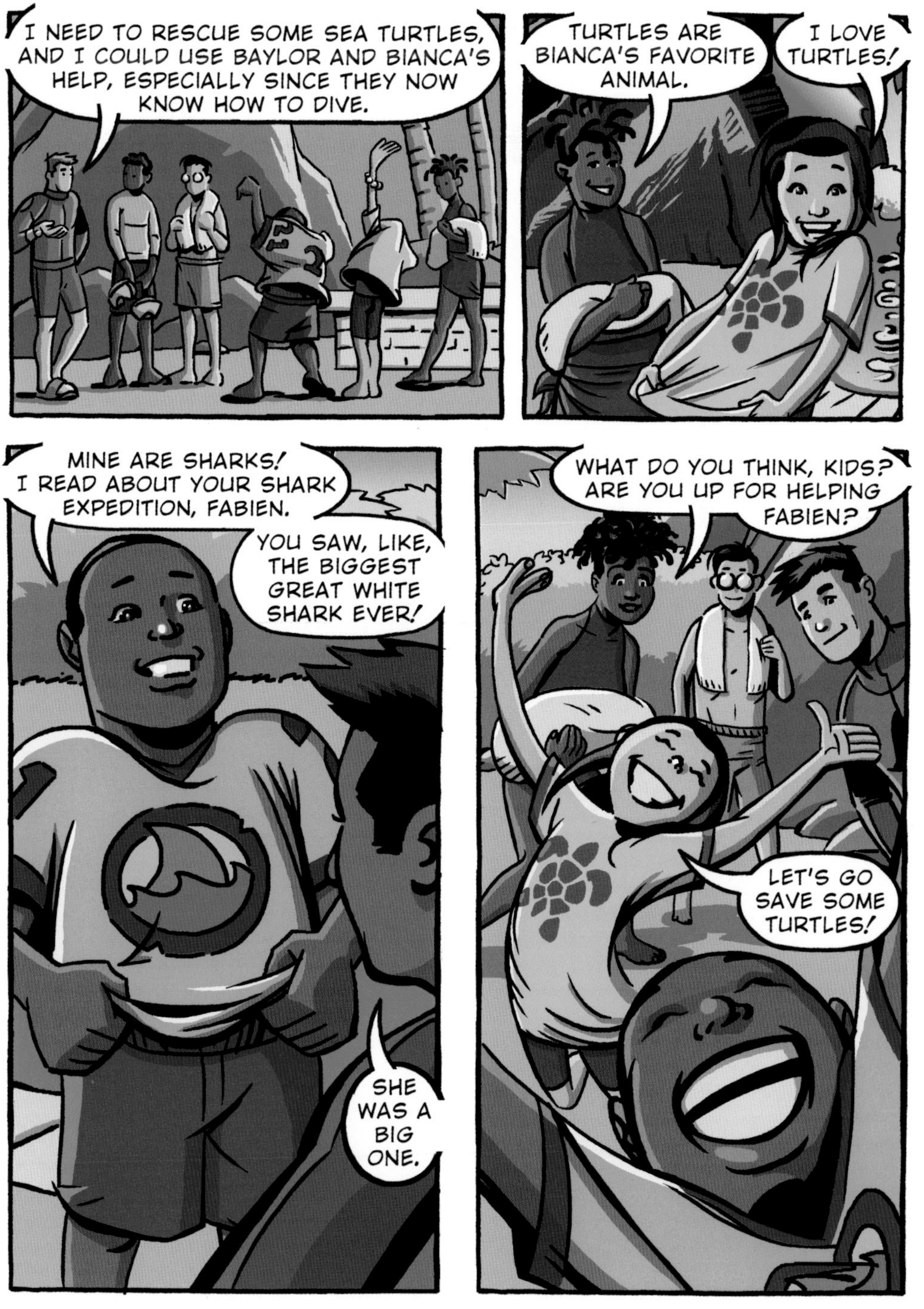
I NEED TO RESCUE SOME SEA TURTLES, AND I COULD USE BAYLOR AND BIANCA'S HELP, ESPECIALLY SINCE THEY NOW KNOW HOW TO DIVE.
TURTLES ARE BIANCA'S FAVORITE ANIMAL.
I LOVE TURTLES!
MINE ARE SHARKS! I READ ABOUT YOUR SHARK EXPEDITION, FABIEN.
YOU SAW, LIKE, THE BIGGEST GREAT WHITE SHARK EVER!
SHE WAS A BIG ONE.
WHAT DO YOU THINK, KIDS? ARE YOU UP FOR HELPING FABIEN?
LET'S GO SAVE SOME TURTLES!

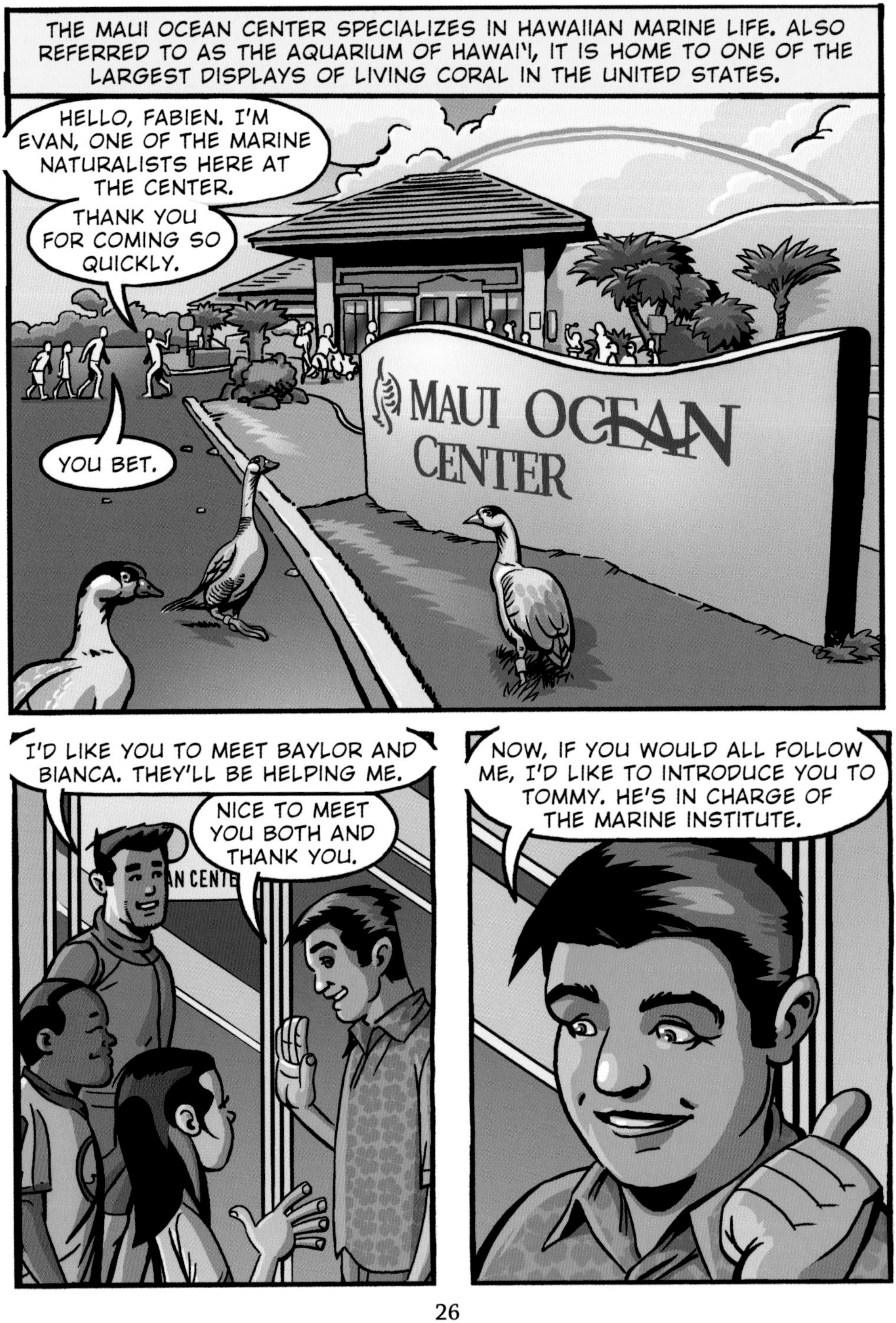
THE MAUI OCEAN CENTER SPECIALIZES IN HAWAIIAN MARINE LIFE. ALSO REFERRED TO AS THE AQUARIUM OF HAWAI'I, IT IS HOME TO ONE OF THE LARGEST DISPLAYS OF LIVING CORAL IN THE UNITED STATES.
HELLO, FABIEN. I'M EVAN, ONE OF THE MARINE NATURALISTS HERE AT THE CENTER.
THANK YOU FOR COMING SO QUICKLY.
YOU BET.
MAUI OCEAN CENTER
I'D LIKE YOU TO MEET BAYLOR AND BIANCA. THEY'LL BE HELPING ME.
NICE TO MEET YOU BOTH AND THANK YOU.
NOW, IF YOU WOULD ALL FOLLOW ME, I'D LIKE TO INTRODUCE YOU TO TOMMY. HE'S IN CHARGE OF THE MARINE INSTITUTE.

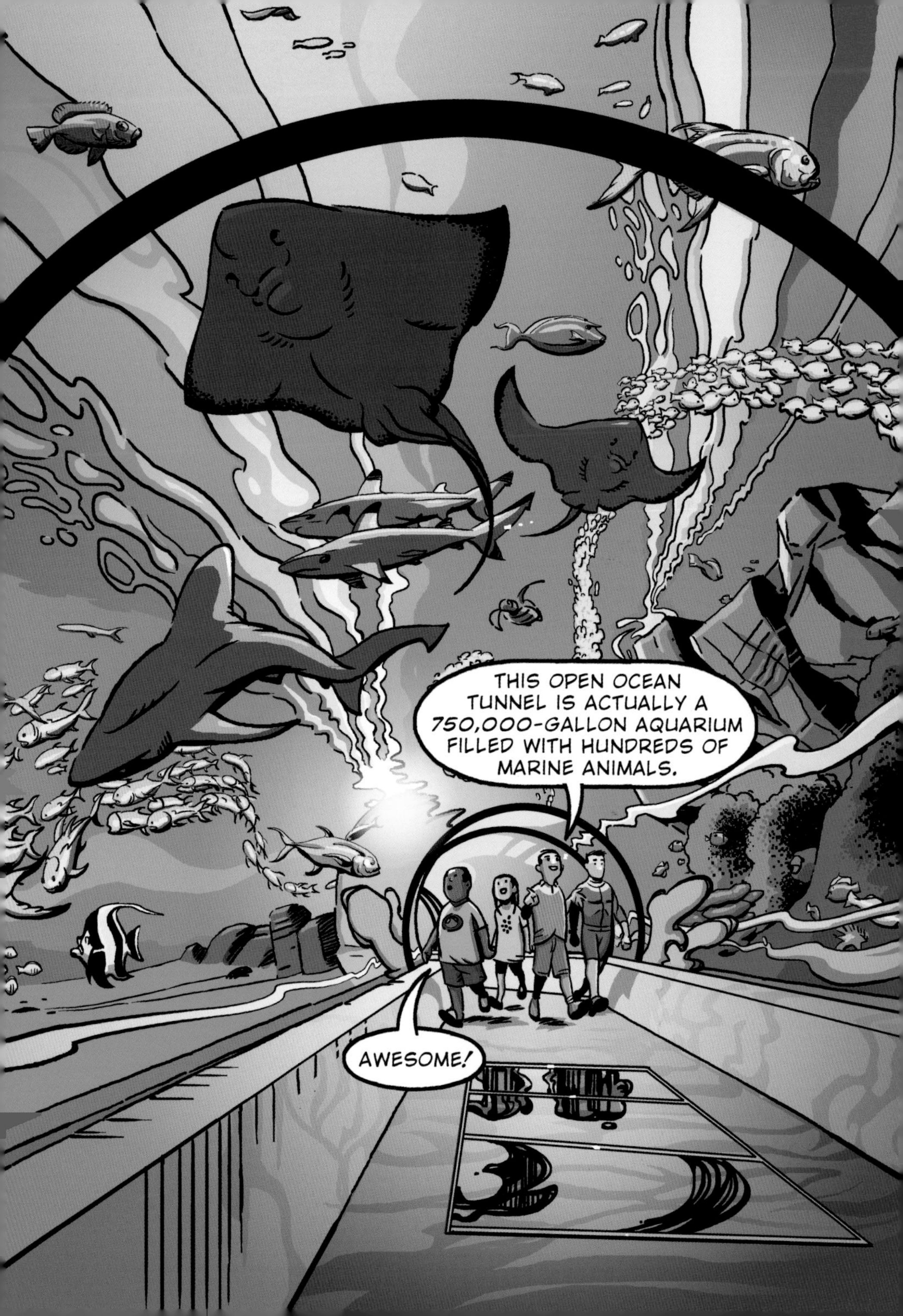
THIS OPEN OCEAN TUNNEL IS ACTUALLY A 750,000-GALLON AQUARIUM FILLED WITH HUNDREDS OF MARINE ANIMALS.
AWESOME!

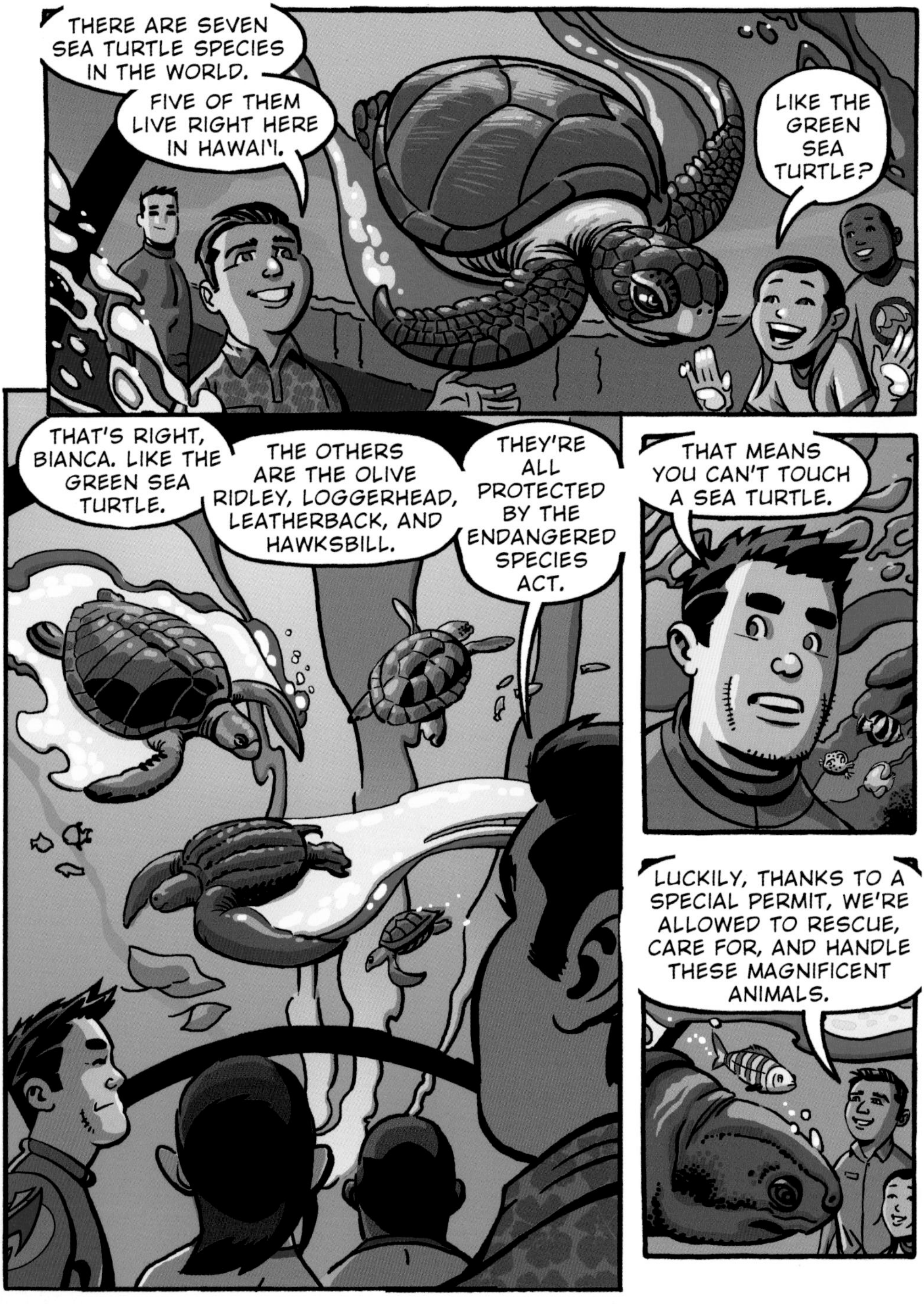
THERE ARE SEVEN SEA TURTLE SPECIES IN THE WORLD.
FIVE OF THEM LIVE RIGHT HERE IN HAWAI'I.
LIKE THE GREEN SEA TURTLE?
THAT'S RIGHT, BIANCA. LIKE THE GREEN SEA TURTLE.
THE OTHERS ARE THE OLIVE RIDLEY, LOGGERHEAD, LEATHERBACK, AND HAWKSBILL.
THEY'RE ALL PROTECTED BY THE ENDANGERED SPECIES ACT.
THAT MEANS YOU CAN'T TOUCH A SEA TURTLE.
LUCKILY, THANKS TO A SPECIAL PERMIT, WE'RE ALLOWED TO RESCUE, CARE FOR, AND HANDLE THESE MAGNIFICENT ANIMALS.

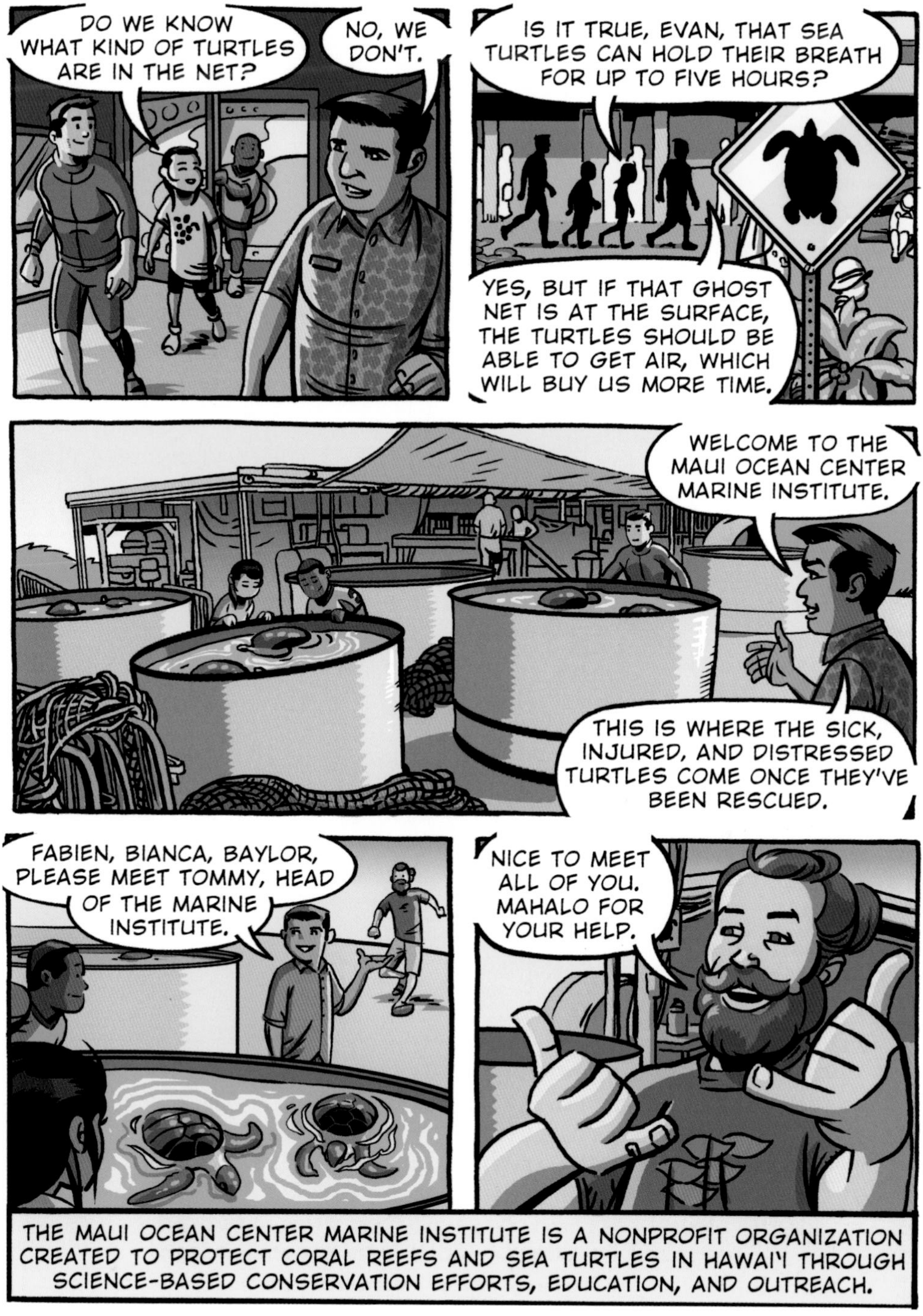
DO WE KNOW WHAT KIND OF TURTLES ARE IN THE NET?
NO, WE DON'T.
IS IT TRUE, EVAN, THAT SEA TURTLES CAN HOLD THEIR BREATH FOR UP TO FIVE HOURS?
YES, BUT IF THAT GHOST NET IS AT THE SURFACE, THE TURTLES SHOULD BE ABLE TO GET AIR, WHICH WILL BUY US MORE TIME.
WELCOME TO THE MAUI OCEAN CENTER MARINE INSTITUTE.
THIS IS WHERE THE SICK, INJURED, AND DISTRESSED TURTLES COME ONCE THEY'VE BEEN RESCUED.
FABIEN, BIANCA, BAYLOR, PLEASE MEET TOMMY, HEAD OF THE MARINE INSTITUTE.
NICE TO MEET ALL OF YOU. MAHALO FOR YOUR HELP.
THE MAUI OCEAN CENTER MARINE INSTITUTE IS A NONPROFIT ORGANIZATION CREATED TO PROTECT CORAL REEFS AND SEA TURTLES IN HAWAI'I THROUGH SCIENCE-BASED CONSERVATION EFFORTS, EDUCATION, AND OUTREACH.

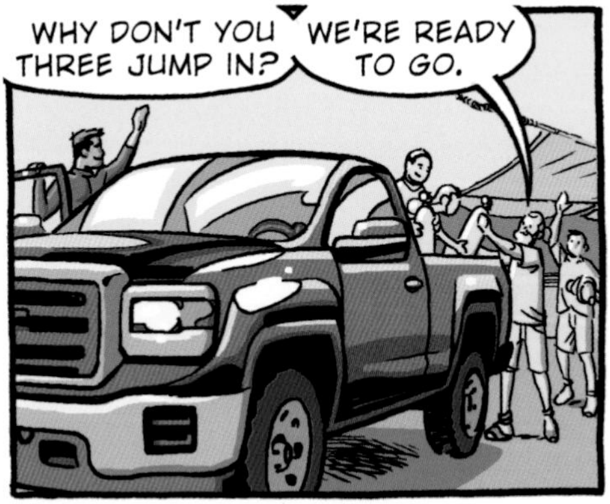
WHY DON'T YOU THREE JUMP IN?
WE'RE READY TO GO.

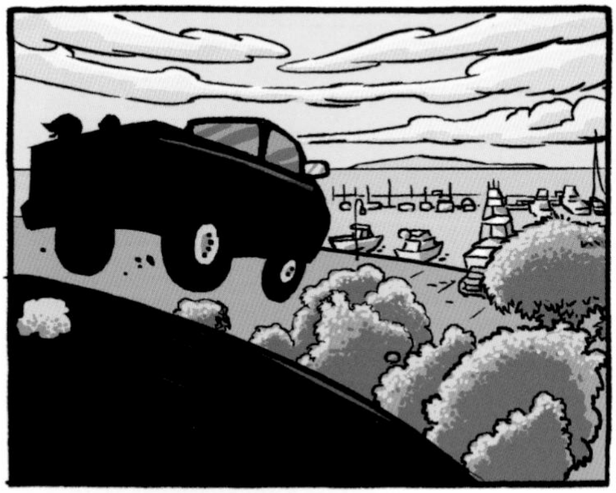

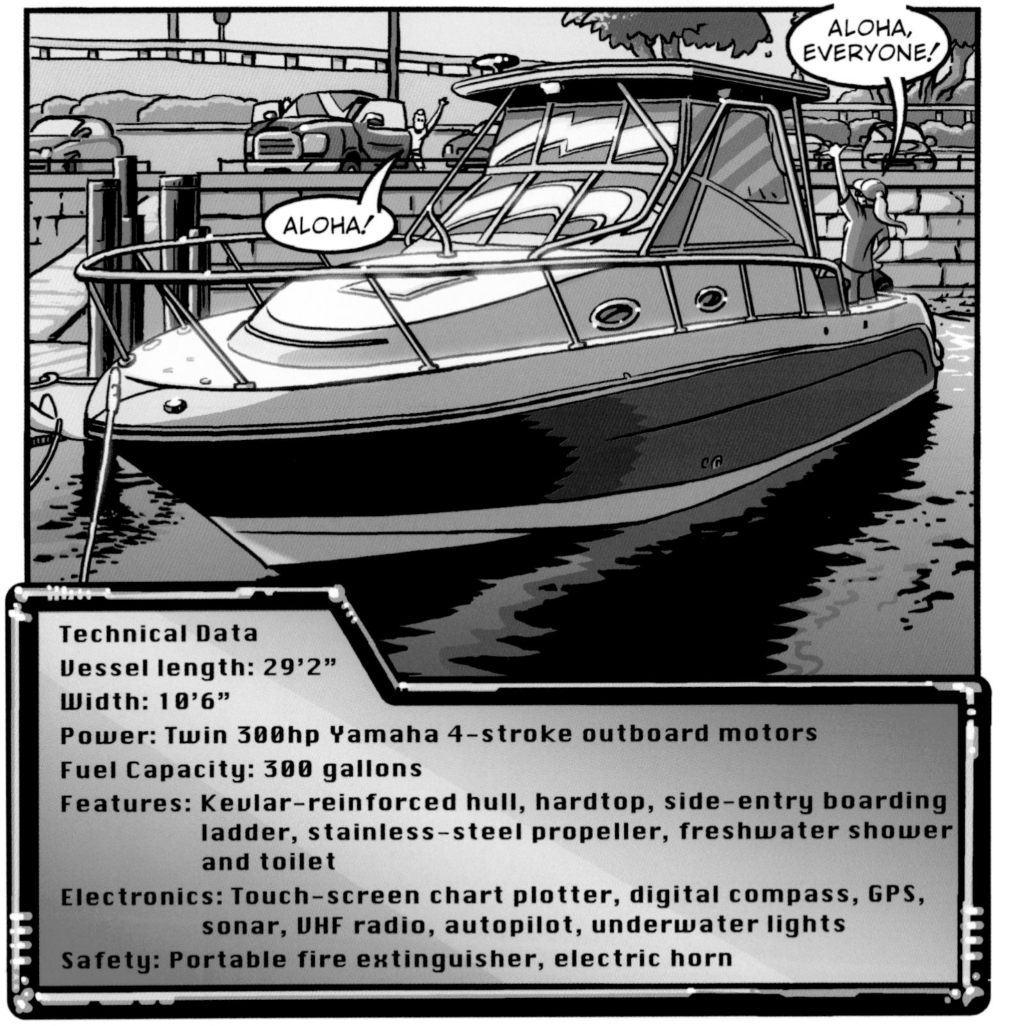
ALOHA, EVERYONE!
ALOHA!

Technical Data

Vessel length: 29'2"

Width: 10'6"

Power: Twin 300hp Yamaha 4-stroke outboard motors

Fuel Capacity: 300 gallons

Features: Kevlar-reinforced hull, hardtop, side-entry boarding ladder, stainless-steel propeller, freshwater shower and toilet

Electronics: Touch-screen chart plotter, digital compass, GPS, sonar, VHF radio, autopilot, underwater lights

Safety: Portable fire extinguisher, electric horn

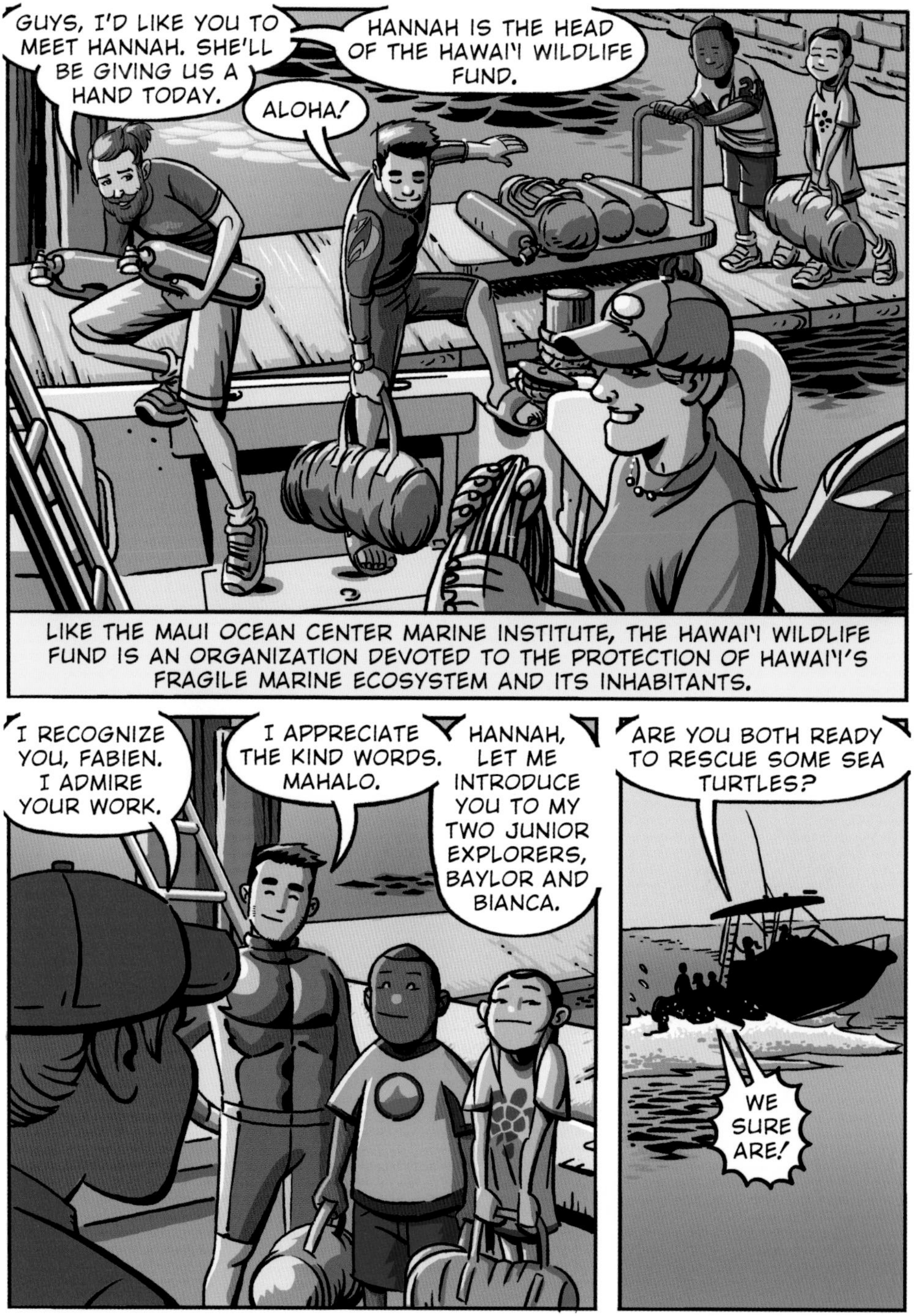
GUYS, I'D LIKE YOU TO MEET HANNAH. SHE'LL BE GIVING US A HAND TODAY.
HANNAH IS THE HEAD OF THE HAWAI'I WILDLIFE FUND.
ALOHA!
LIKE THE MAUI OCEAN CENTER MARINE INSTITUTE, THE HAWAI'I WILDLIFE FUND IS AN ORGANIZATION DEVOTED TO THE PROTECTION OF HAWAI'I'S FRAGILE MARINE ECOSYSTEM AND ITS INHABITANTS.
I RECOGNIZE YOU, FABIEN. I ADMIRE YOUR WORK.
I APPRECIATE THE KIND WORDS. MAHALO.
HANNAH, LET ME INTRODUCE YOU TO MY TWO JUNIOR EXPLORERS, BAYLOR AND BIANCA.
ARE YOU BOTH READY TO RESCUE SOME SEA TURTLES?
WE SURE ARE!

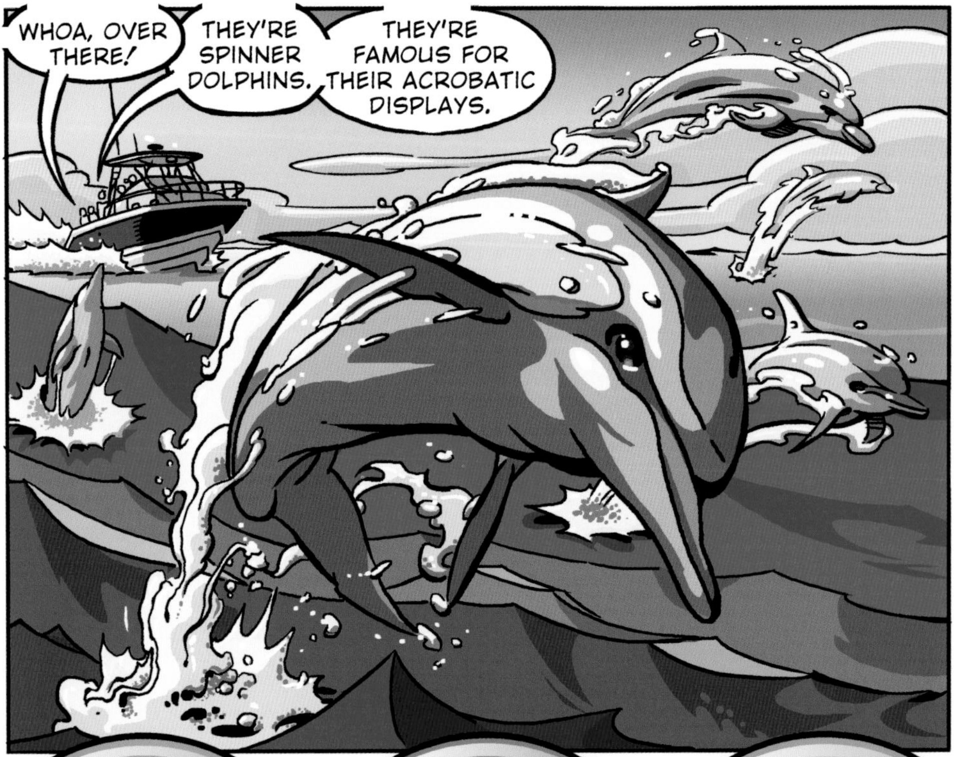
WHOA, OVER THERE!
THEY'RE SPINNER DOLPHINS.
THEY'RE FAMOUS FOR THEIR ACROBATIC DISPLAYS.

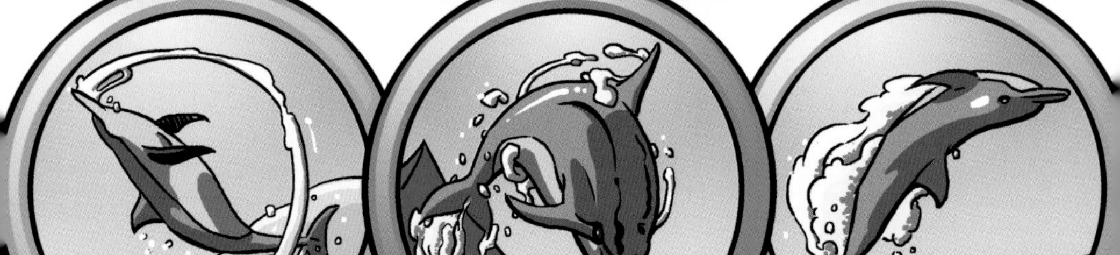

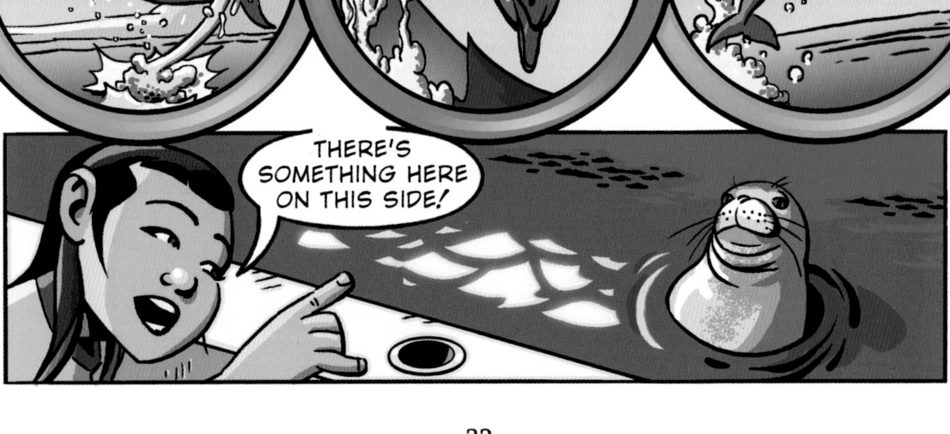
THERE'S SOMETHING HERE ON THIS SIDE!

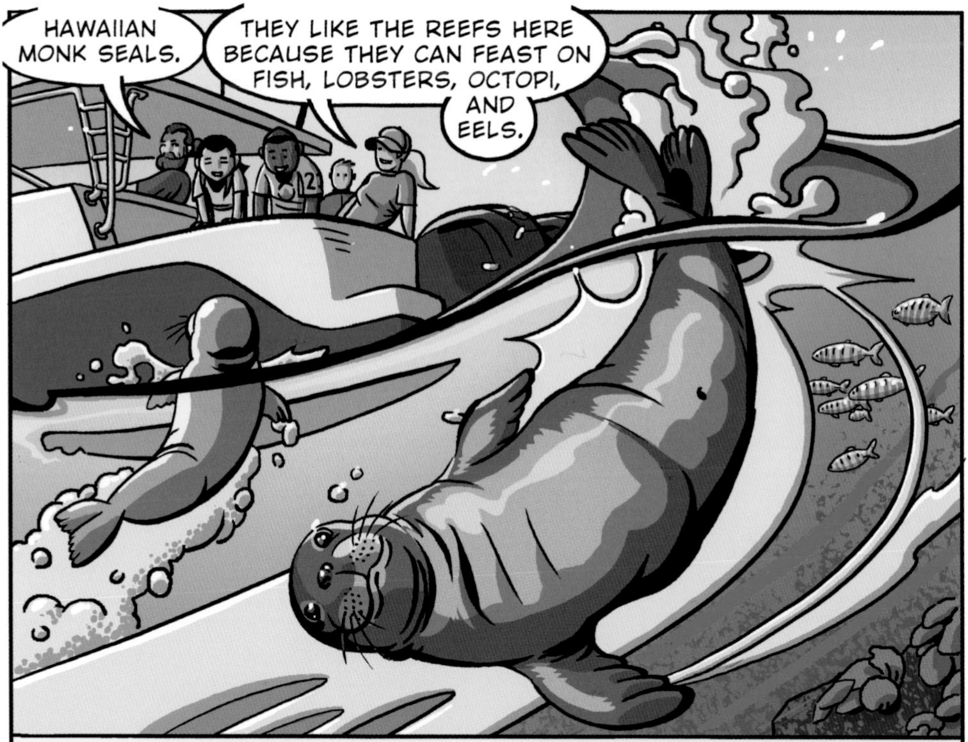
HAWAIIAN MONK SEALS.
THEY LIKE THE REEFS HERE BECAUSE THEY CAN FEAST ON FISH, LOBSTERS, OCTOPI, AND EELS.

THE HAWAIIAN MONK SEAL IS AN ENDANGERED SPECIES NATIVE TO THE HAWAIIAN ISLANDS. ONLY ABOUT 1,000 REMAIN IN THE WILD.

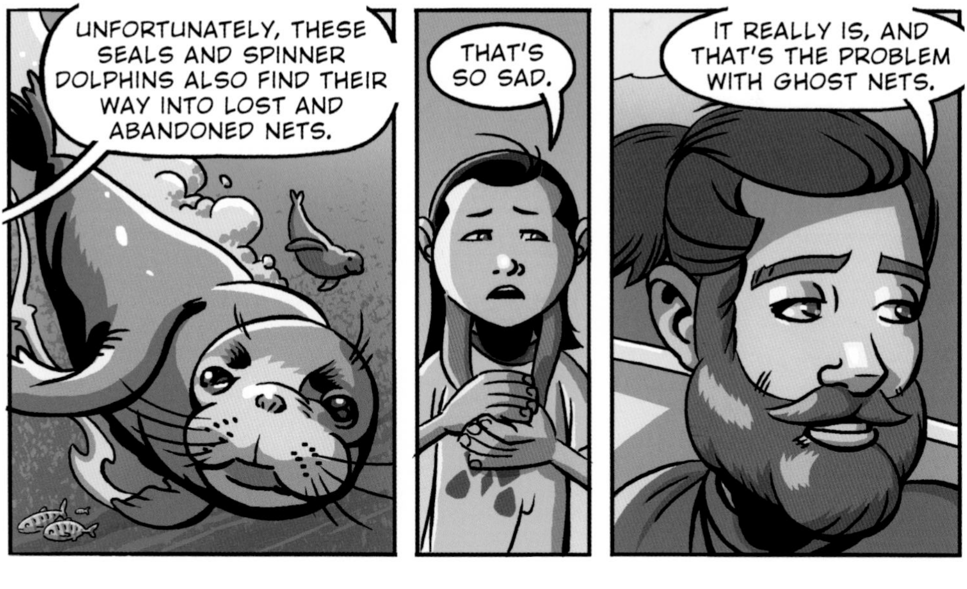
UNFORTUNATELY, THESE SEALS AND SPINNER DOLPHINS ALSO FIND THEIR WAY INTO LOST AND ABANDONED NETS.
THAT'S SO SAD.
IT REALLY IS, AND THAT'S THE PROBLEM WITH GHOST NETS.

"JUST BECAUSE A FISHING NET IS NO LONGER USED DOESN'T MEAN IT STOPS WORKING."

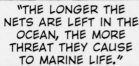

"THE LONGER THE NETS ARE LEFT IN THE OCEAN, THE MORE THREAT THEY CAUSE TO MARINE LIFE."

"I BET A GHOST NET IS SCARIER FOR A SEA TURTLE THAN THEIR MOST FEARED PREDATOR."

"YOU'RE ABSOLUTELY RIGHT ABOUT THAT, FABIEN."

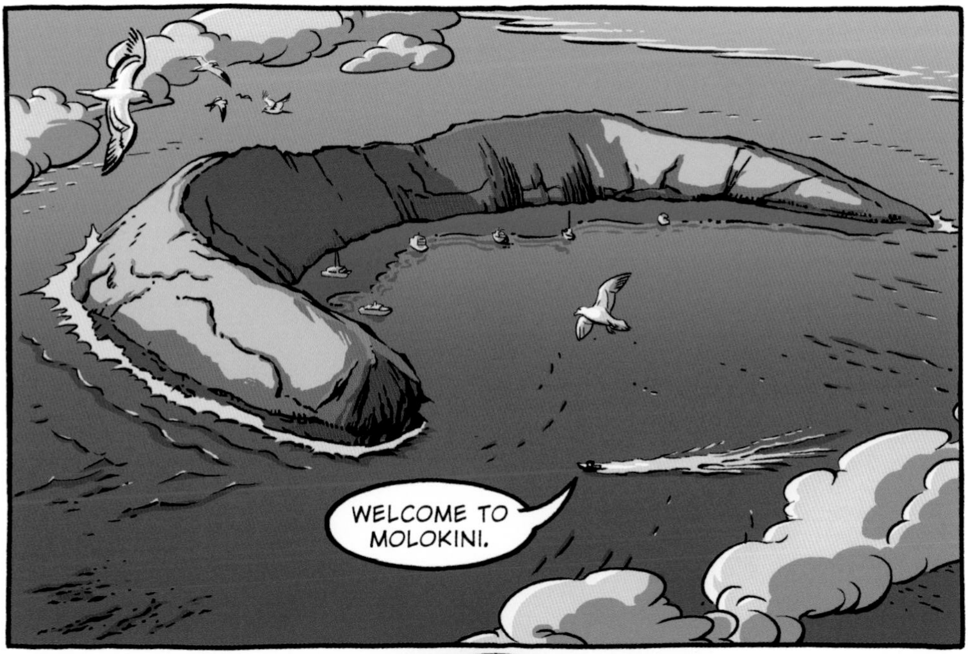
WELCOME TO MOLOKINI.

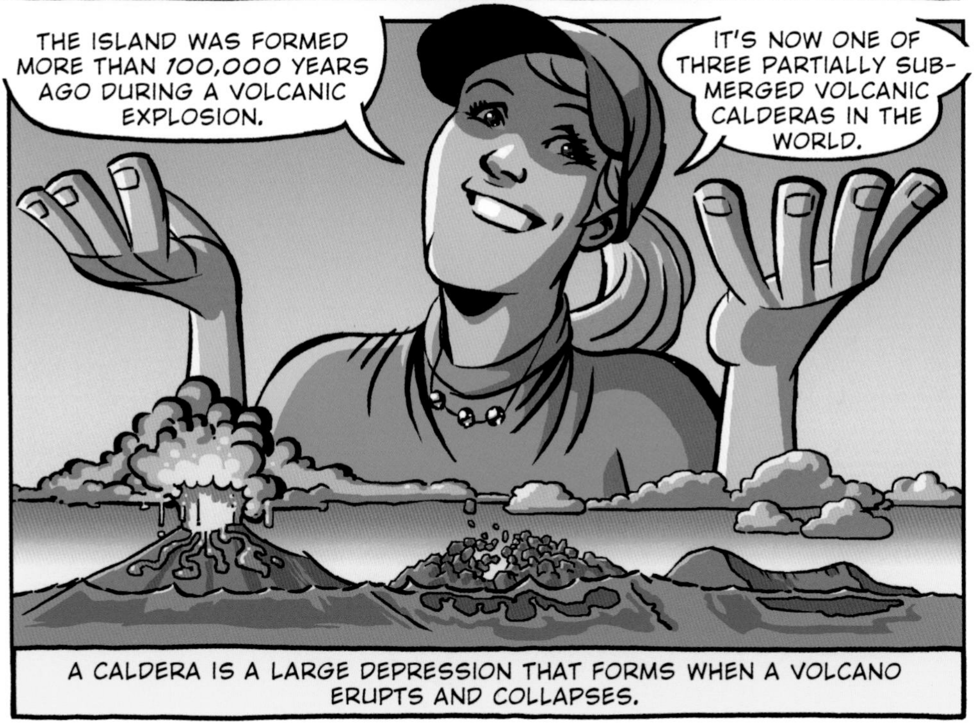
THE ISLAND WAS FORMED MORE THAN *100,000* YEARS AGO DURING A VOLCANIC EXPLOSION.
IT'S NOW ONE OF THREE PARTIALLY SUB-MERGED VOLCANIC CALDERAS IN THE WORLD.
A CALDERA IS A LARGE DEPRESSION THAT FORMS WHEN A VOLCANO ERUPTS AND COLLAPSES.

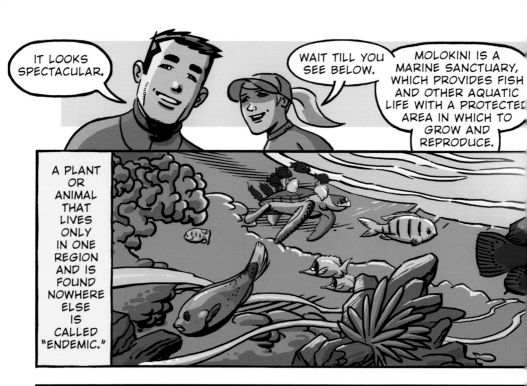

IT LOOKS SPECTACULAR.

WAIT TILL YOU SEE BELOW.

MOLOKINI IS A MARINE SANCTUARY, WHICH PROVIDES FISH AND OTHER AQUATIC LIFE WITH A PROTECTED AREA IN WHICH TO GROW AND REPRODUCE.

A PLANT OR ANIMAL THAT LIVES ONLY IN ONE REGION AND IS FOUND NOWHERE ELSE IS CALLED "ENDEMIC."

MOLOKINI'S UNIQUE SHAPE DOES HAVE A DRAWBACK.

THIS HORSESHOE-SHAPED ISLAND ACTS LIKE A CATCHER'S MITT, TRAPPING ALL SORTS OF PLASTIC AND OCEAN DEBRIS.

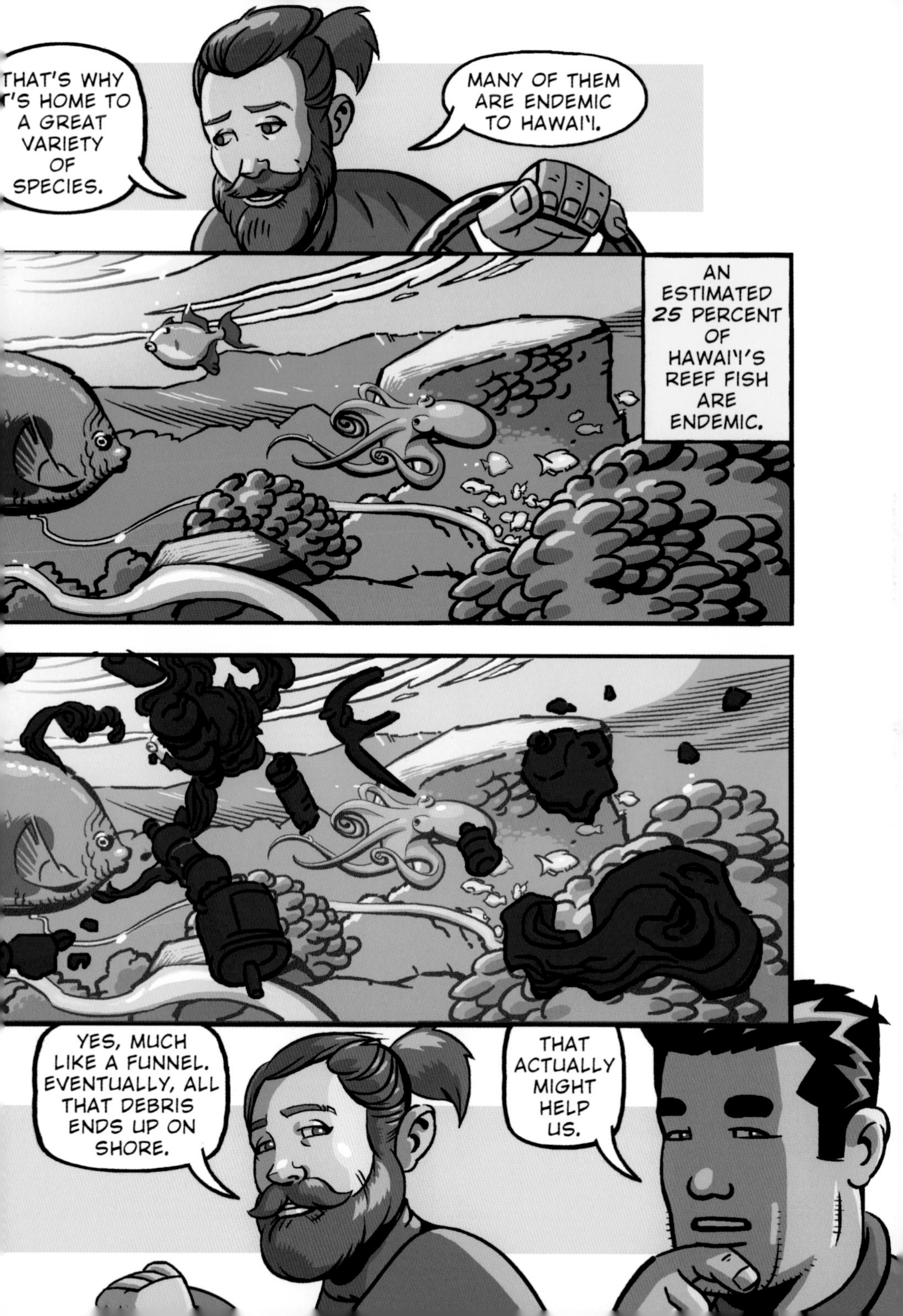

THAT'S WHY IT'S HOME TO A GREAT VARIETY OF SPECIES.
MANY OF THEM ARE ENDEMIC TO HAWAI'I.
AN ESTIMATED 25 PERCENT OF HAWAI'I'S REEF FISH ARE ENDEMIC.
YES, MUCH LIKE A FUNNEL. EVENTUALLY, ALL THAT DEBRIS ENDS UP ON SHORE.
THAT ACTUALLY MIGHT HELP US.

HOW SO?

IF THAT GHOST NET WITH THE TURTLES IS ANYWHERE NEAR, IT SHOULD WORK ITS WAY INSIDE THIS CALDERA, ENDING UP ON THE SHORELINE AS WELL.

I LIKE YOUR THEORY.

WE'RE JUST INSIDE THE 'ALALĀKEIKI CHANNEL, WHERE THE DIVE BOAT SPOTTED THE NET.

GREAT. I SUGGEST WE START HERE AND ZIGZAG OUR WAY INSIDE.

SOUNDS GOOD, FABIEN.

HANNAH AND I CAN SCAN THE SURFACE WHILE YOU THREE SEARCH BELOW.

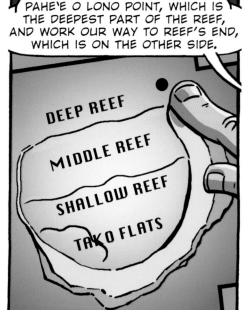

WE CAN BEGIN HERE AT PAHE'E O LONO POINT, WHICH IS THE DEEPEST PART OF THE REEF, AND WORK OUR WAY TO REEF'S END, WHICH IS ON THE OTHER SIDE.

DEEP REEF

MIDDLE REEF

SHALLOW REEF

TAKO FLATS

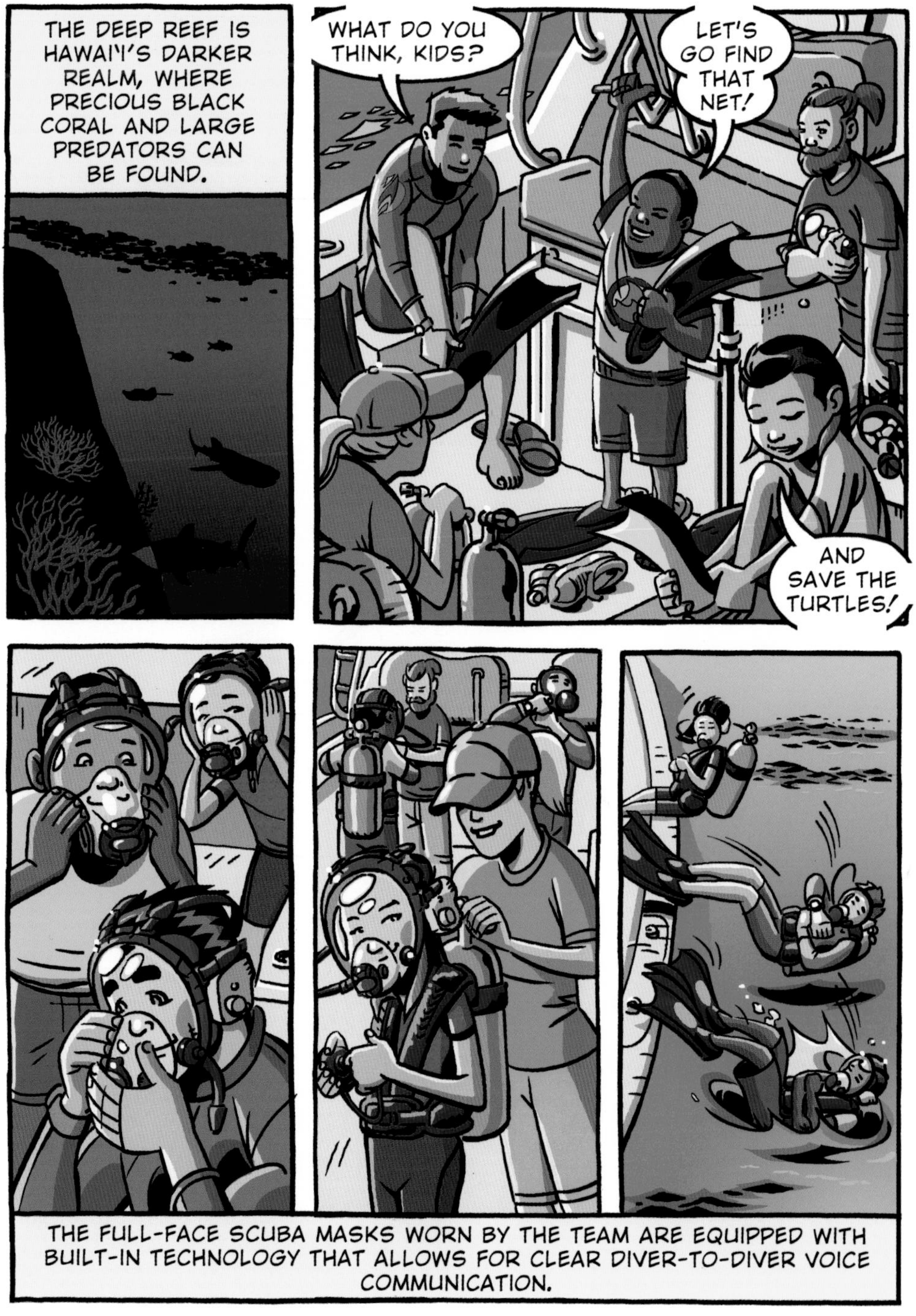
THE DEEP REEF IS HAWAI'I'S DARKER REALM, WHERE PRECIOUS BLACK CORAL AND LARGE PREDATORS CAN BE FOUND.
WHAT DO YOU THINK, KIDS?
LET'S GO FIND THAT NET!
AND SAVE THE TURTLES!
THE FULL-FACE SCUBA MASKS WORN BY THE TEAM ARE EQUIPPED WITH BUILT-IN TECHNOLOGY THAT ALLOWS FOR CLEAR DIVER-TO-DIVER VOICE COMMUNICATION.

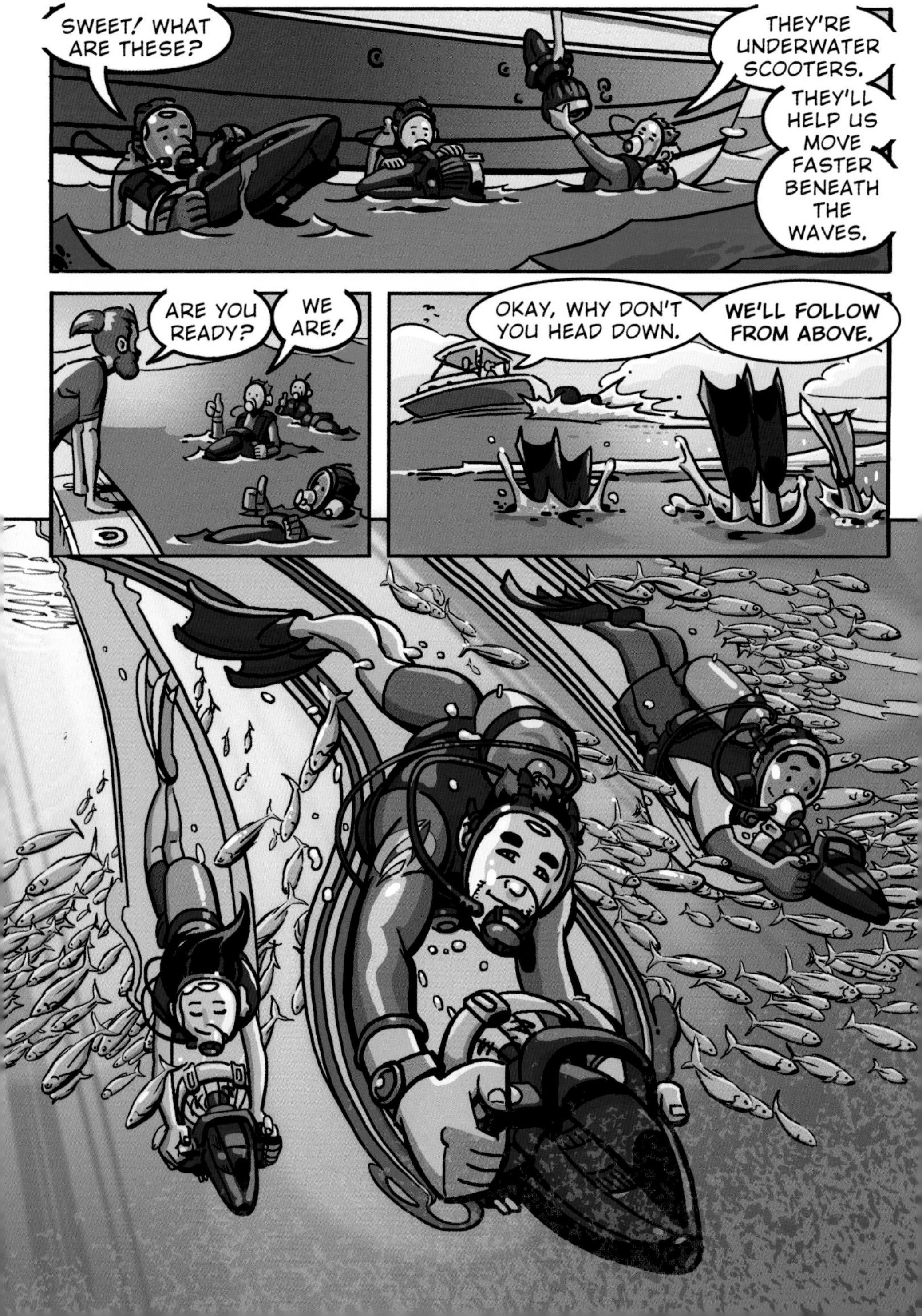
SWEET! WHAT ARE THESE?
THEY'RE UNDERWATER SCOOTERS.
THEY'LL HELP US MOVE FASTER BENEATH THE WAVES.
ARE YOU READY?
WE ARE!
OKAY, WHY DON'T YOU HEAD DOWN.
WE'LL FOLLOW FROM ABOVE.

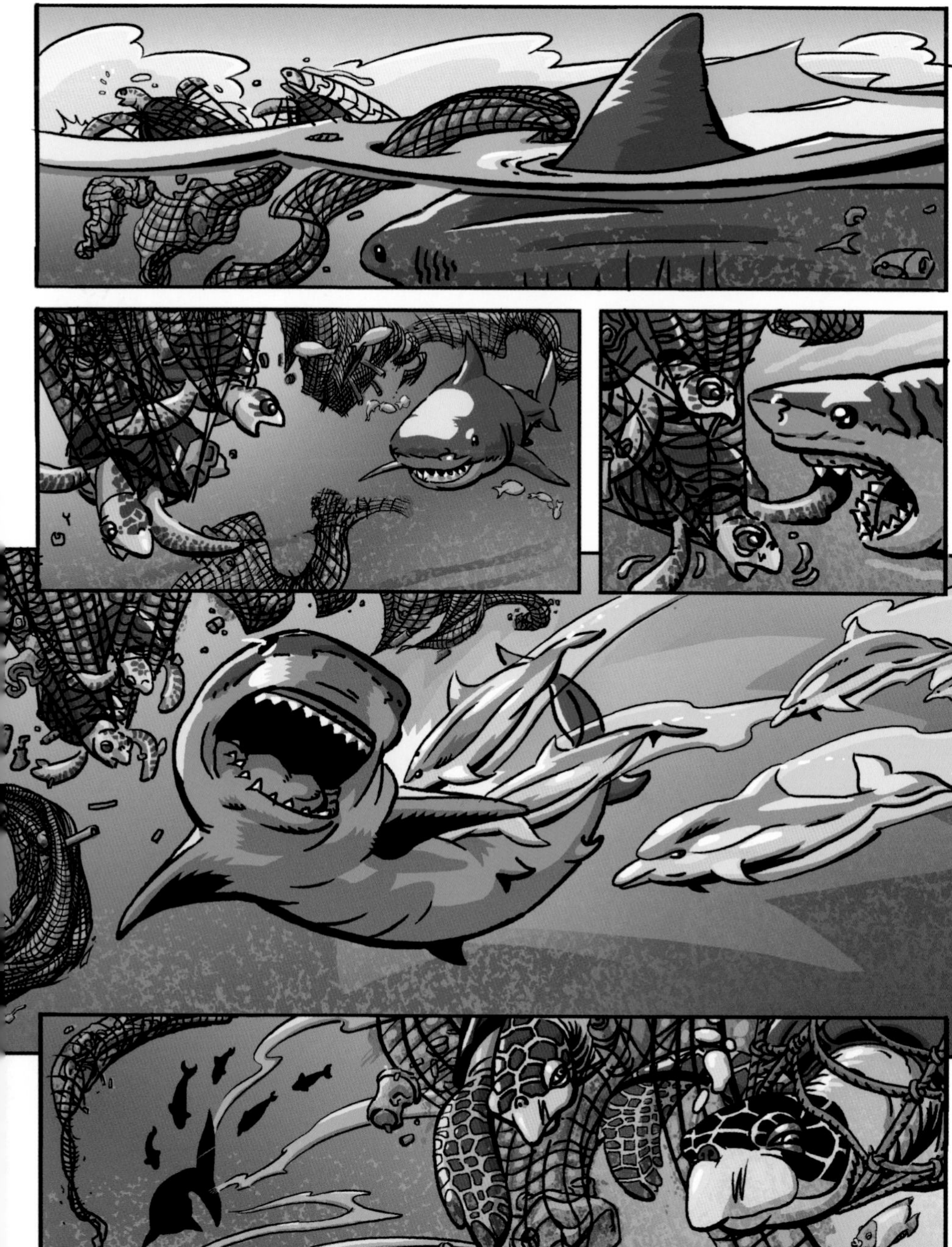

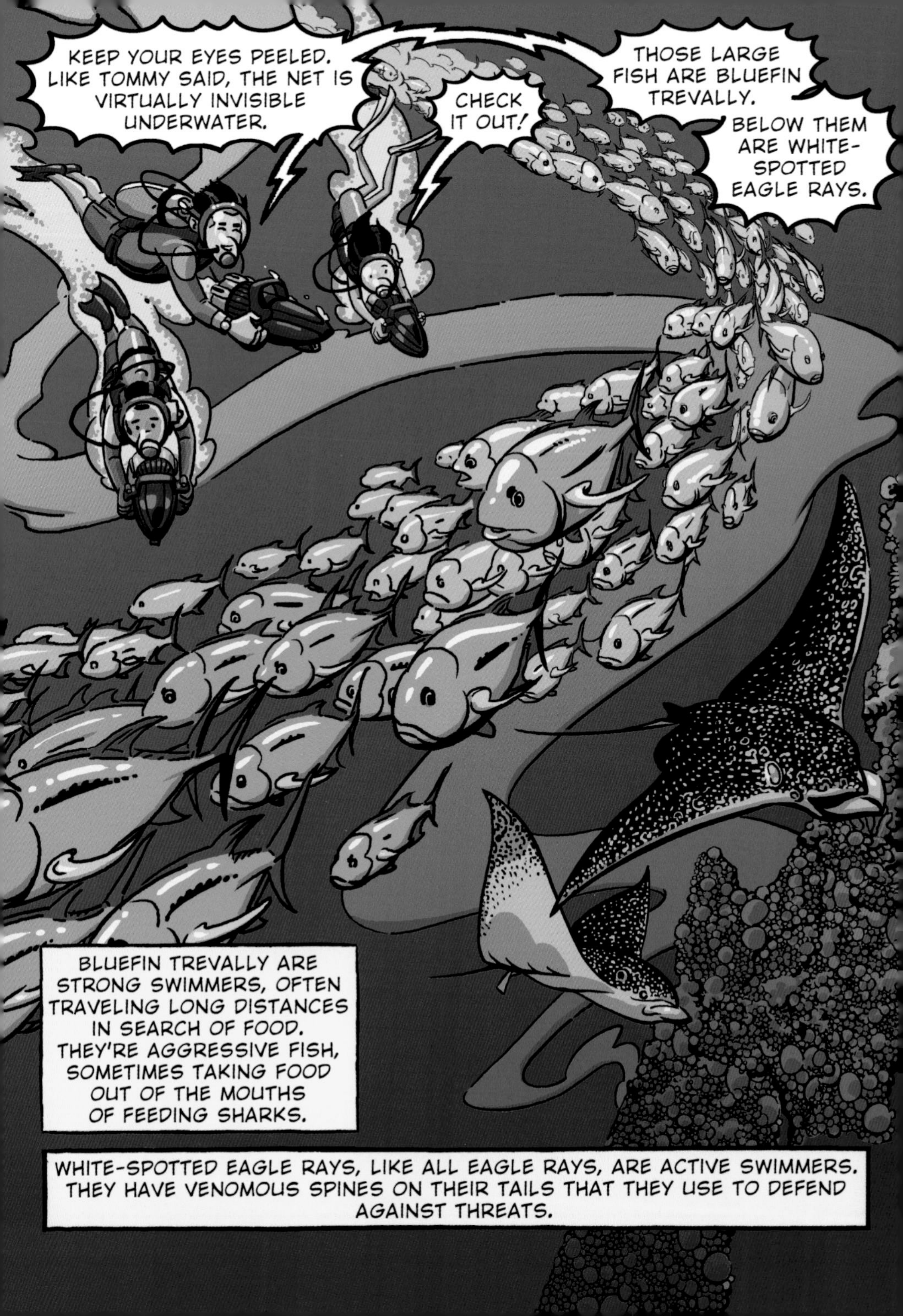
KEEP YOUR EYES PEELED. LIKE TOMMY SAID, THE NET IS VIRTUALLY INVISIBLE UNDERWATER.
CHECK IT OUT!
THOSE LARGE FISH ARE BLUEFIN TREVALLY.
BELOW THEM ARE WHITE-SPOTTED EAGLE RAYS.
BLUEFIN TREVALLY ARE STRONG SWIMMERS, OFTEN TRAVELING LONG DISTANCES IN SEARCH OF FOOD. THEY'RE AGGRESSIVE FISH, SOMETIMES TAKING FOOD OUT OF THE MOUTHS OF FEEDING SHARKS.
WHITE-SPOTTED EAGLE RAYS, LIKE ALL EAGLE RAYS, ARE ACTIVE SWIMMERS. THEY HAVE VENOMOUS SPINES ON THEIR TAILS THAT THEY USE TO DEFEND AGAINST THREATS.

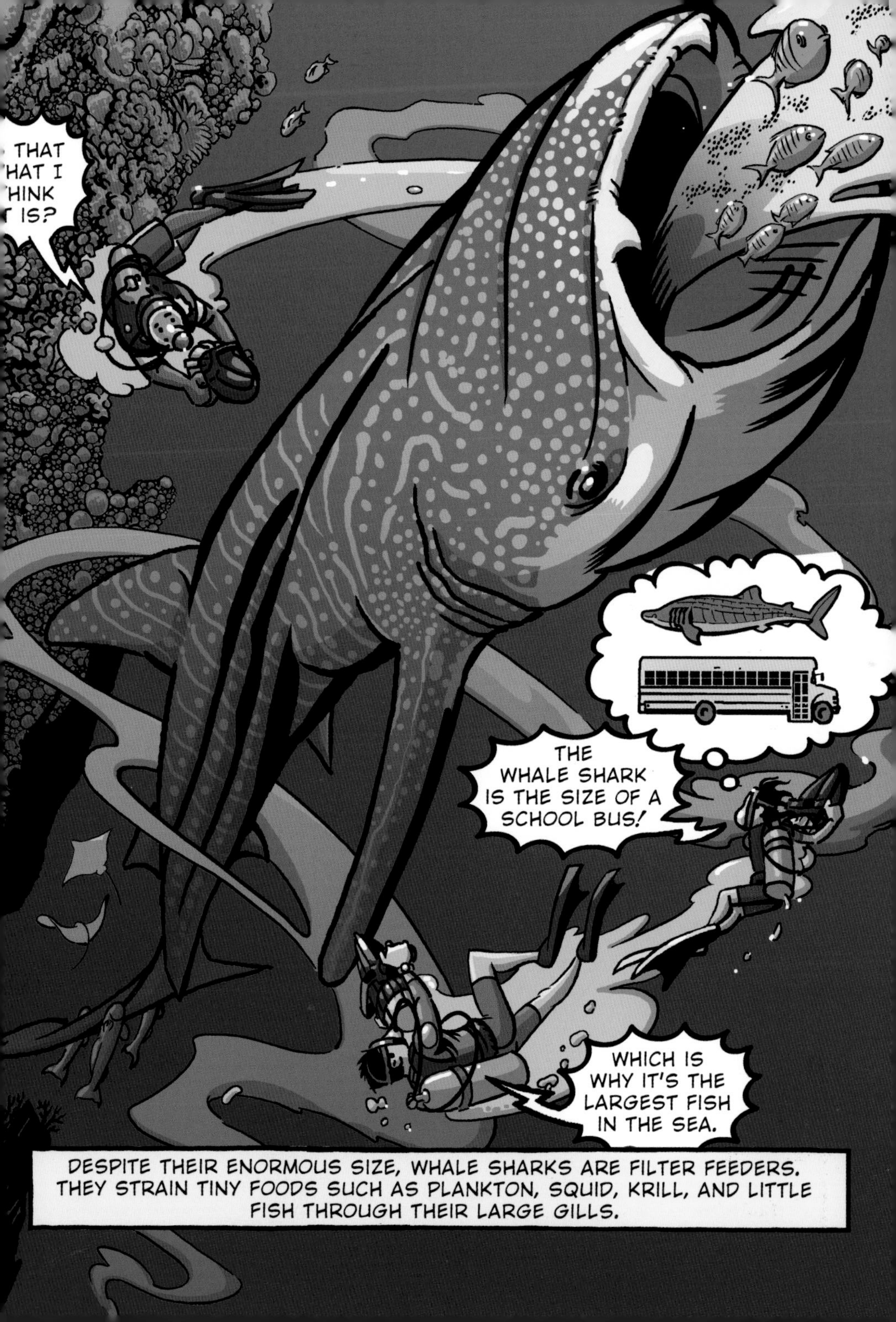
THAT
HAT I
HINK
IS?
THE WHALE SHARK IS THE SIZE OF A SCHOOL BUS!
WHICH IS WHY IT'S THE LARGEST FISH IN THE SEA.
DESPITE THEIR ENORMOUS SIZE, WHALE SHARKS ARE FILTER FEEDERS. THEY STRAIN TINY FOODS SUCH AS PLANKTON, SQUID, KRILL, AND LITTLE FISH THROUGH THEIR LARGE GILLS.

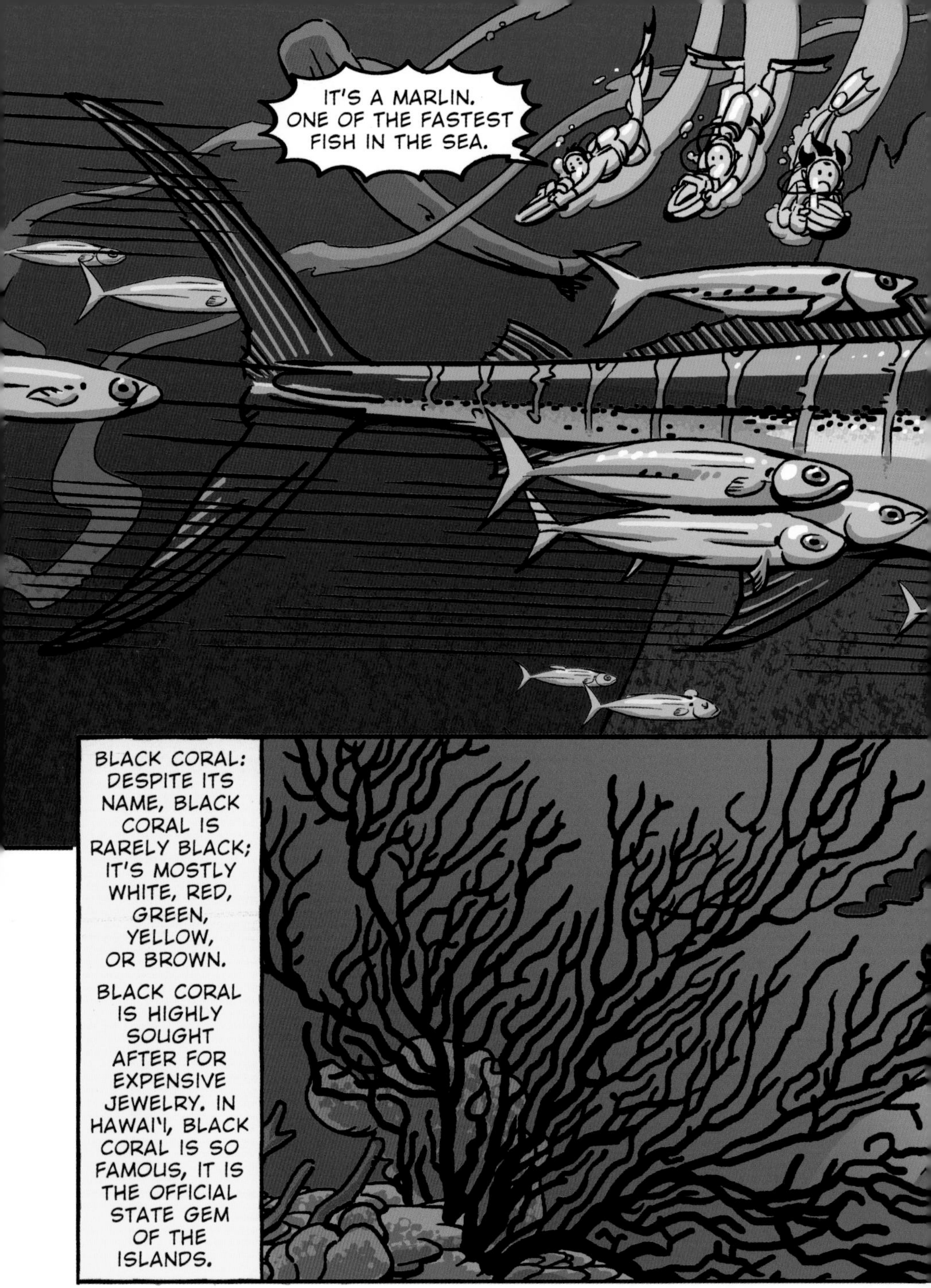
IT'S A MARLIN. ONE OF THE FASTEST FISH IN THE SEA.
BLACK CORAL: DESPITE ITS NAME, BLACK CORAL IS RARELY BLACK; IT'S MOSTLY WHITE, RED, GREEN, YELLOW, OR BROWN.
BLACK CORAL IS HIGHLY SOUGHT AFTER FOR EXPENSIVE JEWELRY. IN HAWAI'I, BLACK CORAL IS SO FAMOUS, IT IS THE OFFICIAL STATE GEM OF THE ISLANDS.

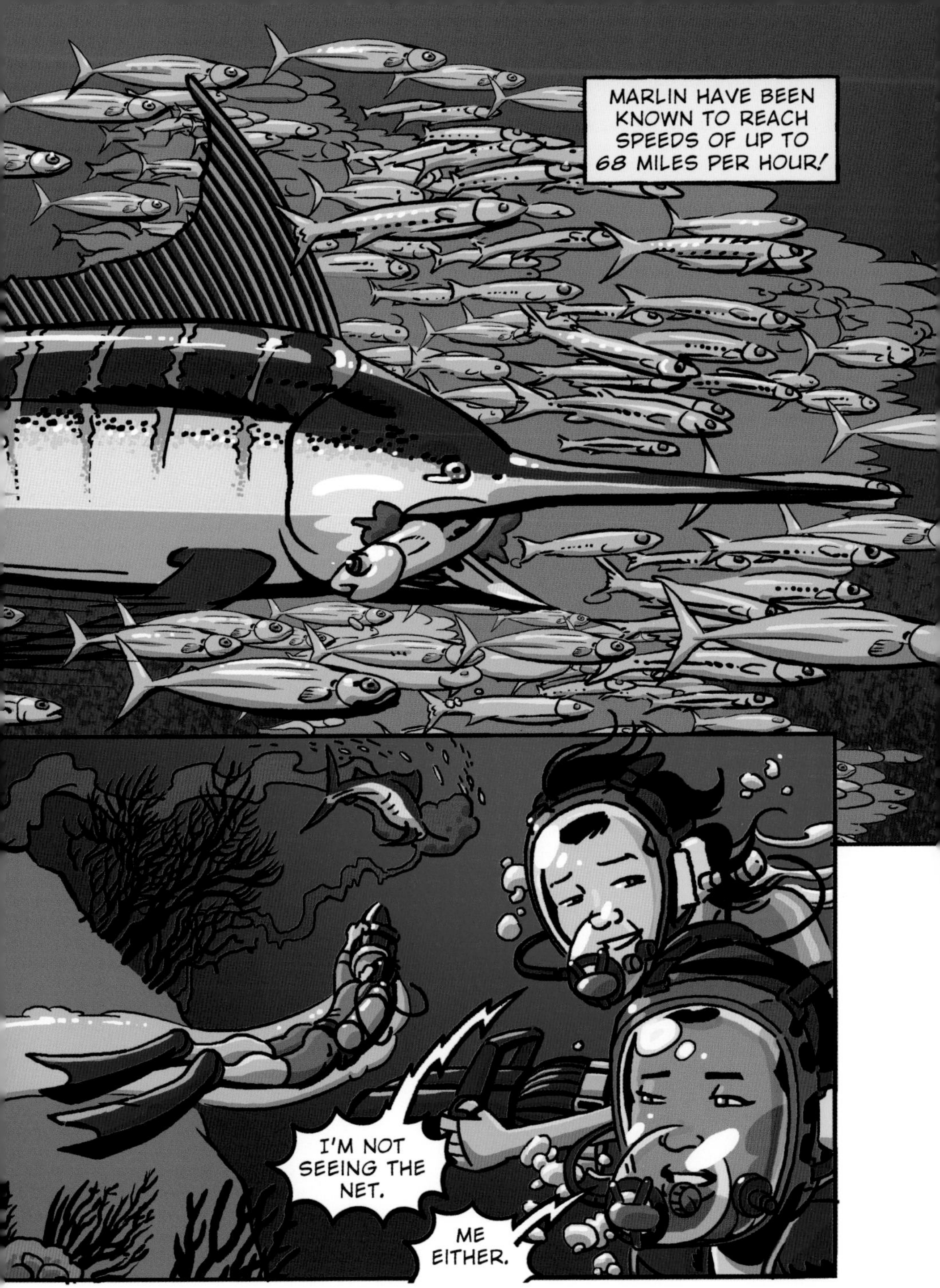
MARLIN HAVE BEEN KNOWN TO REACH SPEEDS OF UP TO 68 MILES PER HOUR!
I'M NOT SEEING THE NET.
ME EITHER.

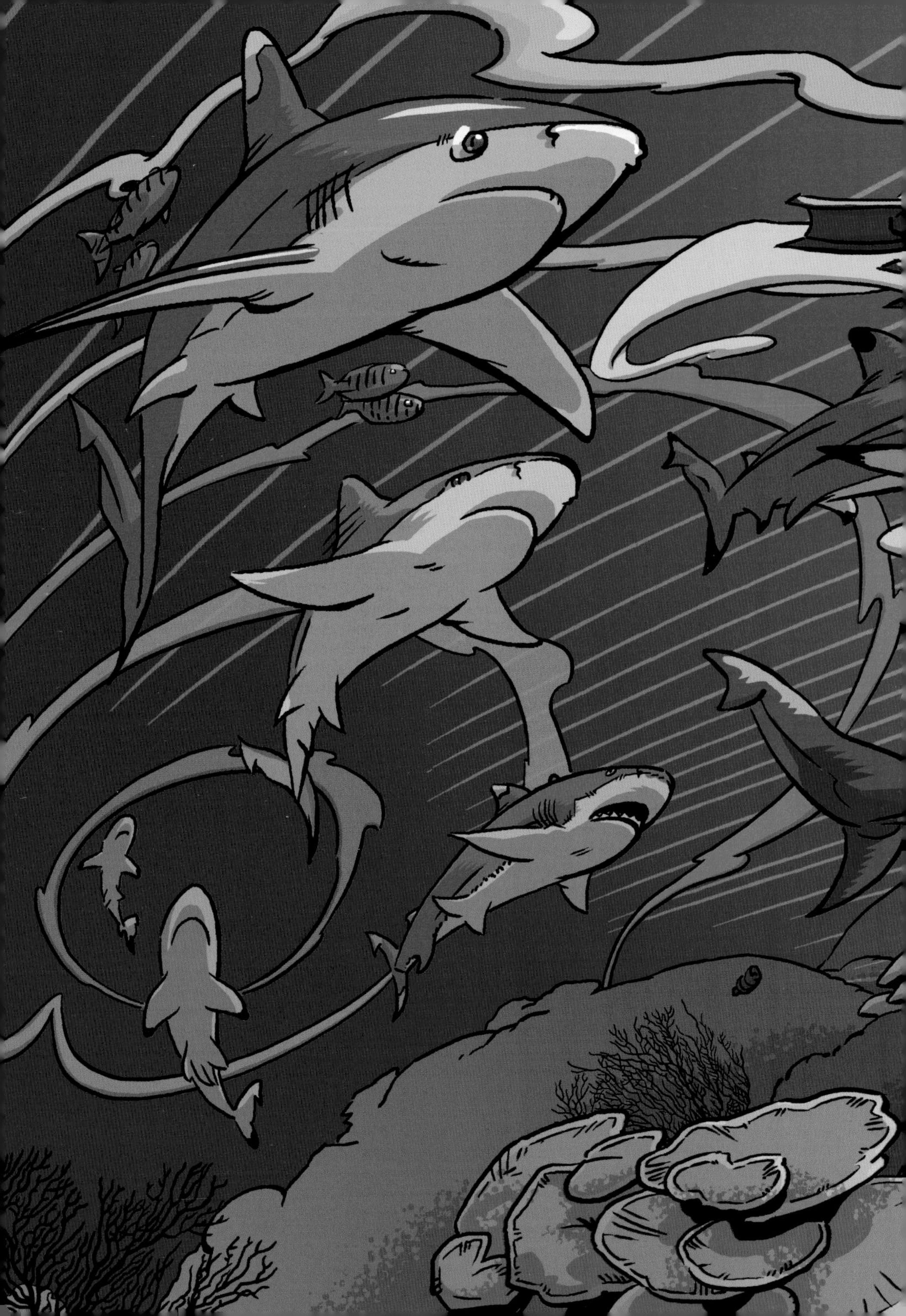

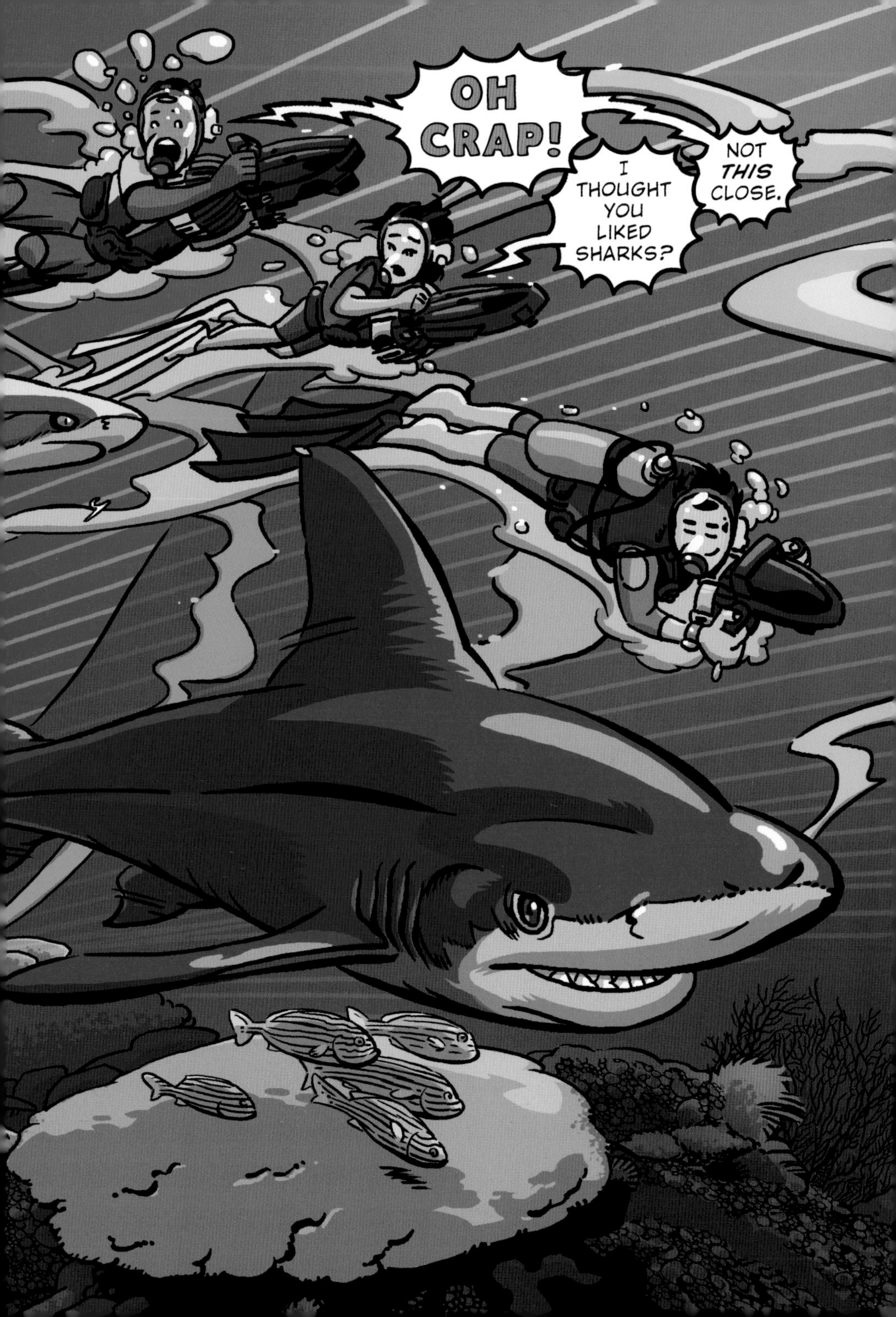
OH CRAP!
I THOUGHT YOU LIKED SHARKS?
NOT *THIS* CLOSE.

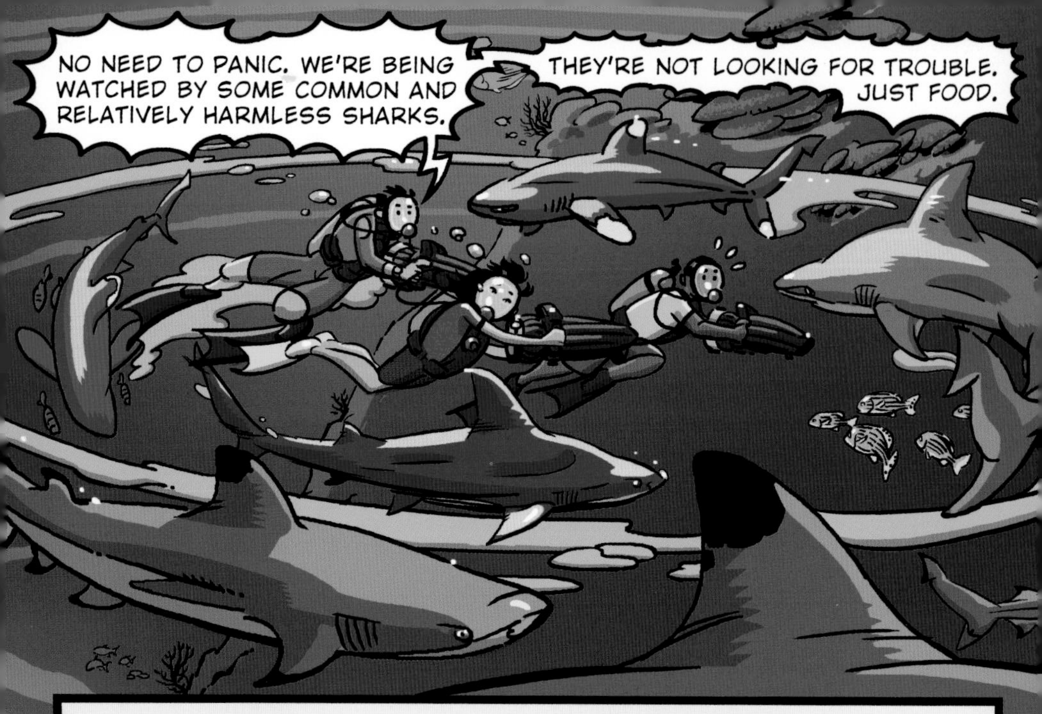
NO NEED TO PANIC. WE'RE BEING WATCHED BY SOME COMMON AND RELATIVELY HARMLESS SHARKS.
THEY'RE NOT LOOKING FOR TROUBLE. JUST FOOD.

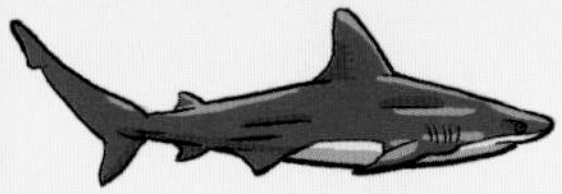

SANDBAR SHARK

REACHING 5 TO 6 FEET IN LENGTH, THIS SHARK FEEDS ON REEF FISH AND CRUSTACEANS.

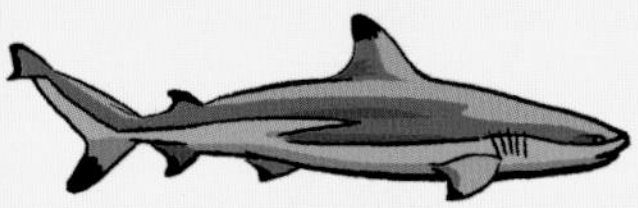

BLACKTIP SHARK

REACHING 8 FEET IN LENGTH AND KNOWN FOR THE BLACK TIPS ON ITS FINS, THIS SHARK PREFERS TO EAT BONY FISH AND THE OCCASIONAL OCTOPUS OR SQUID.

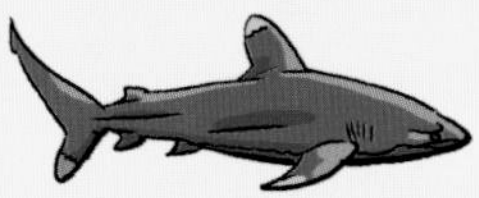

WHITETIP REEF SHARK

REACHING 6 FEET IN LENGTH AND KNOWN FOR THE WHITE TIPS ON ITS FINS, THIS SHARK DOES ENJOY OCTOPUS AND SQUID, ALONG WITH REEF FISH.

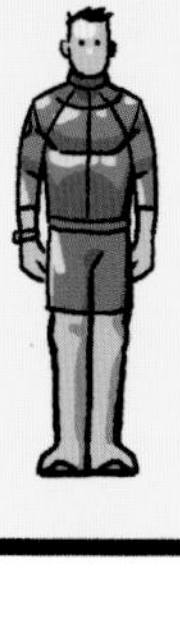

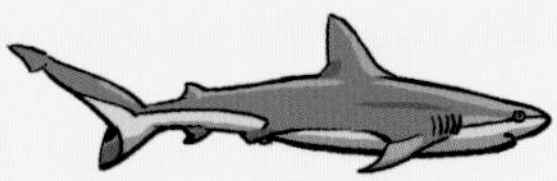

GREY REEF SHARK

REACHING 7 FEET IN LENGTH, THIS SHARK, LIKE THE OTHERS, PREFERS REEF FISH AND THE LESS FREQUENT OCTOPUS OR SQUID.

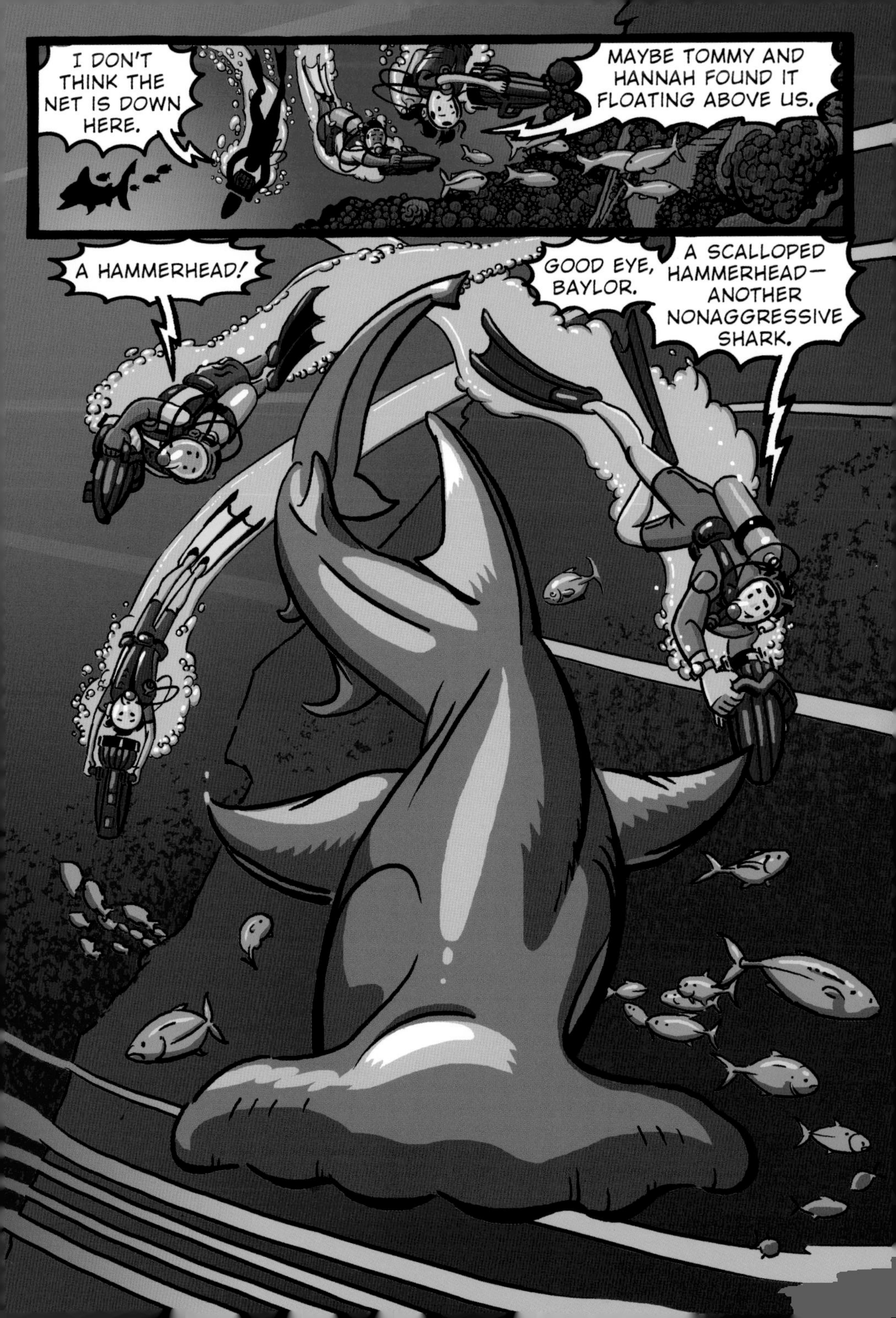
I DON'T THINK THE NET IS DOWN HERE.
MAYBE TOMMY AND HANNAH FOUND IT FLOATING ABOVE US.
A HAMMERHEAD!
GOOD EYE, BAYLOR.
A SCALLOPED HAMMERHEAD—ANOTHER NONAGGRESSIVE SHARK.

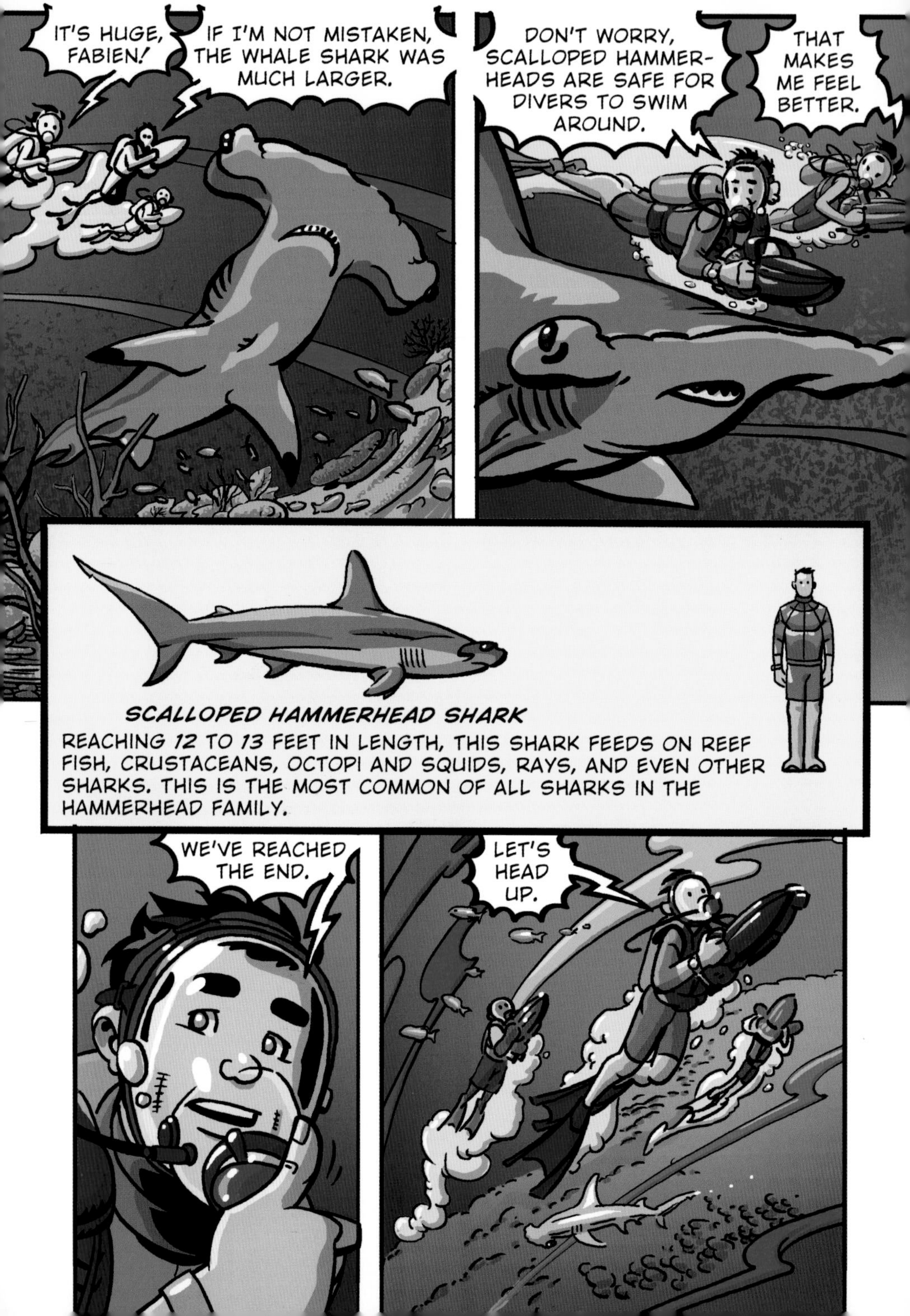
IT'S HUGE, FABIEN!
IF I'M NOT MISTAKEN, THE WHALE SHARK WAS MUCH LARGER.
DON'T WORRY, SCALLOPED HAMMER-HEADS ARE SAFE FOR DIVERS TO SWIM AROUND.
THAT MAKES ME FEEL BETTER.
SCALLOPED HAMMERHEAD SHARK
REACHING 12 TO 13 FEET IN LENGTH, THIS SHARK FEEDS ON REEF FISH, CRUSTACEANS, OCTOPI AND SQUIDS, RAYS, AND EVEN OTHER SHARKS. THIS IS THE MOST COMMON OF ALL SHARKS IN THE HAMMERHEAD FAMILY.
WE'VE REACHED THE END.
LET'S HEAD UP.

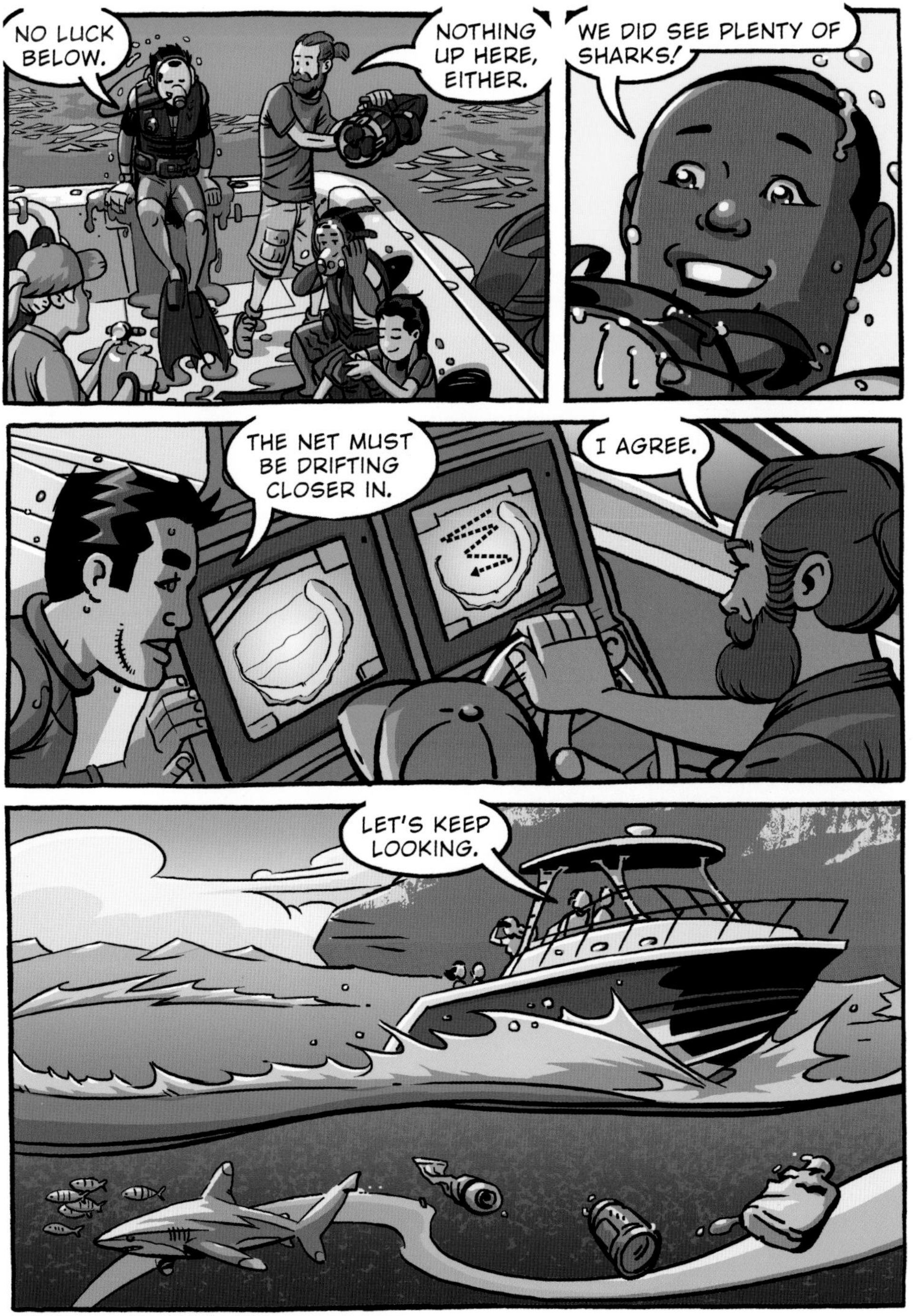
NO LUCK BELOW.
NOTHING UP HERE, EITHER.
WE DID SEE PLENTY OF SHARKS!
THE NET MUST BE DRIFTING CLOSER IN.
I AGREE.
LET'S KEEP LOOKING.

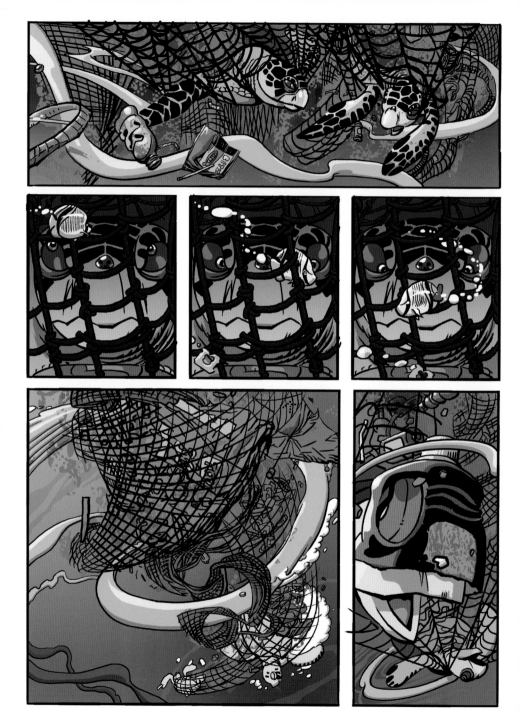

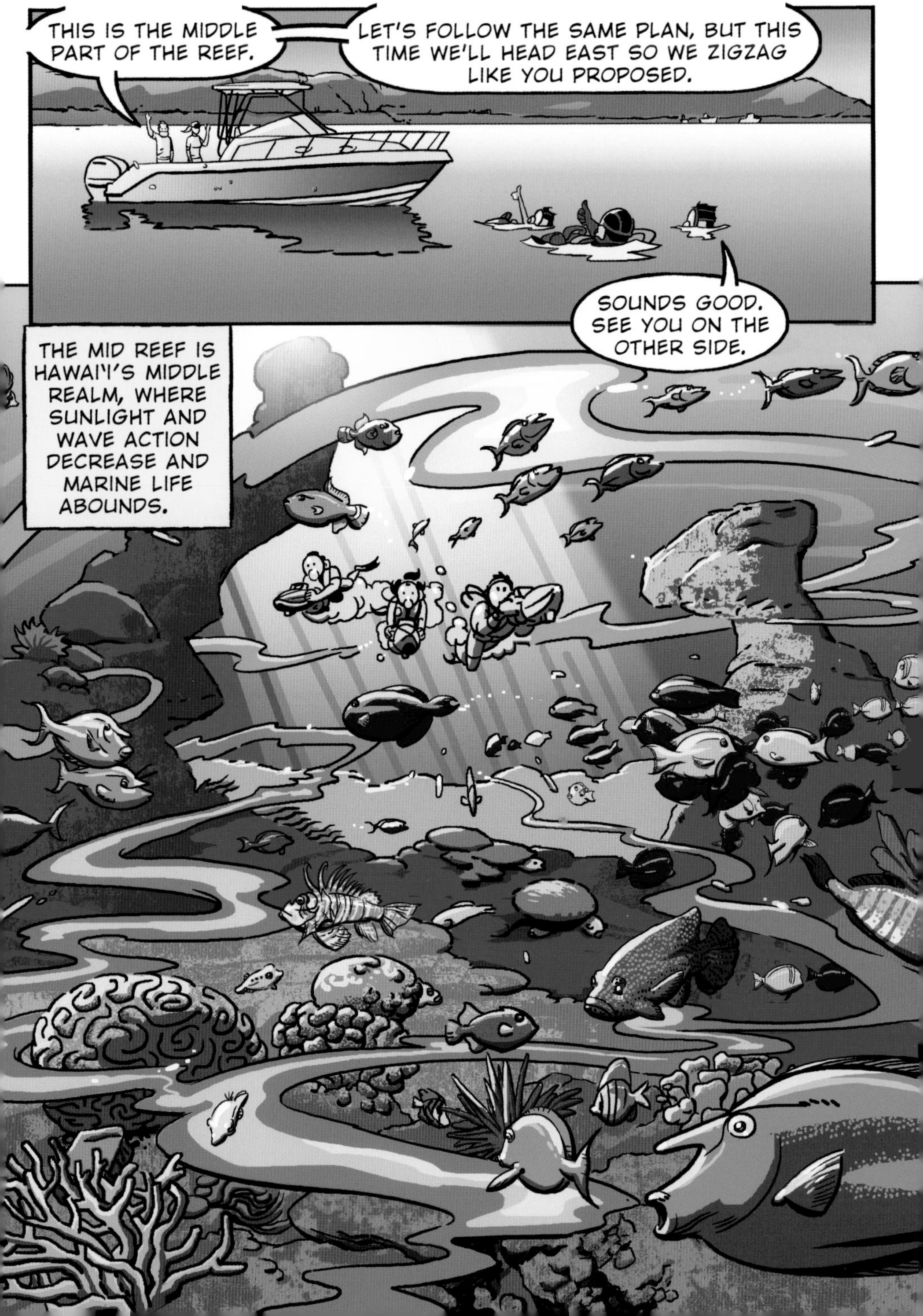

THIS IS THE MIDDLE PART OF THE REEF.
LET'S FOLLOW THE SAME PLAN, BUT THIS TIME WE'LL HEAD EAST SO WE ZIGZAG LIKE YOU PROPOSED.
SOUNDS GOOD. SEE YOU ON THE OTHER SIDE.
THE MID REEF IS HAWAI'I'S MIDDLE REALM, WHERE SUNLIGHT AND WAVE ACTION DECREASE AND MARINE LIFE ABOUNDS.

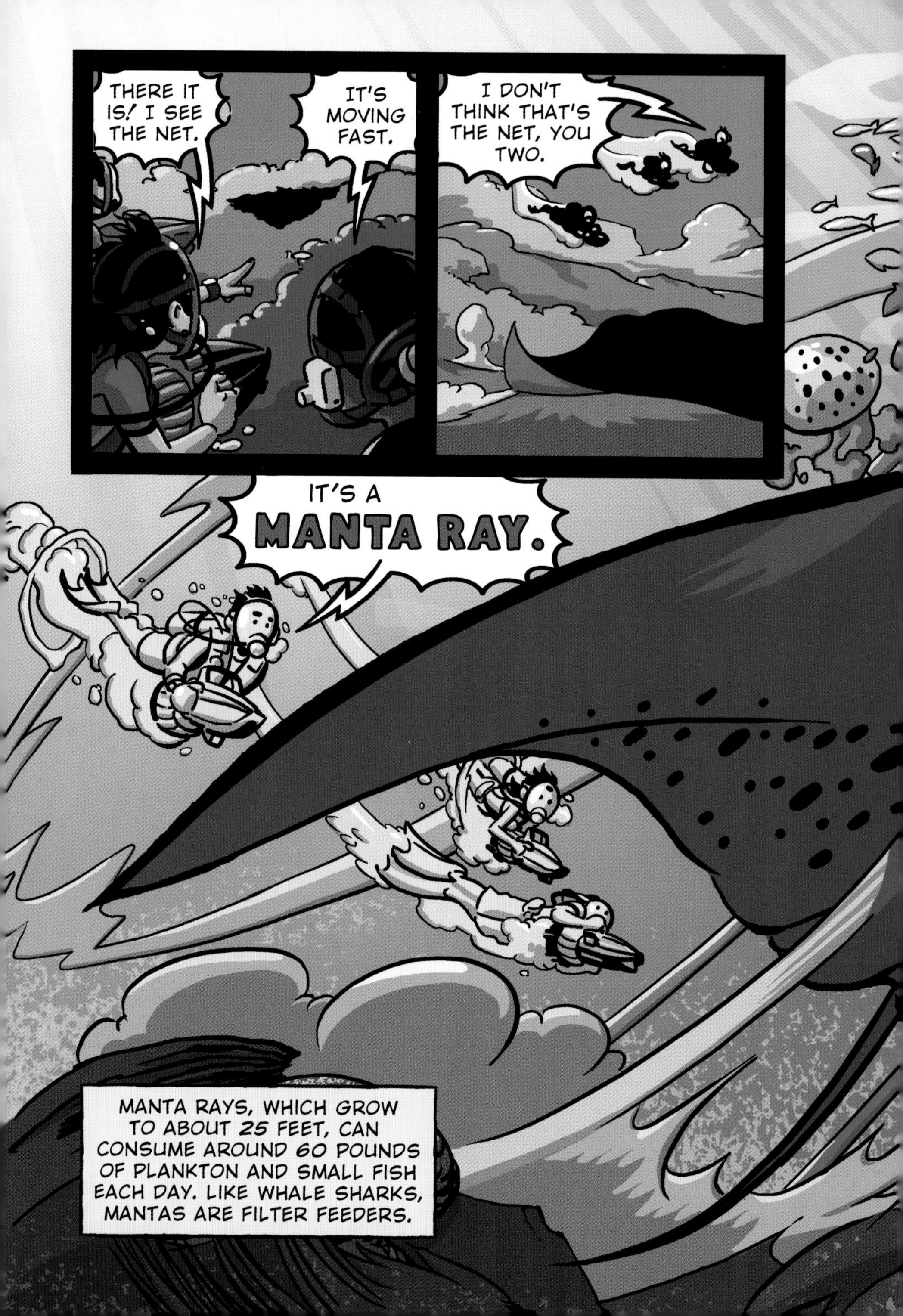
THERE IT IS! I SEE THE NET.
IT'S MOVING FAST.
I DON'T THINK THAT'S THE NET, YOU TWO.
IT'S A MANTA RAY.
MANTA RAYS, WHICH GROW TO ABOUT 25 FEET, CAN CONSUME AROUND 60 POUNDS OF PLANKTON AND SMALL FISH EACH DAY. LIKE WHALE SHARKS, MANTAS ARE FILTER FEEDERS.

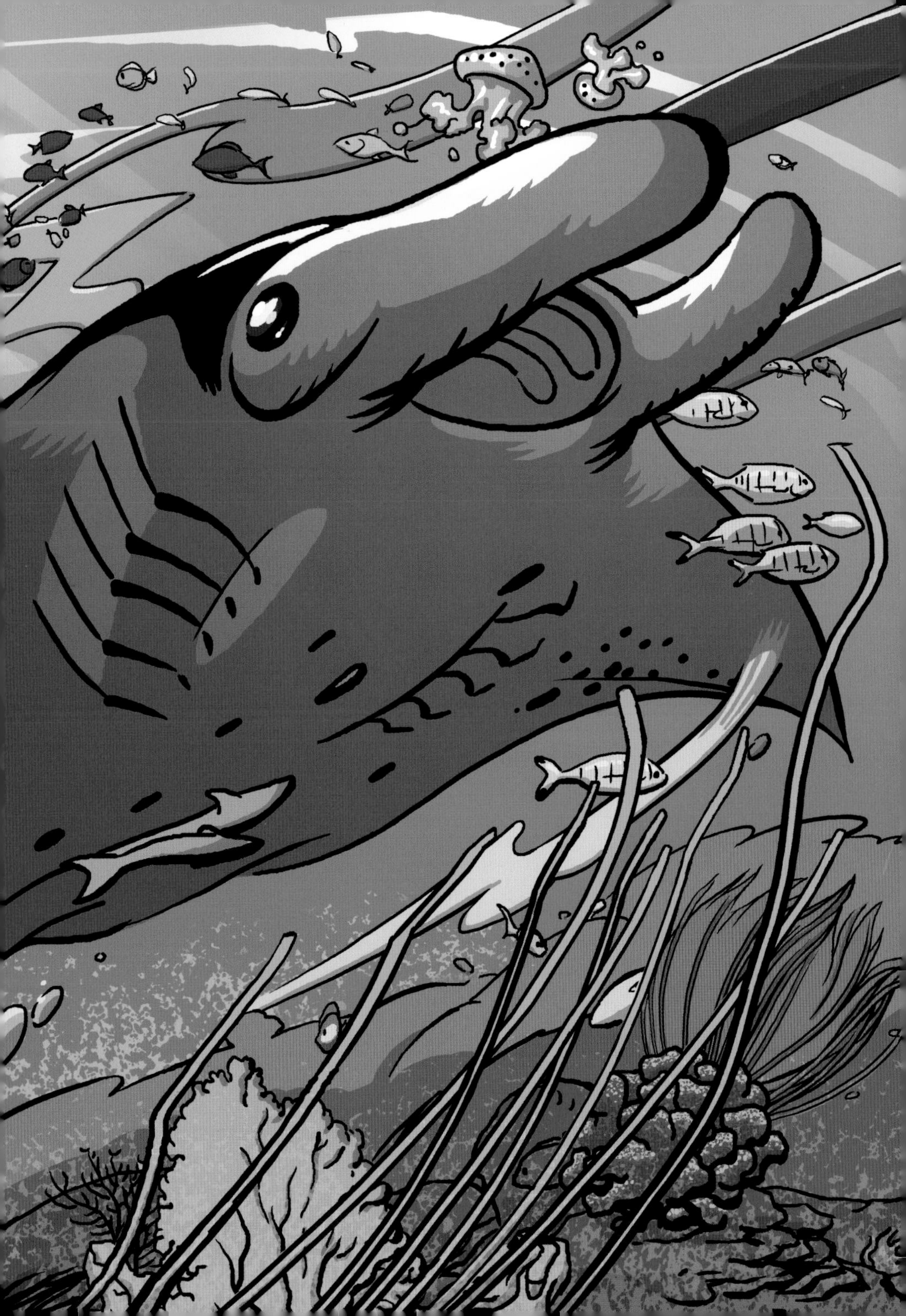

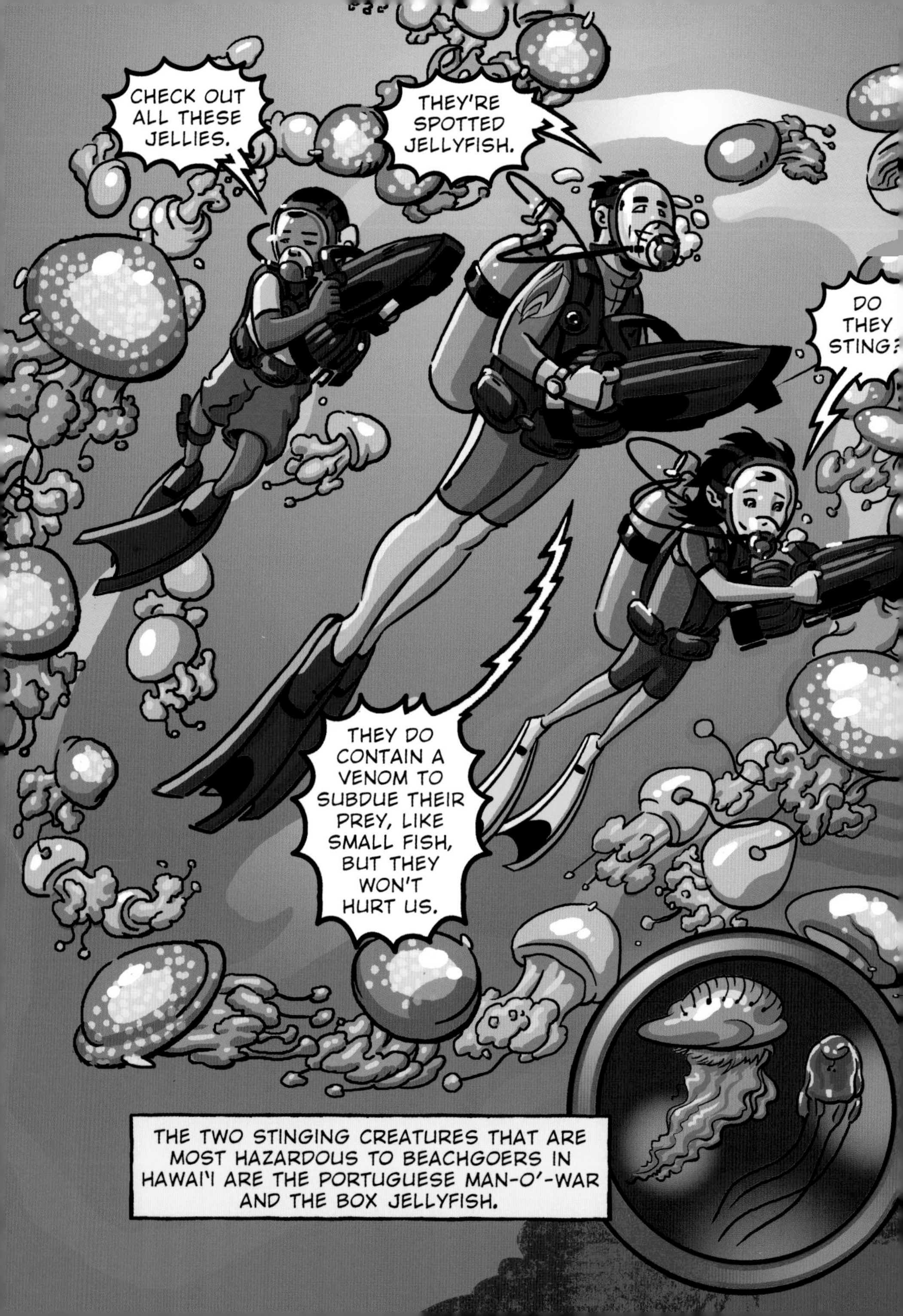
CHECK OUT ALL THESE JELLIES.
THEY'RE SPOTTED JELLYFISH.
DO THEY STING?
THEY DO CONTAIN A VENOM TO SUBDUE THEIR PREY, LIKE SMALL FISH, BUT THEY WON'T HURT US.
THE TWO STINGING CREATURES THAT ARE MOST HAZARDOUS TO BEACHGOERS IN HAWAI'I ARE THE PORTUGUESE MAN-O'-WAR AND THE BOX JELLYFISH.

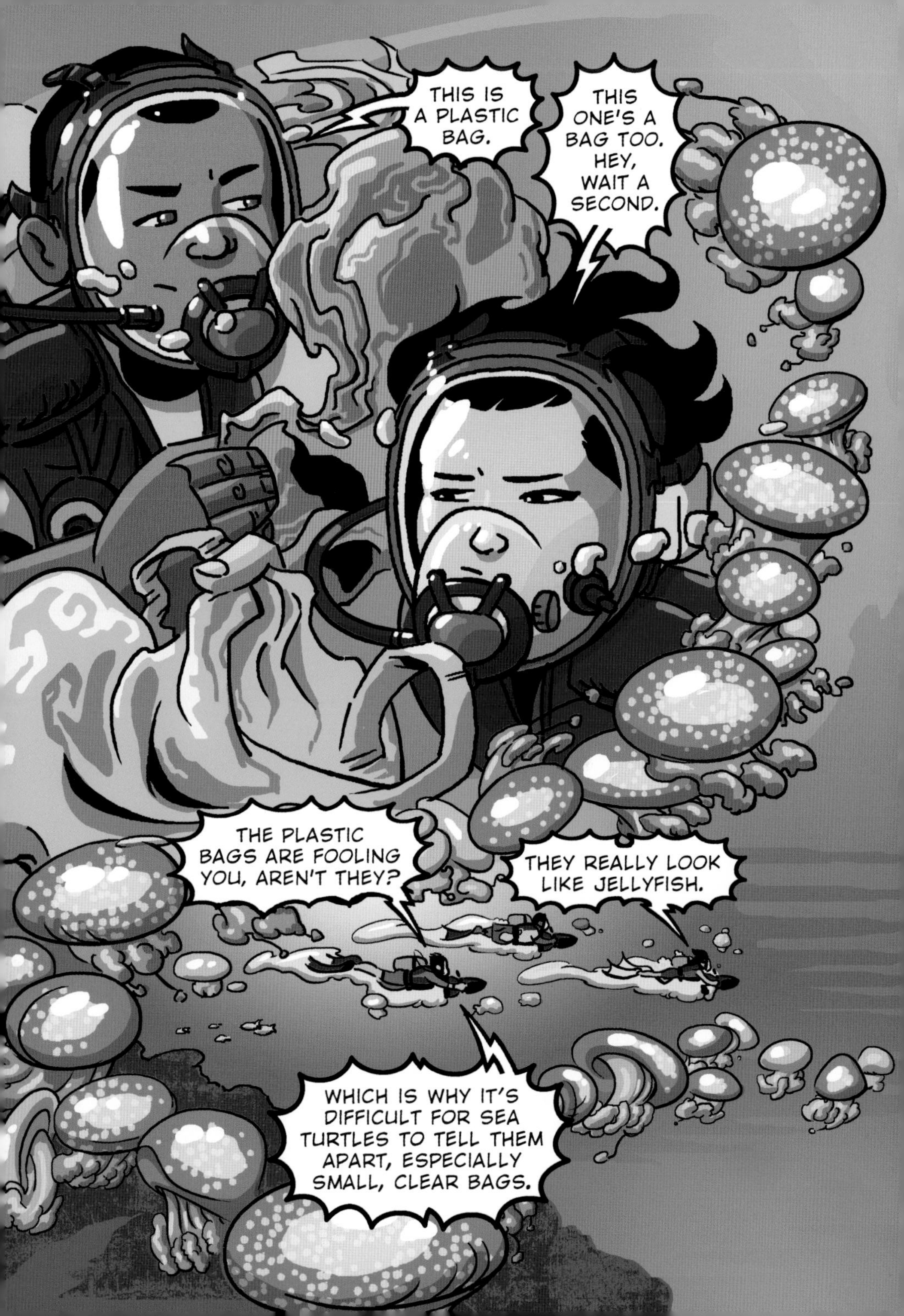
THIS IS A PLASTIC BAG.
THIS ONE'S A BAG TOO. HEY, WAIT A SECOND.
THE PLASTIC BAGS ARE FOOLING YOU, AREN'T THEY?
THEY REALLY LOOK LIKE JELLYFISH.
WHICH IS WHY IT'S DIFFICULT FOR SEA TURTLES TO TELL THEM APART, ESPECIALLY SMALL, CLEAR BAGS.

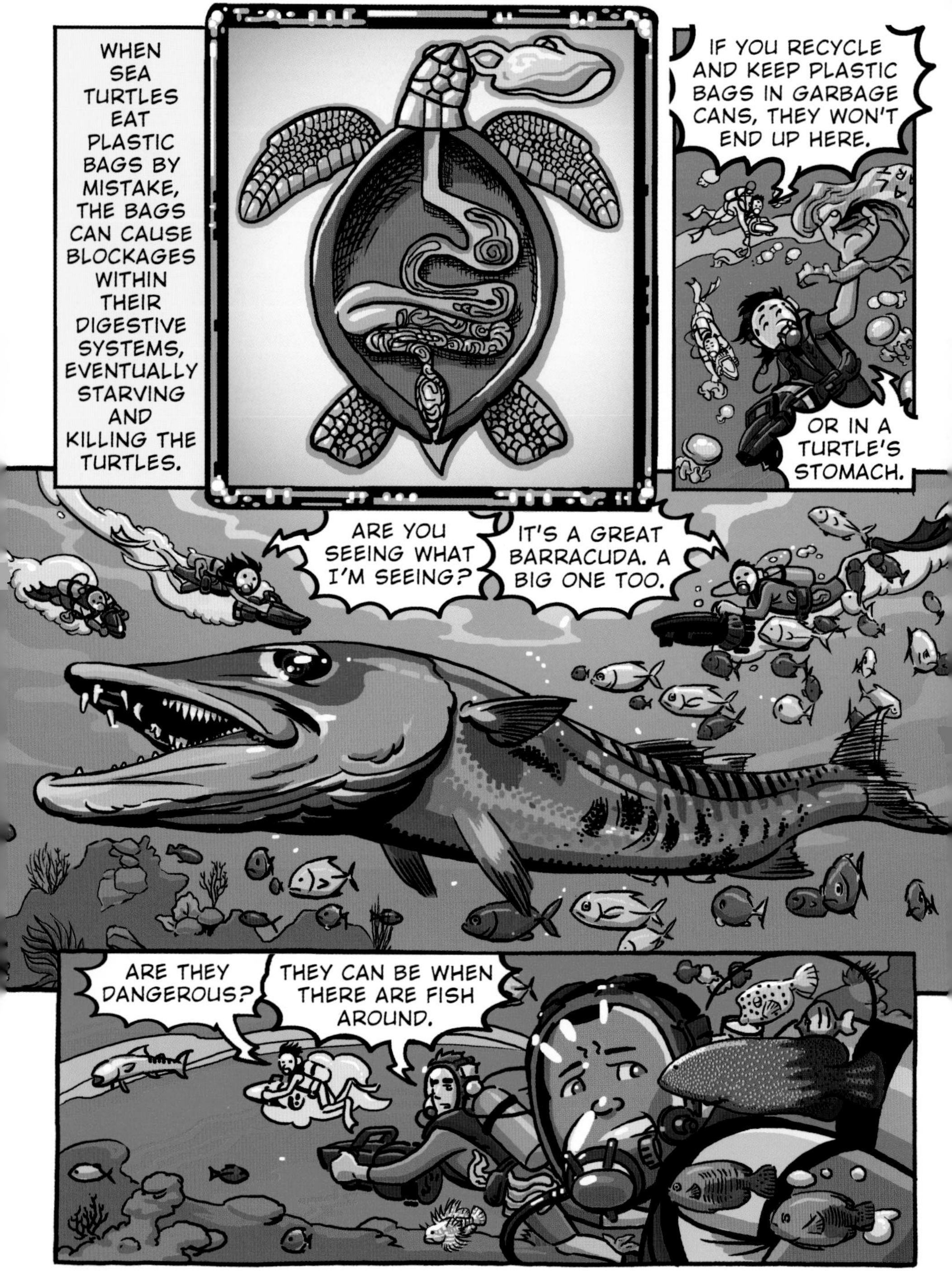
WHEN SEA TURTLES EAT PLASTIC BAGS BY MISTAKE, THE BAGS CAN CAUSE BLOCKAGES WITHIN THEIR DIGESTIVE SYSTEMS, EVENTUALLY STARVING AND KILLING THE TURTLES.
IF YOU RECYCLE AND KEEP PLASTIC BAGS IN GARBAGE CANS, THEY WON'T END UP HERE.
OR IN A TURTLE'S STOMACH.
ARE YOU SEEING WHAT I'M SEEING?
IT'S A GREAT BARRACUDA. A BIG ONE TOO.
ARE THEY DANGEROUS?
THEY CAN BE WHEN THERE ARE FISH AROUND.

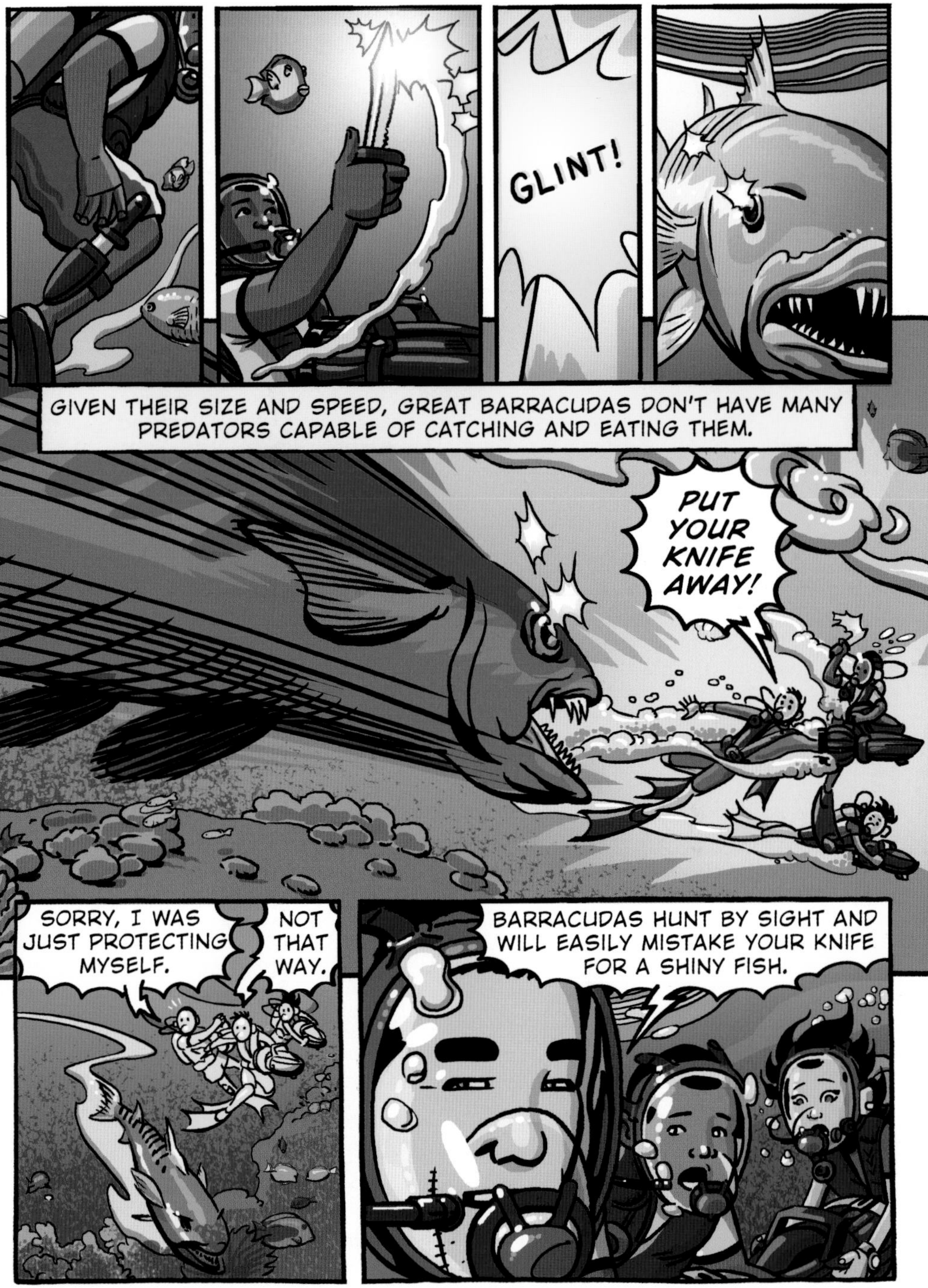
GLINT!
GIVEN THEIR SIZE AND SPEED, GREAT BARRACUDAS DON'T HAVE MANY PREDATORS CAPABLE OF CATCHING AND EATING THEM.
PUT YOUR KNIFE AWAY!
SORRY, I WAS JUST PROTECTING MYSELF.
NOT THAT WAY.
BARRACUDAS HUNT BY SIGHT AND WILL EASILY MISTAKE YOUR KNIFE FOR A SHINY FISH.

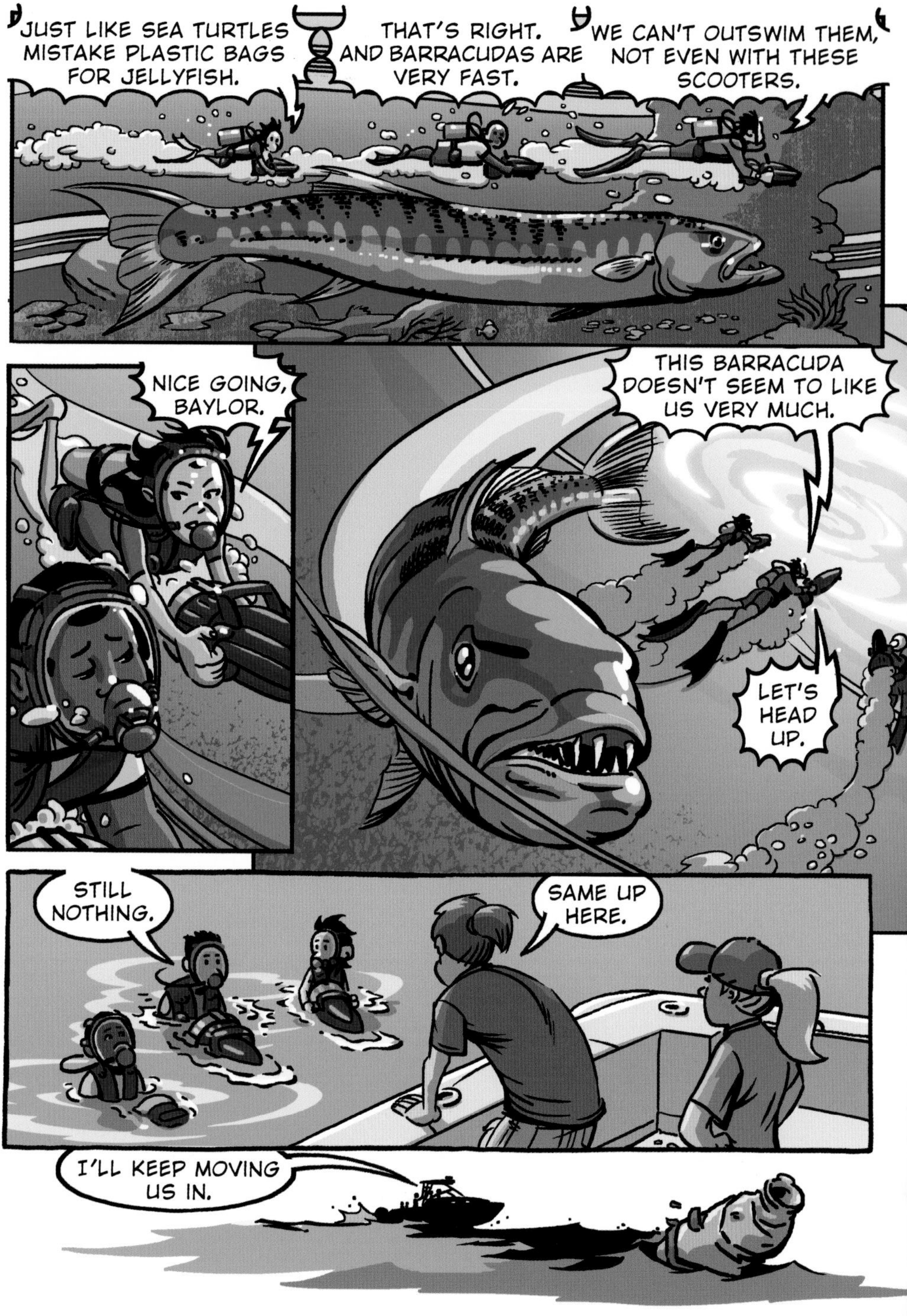
JUST LIKE SEA TURTLES MISTAKE PLASTIC BAGS FOR JELLYFISH.
THAT'S RIGHT. AND BARRACUDAS ARE VERY FAST.
WE CAN'T OUTSWIM THEM, NOT EVEN WITH THESE SCOOTERS.
NICE GOING, BAYLOR.
THIS BARRACUDA DOESN'T SEEM TO LIKE US VERY MUCH.
LET'S HEAD UP.
STILL NOTHING.
SAME UP HERE.
I'LL KEEP MOVING US IN.

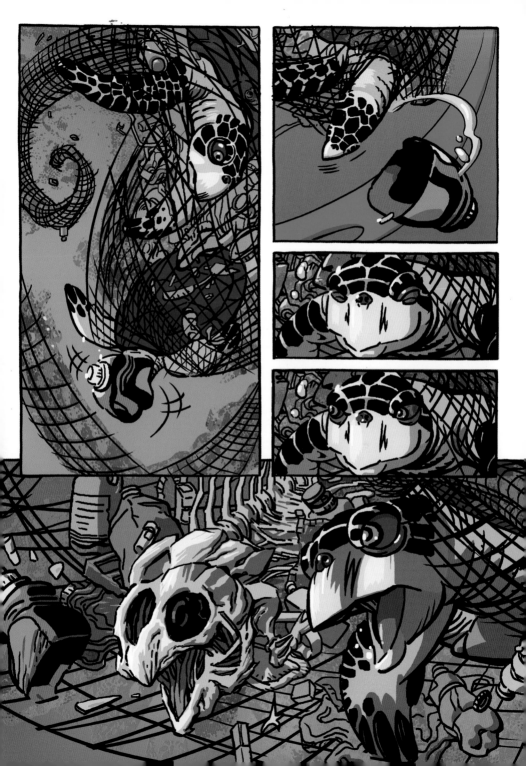

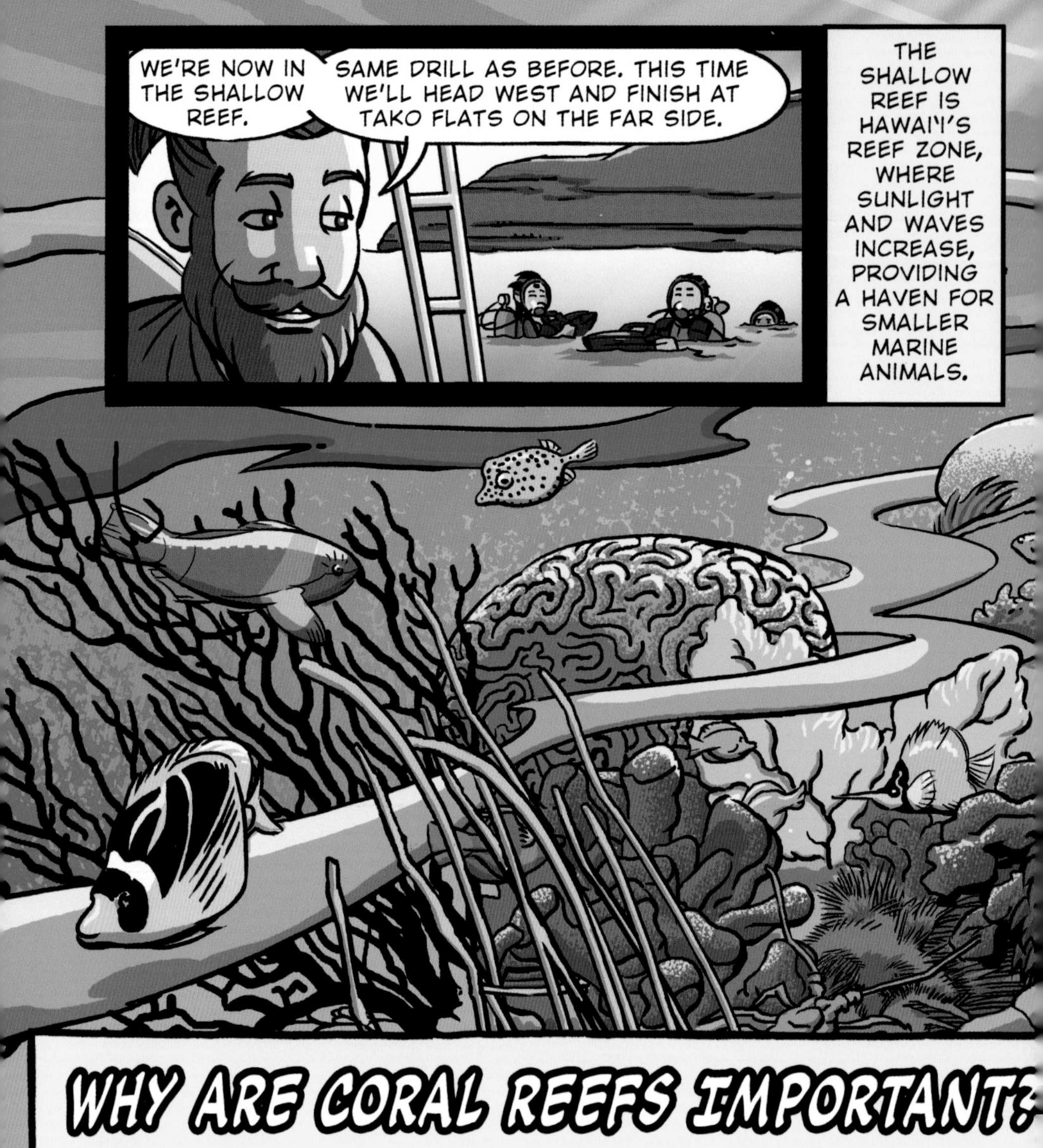

WE'RE NOW IN THE SHALLOW REEF.
SAME DRILL AS BEFORE. THIS TIME WE'LL HEAD WEST AND FINISH AT TAKO FLATS ON THE FAR SIDE.
THE SHALLOW REEF IS HAWAI'I'S REEF ZONE, WHERE SUNLIGHT AND WAVES INCREASE, PROVIDING A HAVEN FOR SMALLER MARINE ANIMALS.

WHY ARE CORAL REEFS IMPORTANT?

HABITAT: CORAL IS A LIVING, GROWING ORGANISM. LIKE UNDERWATER CITIES, CORAL REEFS ARE HOME TO OVER 1 MILLION DIFFERENT MARINE ORGANISMS.

FOOD: FAMILIES AND COMMERCIAL FISHERS HARVEST AND DEPEND ON A LARGE VARIETY AND NUMBER OF FISH AND INVERTEBRATES THAT LIVE ON THE REEF, MAKING REEF FISH AN IMPORTANT PART OF THE FOOD CHAIN.

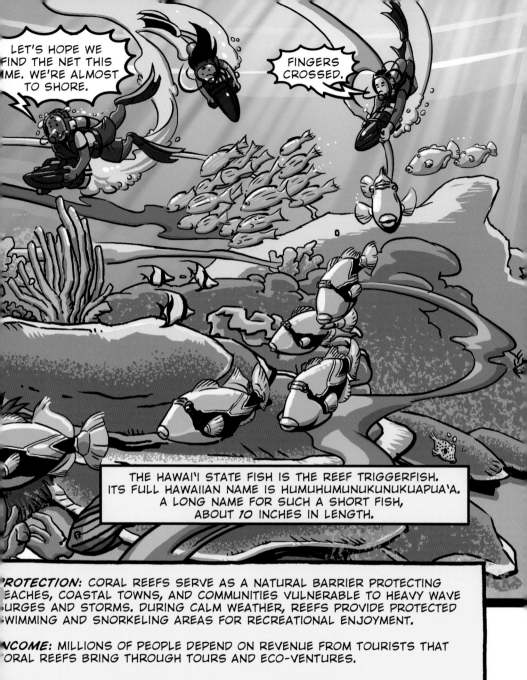

LET'S HOPE WE FIND THE NET THIS TIME. WE'RE ALMOST TO SHORE.

FINGERS CROSSED.

THE HAWAI'I STATE FISH IS THE REEF TRIGGERFISH. ITS FULL HAWAIIAN NAME IS HUMUHUMUNUKUNUKUAPUA'A. A LONG NAME FOR SUCH A SHORT FISH, ABOUT 10 INCHES IN LENGTH.

PROTECTION: CORAL REEFS SERVE AS A NATURAL BARRIER PROTECTING BEACHES, COASTAL TOWNS, AND COMMUNITIES VULNERABLE TO HEAVY WAVE SURGES AND STORMS. DURING CALM WEATHER, REEFS PROVIDE PROTECTED SWIMMING AND SNORKELING AREAS FOR RECREATIONAL ENJOYMENT.

INCOME: MILLIONS OF PEOPLE DEPEND ON REVENUE FROM TOURISTS THAT CORAL REEFS BRING THROUGH TOURS AND ECO-VENTURES.

MEDICINE: CORAL REEFS CAN SAVE LIVES. MANY LIFESAVING DRUGS HAVE BEEN DEVELOPED FROM CHEMICALS FOUND IN REEF ORGANISMS, SUCH AS SPONGES, SNAILS, AND CORALS.

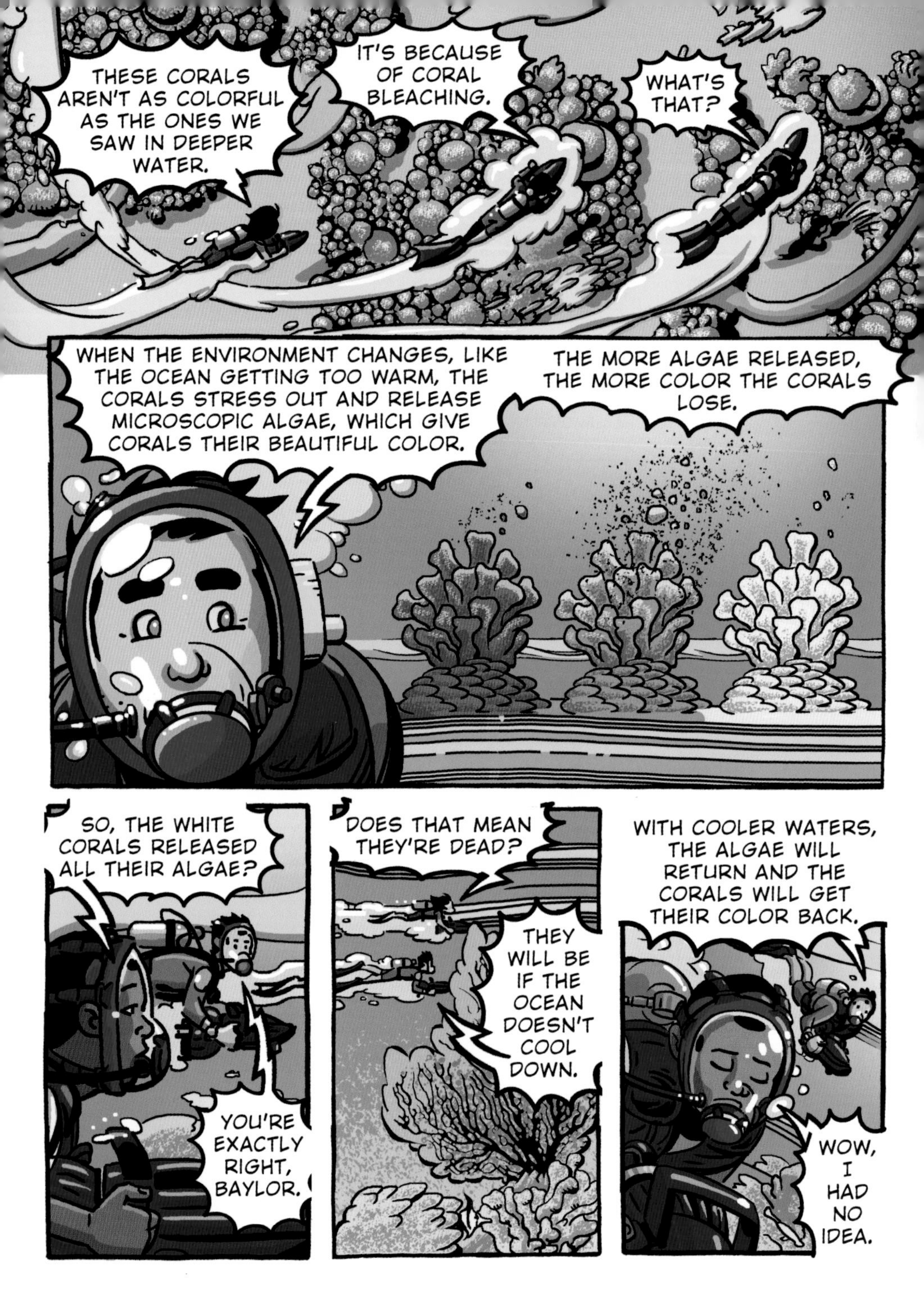
THESE CORALS AREN'T AS COLORFUL AS THE ONES WE SAW IN DEEPER WATER.
IT'S BECAUSE OF CORAL BLEACHING.
WHAT'S THAT?
WHEN THE ENVIRONMENT CHANGES, LIKE THE OCEAN GETTING TOO WARM, THE CORALS STRESS OUT AND RELEASE MICROSCOPIC ALGAE, WHICH GIVE CORALS THEIR BEAUTIFUL COLOR.
THE MORE ALGAE RELEASED, THE MORE COLOR THE CORALS LOSE.
SO, THE WHITE CORALS RELEASED ALL THEIR ALGAE?
YOU'RE EXACTLY RIGHT, BAYLOR.
DOES THAT MEAN THEY'RE DEAD?
THEY WILL BE IF THE OCEAN DOESN'T COOL DOWN.
WITH COOLER WATERS, THE ALGAE WILL RETURN AND THE CORALS WILL GET THEIR COLOR BACK.
WOW, I HAD NO IDEA.

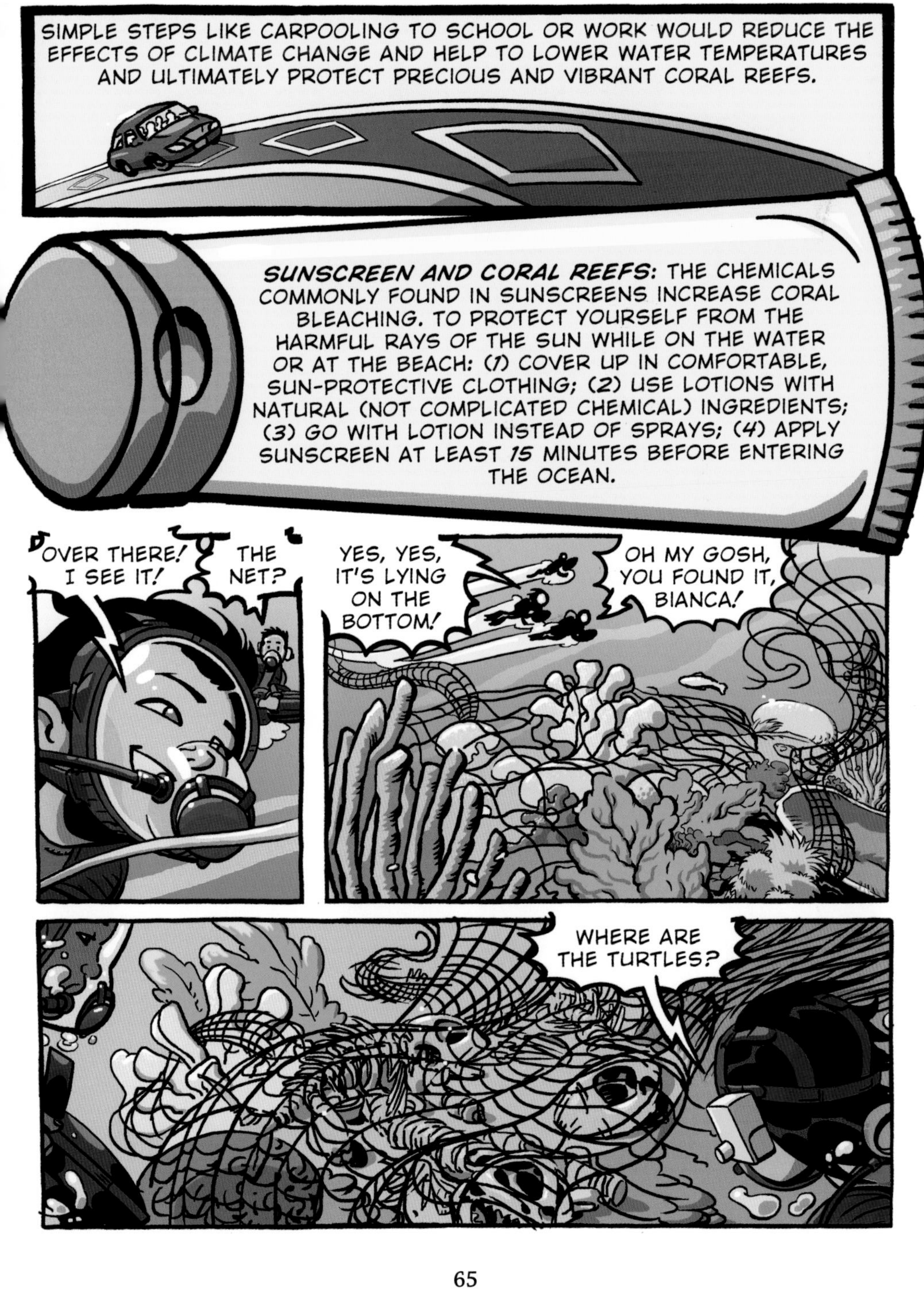
SIMPLE STEPS LIKE CARPOOLING TO SCHOOL OR WORK WOULD REDUCE THE EFFECTS OF CLIMATE CHANGE AND HELP TO LOWER WATER TEMPERATURES AND ULTIMATELY PROTECT PRECIOUS AND VIBRANT CORAL REEFS.
SUNSCREEN AND CORAL REEFS: THE CHEMICALS COMMONLY FOUND IN SUNSCREENS INCREASE CORAL BLEACHING. TO PROTECT YOURSELF FROM THE HARMFUL RAYS OF THE SUN WHILE ON THE WATER OR AT THE BEACH: (1) COVER UP IN COMFORTABLE, SUN-PROTECTIVE CLOTHING; (2) USE LOTIONS WITH NATURAL (NOT COMPLICATED CHEMICAL) INGREDIENTS; (3) GO WITH LOTION INSTEAD OF SPRAYS; (4) APPLY SUNSCREEN AT LEAST 15 MINUTES BEFORE ENTERING THE OCEAN.
OVER THERE! I SEE IT!
THE NET?
YES, YES, IT'S LYING ON THE BOTTOM!
OH MY GOSH, YOU FOUND IT, BIANCA!
WHERE ARE THE TURTLES?

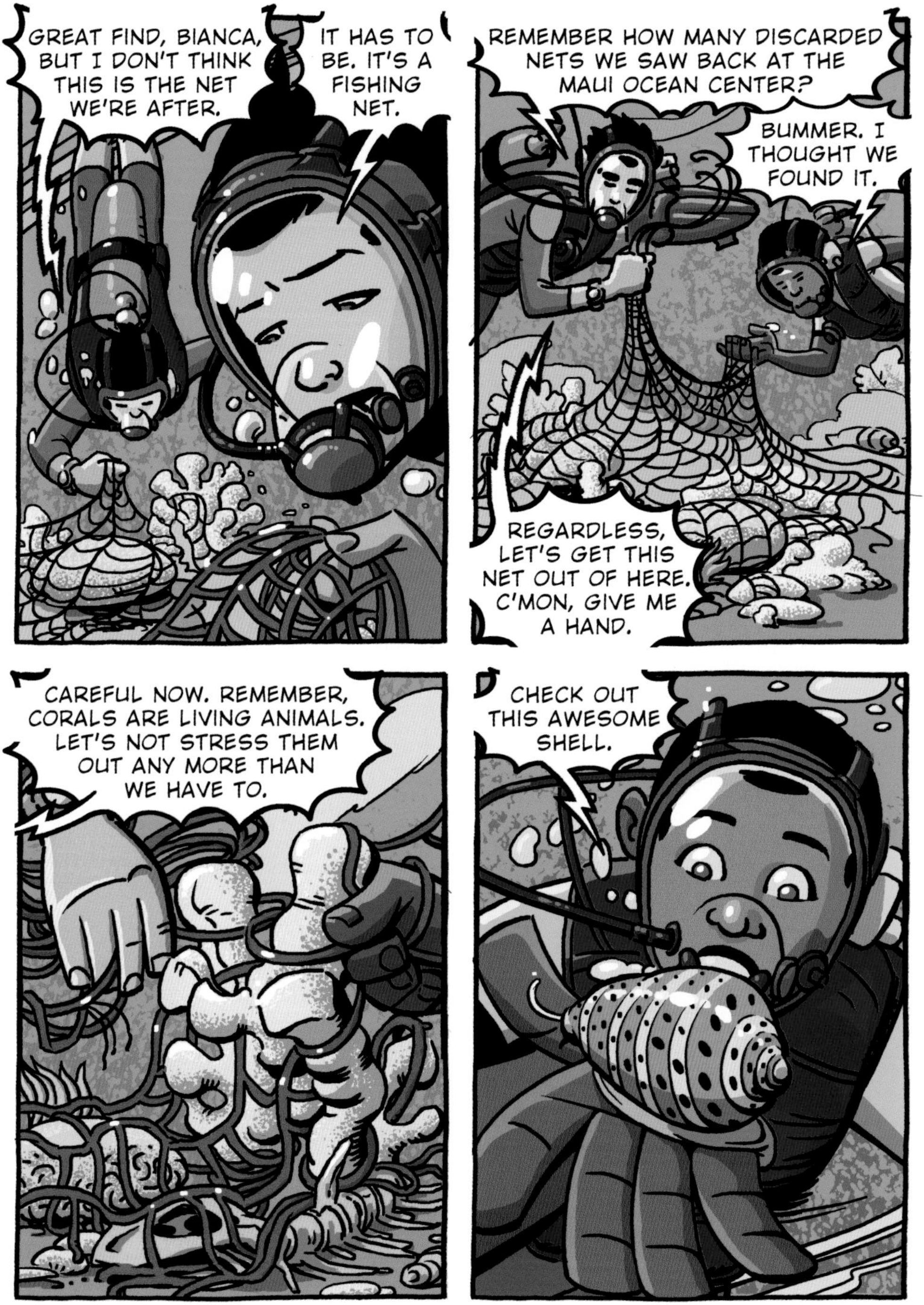
GREAT FIND, BIANCA, BUT I DON'T THINK THIS IS THE NET WE'RE AFTER.
IT HAS TO BE. IT'S A FISHING NET.
REMEMBER HOW MANY DISCARDED NETS WE SAW BACK AT THE MAUI OCEAN CENTER?
BUMMER. I THOUGHT WE FOUND IT.
REGARDLESS, LET'S GET THIS NET OUT OF HERE. C'MON, GIVE ME A HAND.
CAREFUL NOW. REMEMBER, CORALS ARE LIVING ANIMALS. LET'S NOT STRESS THEM OUT ANY MORE THAN WE HAVE TO.
CHECK OUT THIS AWESOME SHELL.

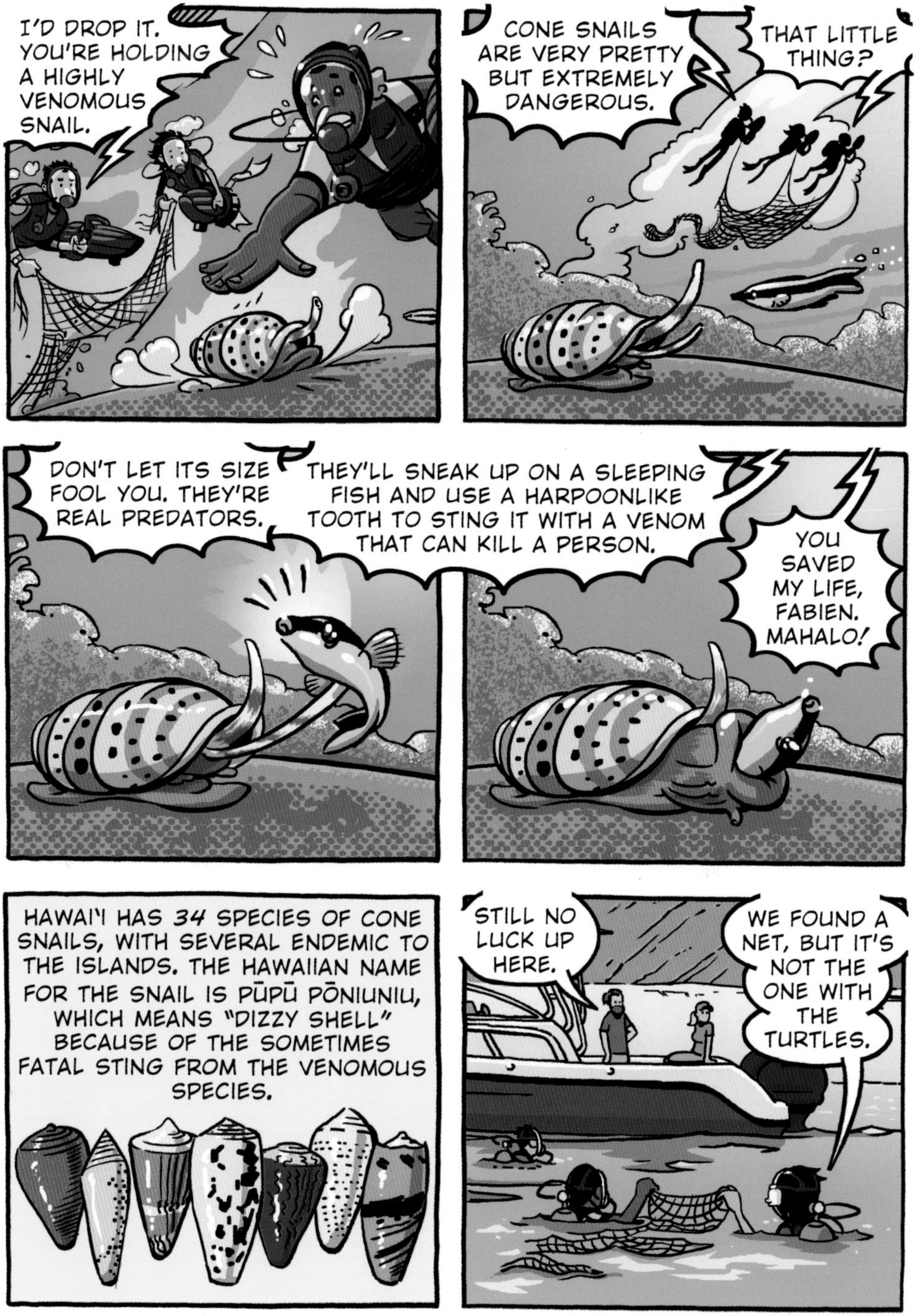
I'D DROP IT. YOU'RE HOLDING A HIGHLY VENOMOUS SNAIL.
CONE SNAILS ARE VERY PRETTY BUT EXTREMELY DANGEROUS.
THAT LITTLE THING?
DON'T LET ITS SIZE FOOL YOU. THEY'RE REAL PREDATORS.
THEY'LL SNEAK UP ON A SLEEPING FISH AND USE A HARPOONLIKE TOOTH TO STING IT WITH A VENOM THAT CAN KILL A PERSON.
YOU SAVED MY LIFE, FABIEN. MAHALO!
HAWAI'I HAS 34 SPECIES OF CONE SNAILS, WITH SEVERAL ENDEMIC TO THE ISLANDS. THE HAWAIIAN NAME FOR THE SNAIL IS PŪPŪ PŌNIUNIU, WHICH MEANS "DIZZY SHELL" BECAUSE OF THE SOMETIMES FATAL STING FROM THE VENOMOUS SPECIES.
STILL NO LUCK UP HERE.
WE FOUND A NET, BUT IT'S NOT THE ONE WITH THE TURTLES.

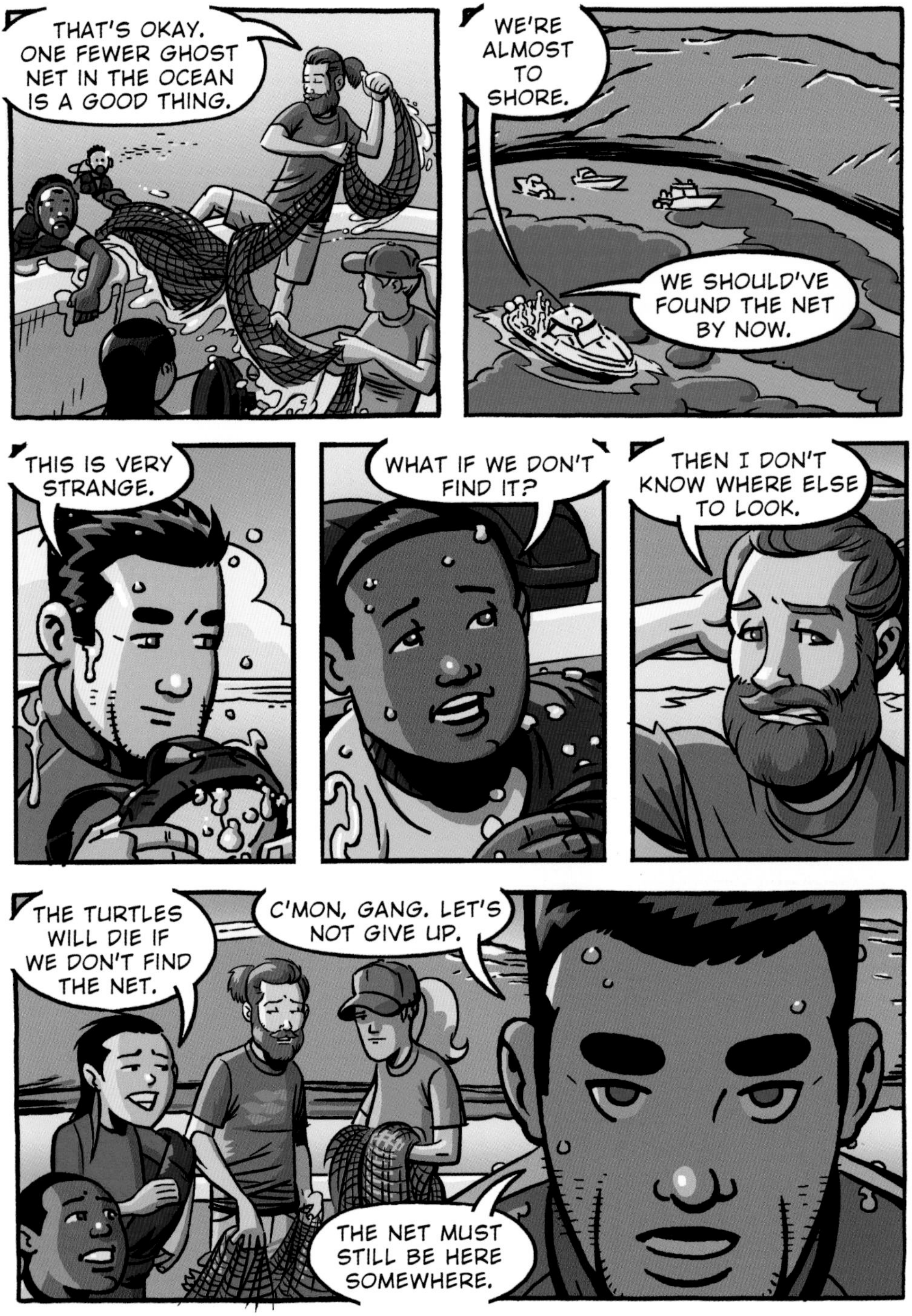
THAT'S OKAY. ONE FEWER GHOST NET IN THE OCEAN IS A GOOD THING.
WE'RE ALMOST TO SHORE.
WE SHOULD'VE FOUND THE NET BY NOW.
THIS IS VERY STRANGE.
WHAT IF WE DON'T FIND IT?
THEN I DON'T KNOW WHERE ELSE TO LOOK.
THE TURTLES WILL DIE IF WE DON'T FIND THE NET.
C'MON, GANG. LET'S NOT GIVE UP.
THE NET MUST STILL BE HERE SOMEWHERE.

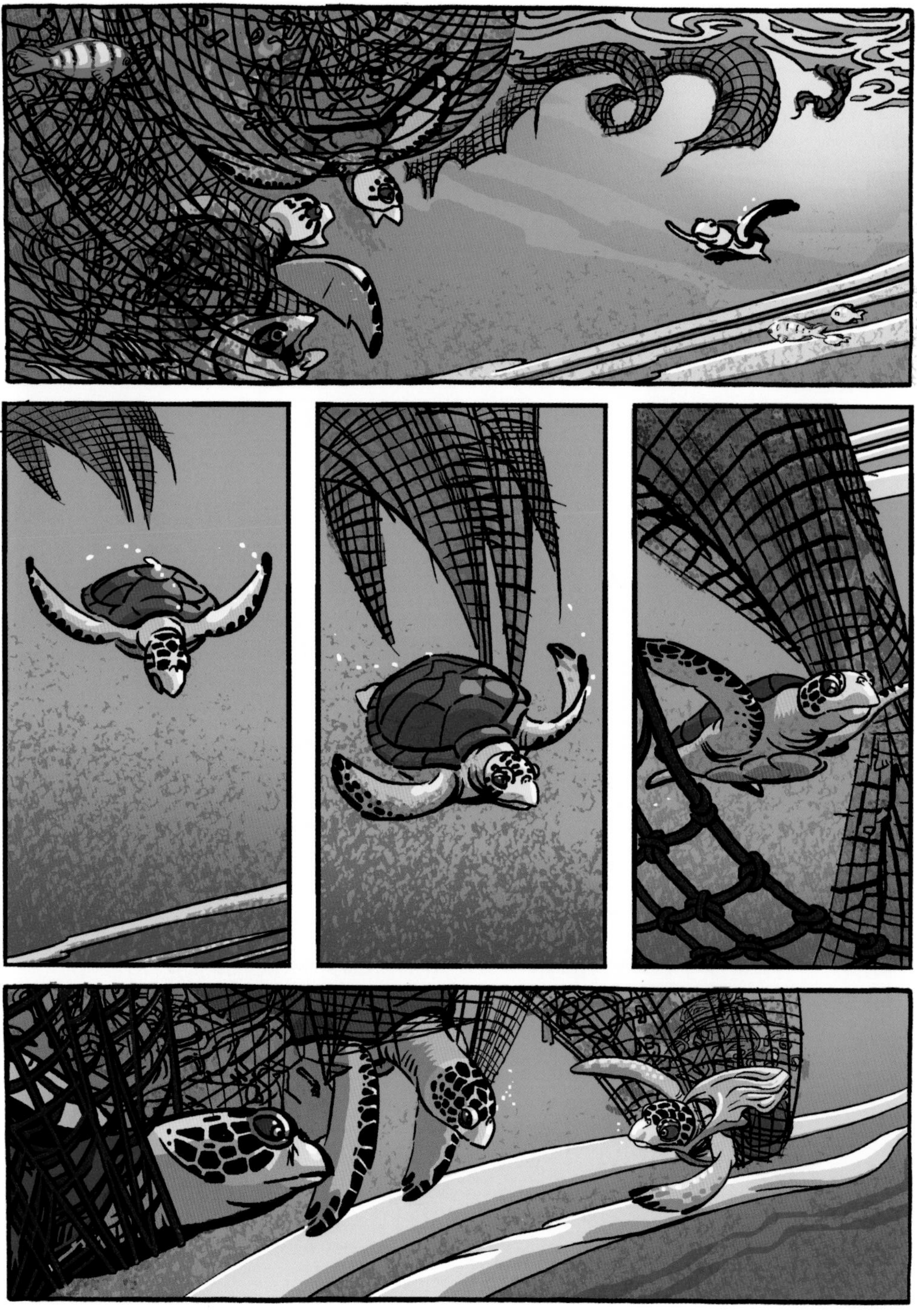

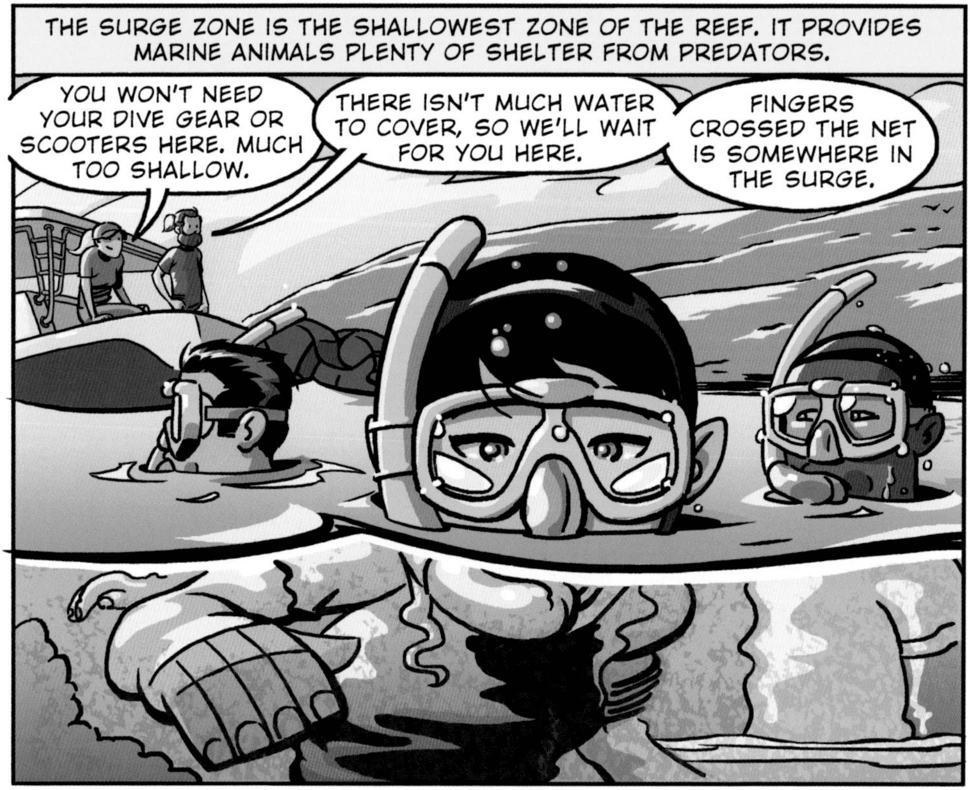
THE SURGE ZONE IS THE SHALLOWEST ZONE OF THE REEF. IT PROVIDES MARINE ANIMALS PLENTY OF SHELTER FROM PREDATORS.
YOU WON'T NEED YOUR DIVE GEAR OR SCOOTERS HERE. MUCH TOO SHALLOW.
THERE ISN'T MUCH WATER TO COVER, SO WE'LL WAIT FOR YOU HERE.
FINGERS CROSSED THE NET IS SOMEWHERE IN THE SURGE.

WAYS TO HELP PROTECT OUR PRECIOUS CORAL REEFS

WATCH YOUR STEP: WHEN SNORKELING OR DIVING, PUT ON GEAR BEFORE ENTERING THE OCEAN AND STAY AFLOAT IN THE WATER. SWIM OVER CORALS FROM A SAFE DISTANCE.

USE A TRASH CAN: WHAT'S ON LAND TODAY WILL BE ON OUR REEFS TOMORROW. KEEP OCEANS AND BEACHES FREE OF LITTER.

CHOOSE WISELY: FISH KEEP THE REEF HEALTHY. DO NOT COLLECT CORAL, FISH, AND SHELLS FROM THE OCEAN.

KEEP POLLUTANTS OUT OF THE OCEAN: POLLUTION CAN COVER AND CHOKE CORAL. CHOOSE ECO-FRIENDLY PRODUCTS SUCH AS BIODEGRADABLE DETERGENTS, LOTIONS, AND GARDEN FERTILIZERS. REMEMBER, ALL DRAINS LEAD TO THE OCEAN.

FISH NEED TO FORAGE: DON'T FEED FISH IN THE WILD. IT'S UNHEALTHY FOR THE REEF ECOSYSTEM.

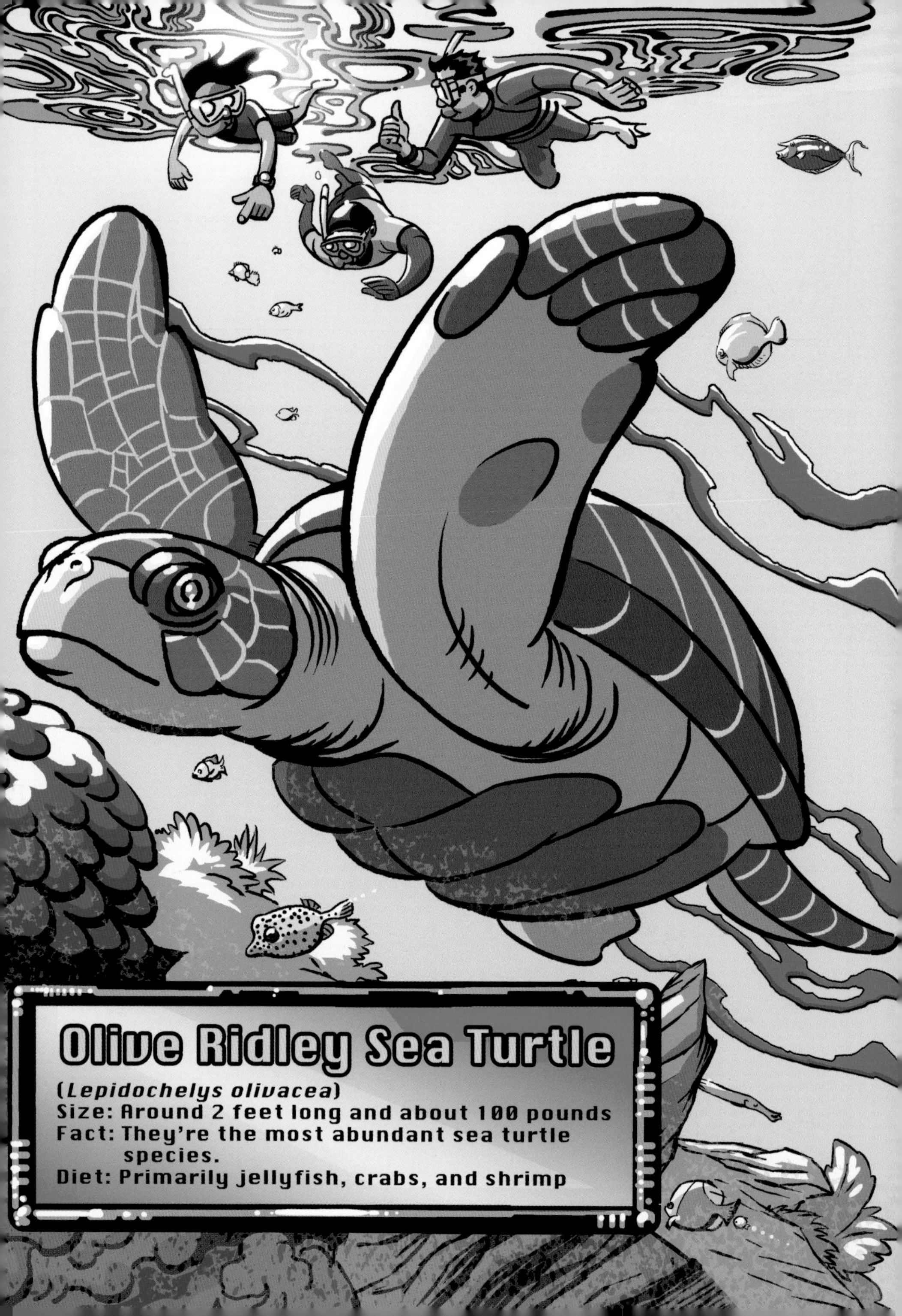

Olive Ridley Sea Turtle

(*Lepidochelys olivacea*)
Size: Around 2 feet long and about 100 pounds
Fact: They're the most abundant sea turtle species.
Diet: Primarily jellyfish, crabs, and shrimp

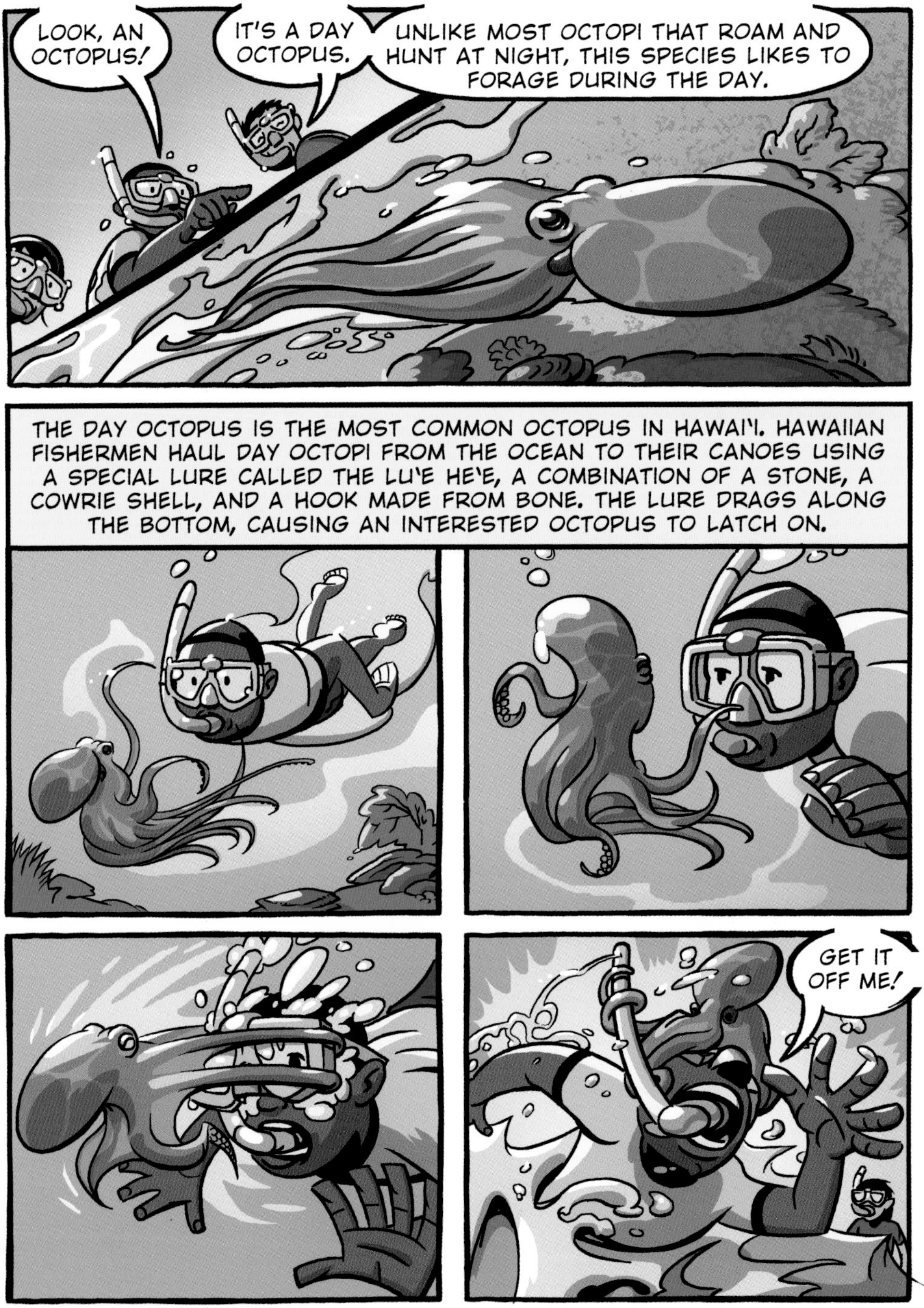
LOOK, AN OCTOPUS!
IT'S A DAY OCTOPUS.
UNLIKE MOST OCTOPI THAT ROAM AND HUNT AT NIGHT, THIS SPECIES LIKES TO FORAGE DURING THE DAY.
THE DAY OCTOPUS IS THE MOST COMMON OCTOPUS IN HAWAIʻI. HAWAIIAN FISHERMEN HAUL DAY OCTOPI FROM THE OCEAN TO THEIR CANOES USING A SPECIAL LURE CALLED THE LUʻE HEʻE, A COMBINATION OF A STONE, A COWRIE SHELL, AND A HOOK MADE FROM BONE. THE LURE DRAGS ALONG THE BOTTOM, CAUSING AN INTERESTED OCTOPUS TO LATCH ON.
GET IT OFF ME!

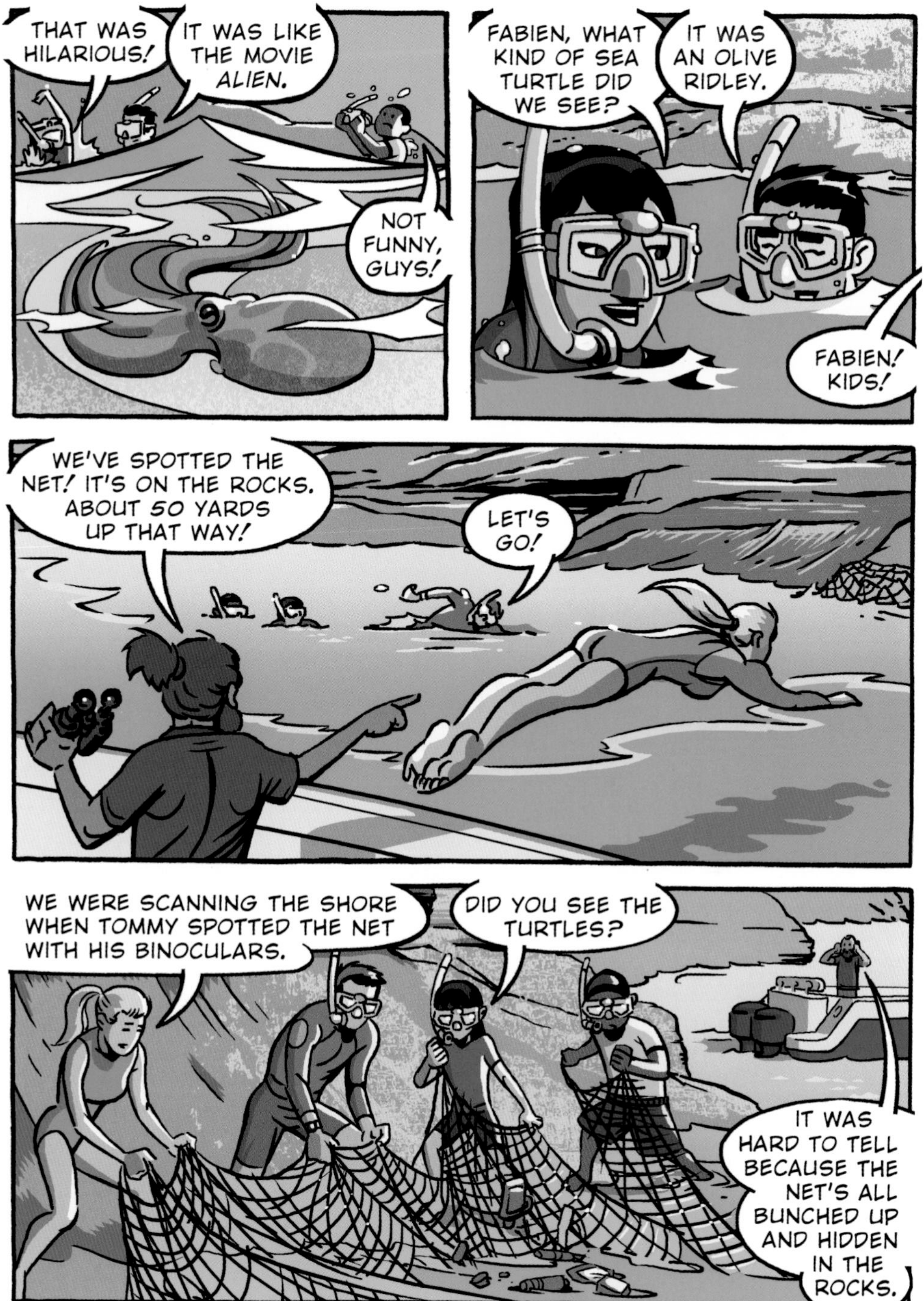
THAT WAS HILARIOUS!
IT WAS LIKE THE MOVIE ALIEN.
NOT FUNNY, GUYS!
FABIEN, WHAT KIND OF SEA TURTLE DID WE SEE?
IT WAS AN OLIVE RIDLEY.
FABIEN! KIDS!
WE'VE SPOTTED THE NET! IT'S ON THE ROCKS. ABOUT 50 YARDS UP THAT WAY!
LET'S GO!
WE WERE SCANNING THE SHORE WHEN TOMMY SPOTTED THE NET WITH HIS BINOCULARS.
DID YOU SEE THE TURTLES?
IT WAS HARD TO TELL BECAUSE THE NET'S ALL BUNCHED UP AND HIDDEN IN THE ROCKS.

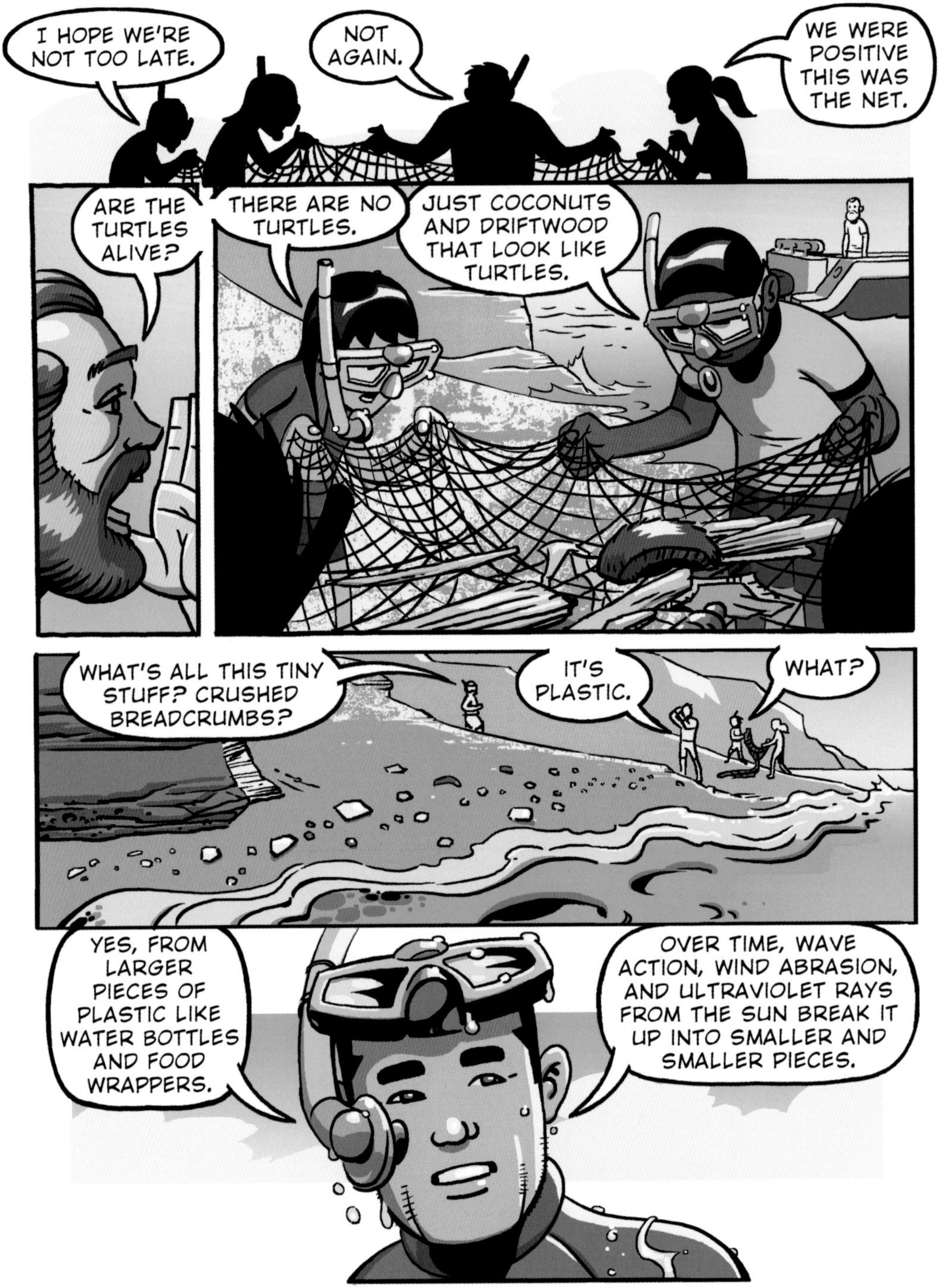

I HOPE WE'RE NOT TOO LATE.
NOT AGAIN.
WE WERE POSITIVE THIS WAS THE NET.
ARE THE TURTLES ALIVE?
THERE ARE NO TURTLES.
JUST COCONUTS AND DRIFTWOOD THAT LOOK LIKE TURTLES.
WHAT'S ALL THIS TINY STUFF? CRUSHED BREADCRUMBS?
IT'S PLASTIC.
WHAT?
YES, FROM LARGER PIECES OF PLASTIC LIKE WATER BOTTLES AND FOOD WRAPPERS.
OVER TIME, WAVE ACTION, WIND ABRASION, AND ULTRAVIOLET RAYS FROM THE SUN BREAK IT UP INTO SMALLER AND SMALLER PIECES.

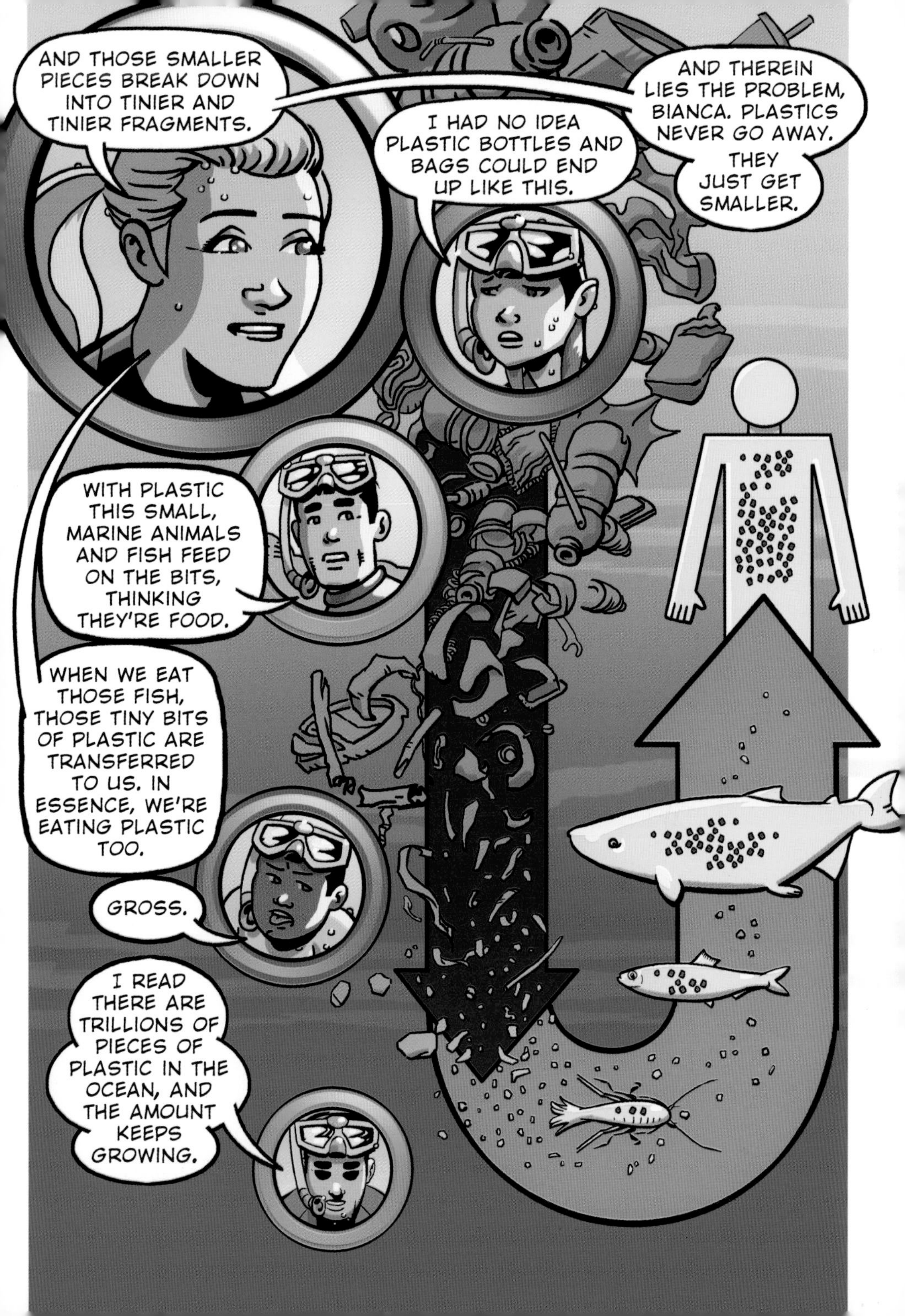
AND THOSE SMALLER PIECES BREAK DOWN INTO TINIER AND TINIER FRAGMENTS.
I HAD NO IDEA PLASTIC BOTTLES AND BAGS COULD END UP LIKE THIS.
AND THEREIN LIES THE PROBLEM, BIANCA. PLASTICS NEVER GO AWAY.
THEY JUST GET SMALLER.
WITH PLASTIC THIS SMALL, MARINE ANIMALS AND FISH FEED ON THE BITS, THINKING THEY'RE FOOD.
WHEN WE EAT THOSE FISH, THOSE TINY BITS OF PLASTIC ARE TRANSFERRED TO US. IN ESSENCE, WE'RE EATING PLASTIC TOO.
GROSS.
I READ THERE ARE TRILLIONS OF PIECES OF PLASTIC IN THE OCEAN, AND THE AMOUNT KEEPS GROWING.

IN ANOTHER THIRTY YEARS OUR OCEANS COULD HAVE MORE PLASTIC THAN FISH.

WOW.

EIGHT MILLION TONS OF PLASTIC DEBRIS ENTER THE EARTH'S OCEANS EVERY YEAR. ONE OF THE LARGEST ACCUMULATIONS OF OCEAN PLASTIC IN THE WORLD IS CURRENTLY LOCATED BETWEEN HAWAI'I AND CALIFORNIA. IT'S KNOWN AS THE GREAT PACIFIC GARBAGE PATCH.

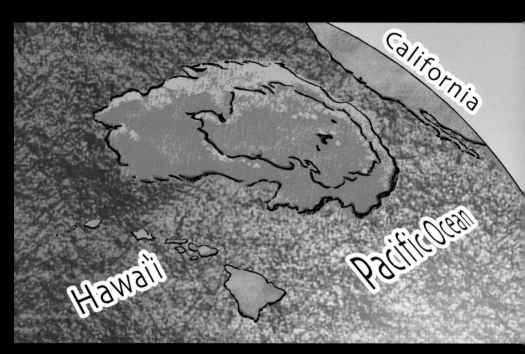

California

Hawai'i

Pacific Ocean

GUYS, OVER THERE!

OH MY!

IT'S A LOGGER-HEAD.

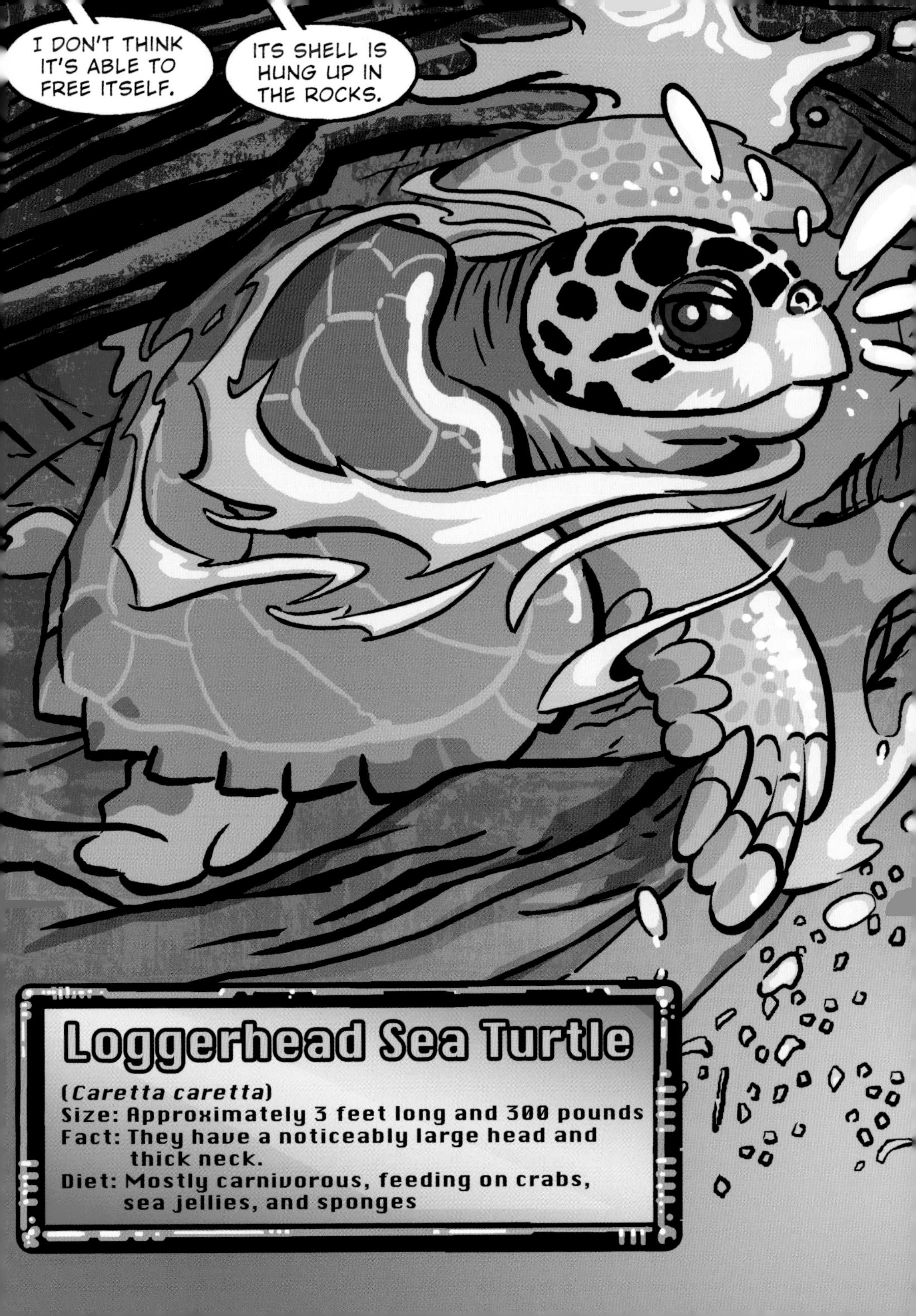
I DON'T THINK IT'S ABLE TO FREE ITSELF.
ITS SHELL IS HUNG UP IN THE ROCKS.
Loggerhead Sea Turtle
(Caretta caretta)
Size: Approximately 3 feet long and 300 pounds
Fact: They have a noticeably large head and thick neck.
Diet: Mostly carnivorous, feeding on crabs, sea jellies, and sponges

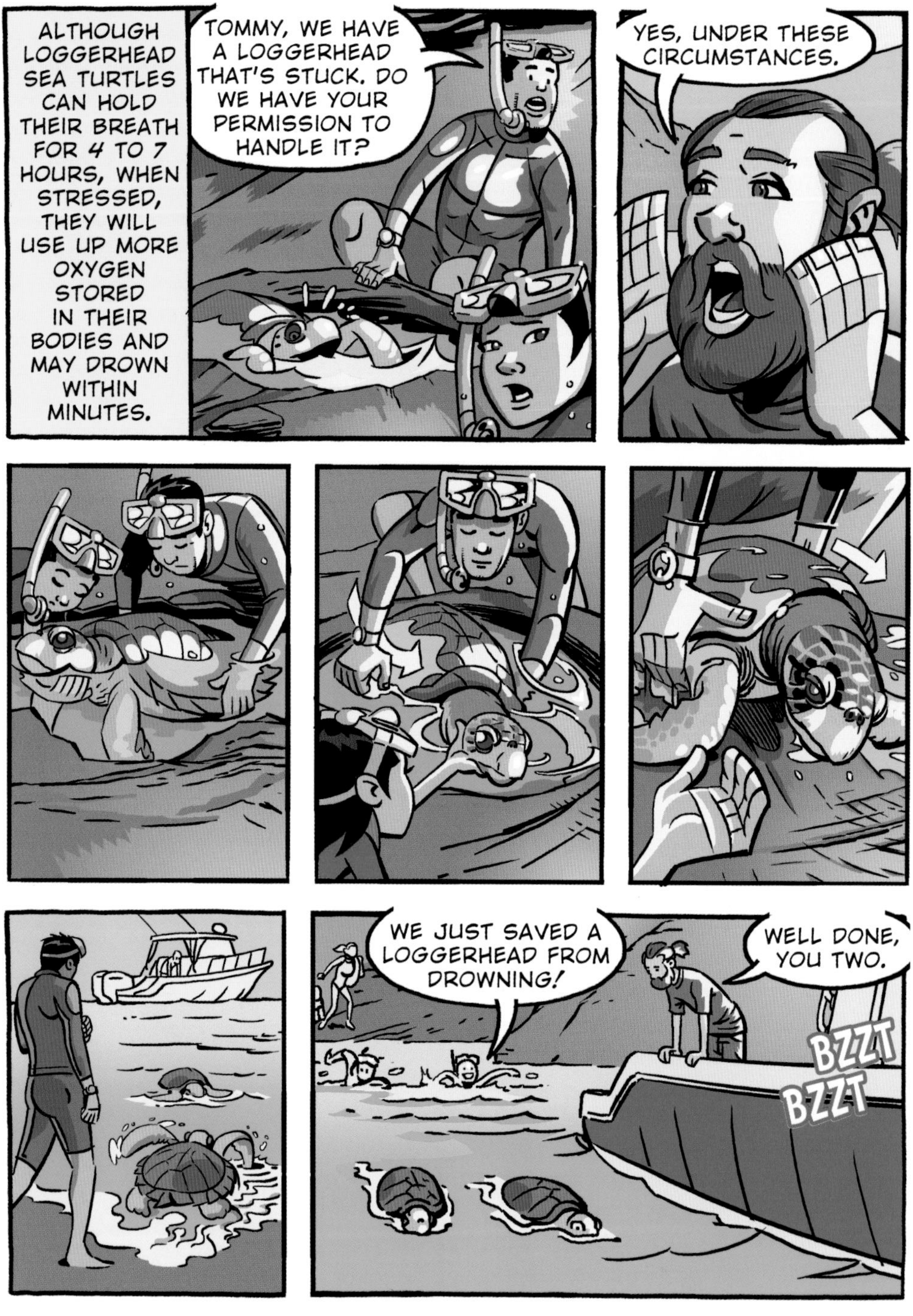
ALTHOUGH LOGGERHEAD SEA TURTLES CAN HOLD THEIR BREATH FOR 4 TO 7 HOURS, WHEN STRESSED, THEY WILL USE UP MORE OXYGEN STORED IN THEIR BODIES AND MAY DROWN WITHIN MINUTES.
TOMMY, WE HAVE A LOGGERHEAD THAT'S STUCK. DO WE HAVE YOUR PERMISSION TO HANDLE IT?
YES, UNDER THESE CIRCUMSTANCES.
WE JUST SAVED A LOGGERHEAD FROM DROWNING!
WELL DONE, YOU TWO.
BZZT
BZZT

SEA TURTLE RESCUE LINE, THIS IS TOMMY...

BZT*

I JUST GOT A CALL. A WHALE-WATCHING BOAT SPOTTED THE NET BETWEEN HERE AND LĀNA'I!

LĀNA'I?

THEY FOUND THE NET. AND THE SEA TURTLES.

YAY!

WHAT'S THE NET DOING WAY OVER THERE?

ALL I CAN THINK OF IS, FROM TIME TO TIME, CYCLONIC EDDIES FORM HERE AT MOLOKINI. AN EDDY MUST'VE FORMED BEFORE WE ARRIVED.

AN EDDY IS A CURRENT OF WATER THAT TRAVELS IN A CIRCULAR MOTION, SIMILAR TO A WHIRLPOOL. WHEN THE EDDY SWIRLS IN A COUNTER-CLOCKWISE DIRECTION IN THE NORTHERN HEMISPHERE, IT'S CALLED A "CYCLONIC EDDY."

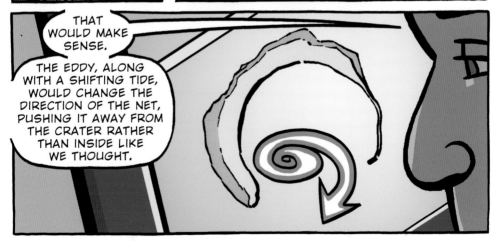

THAT WOULD MAKE SENSE.

THE EDDY, ALONG WITH A SHIFTING TIDE, WOULD CHANGE THE DIRECTION OF THE NET, PUSHING IT AWAY FROM THE CRATER RATHER THAN INSIDE LIKE WE THOUGHT.

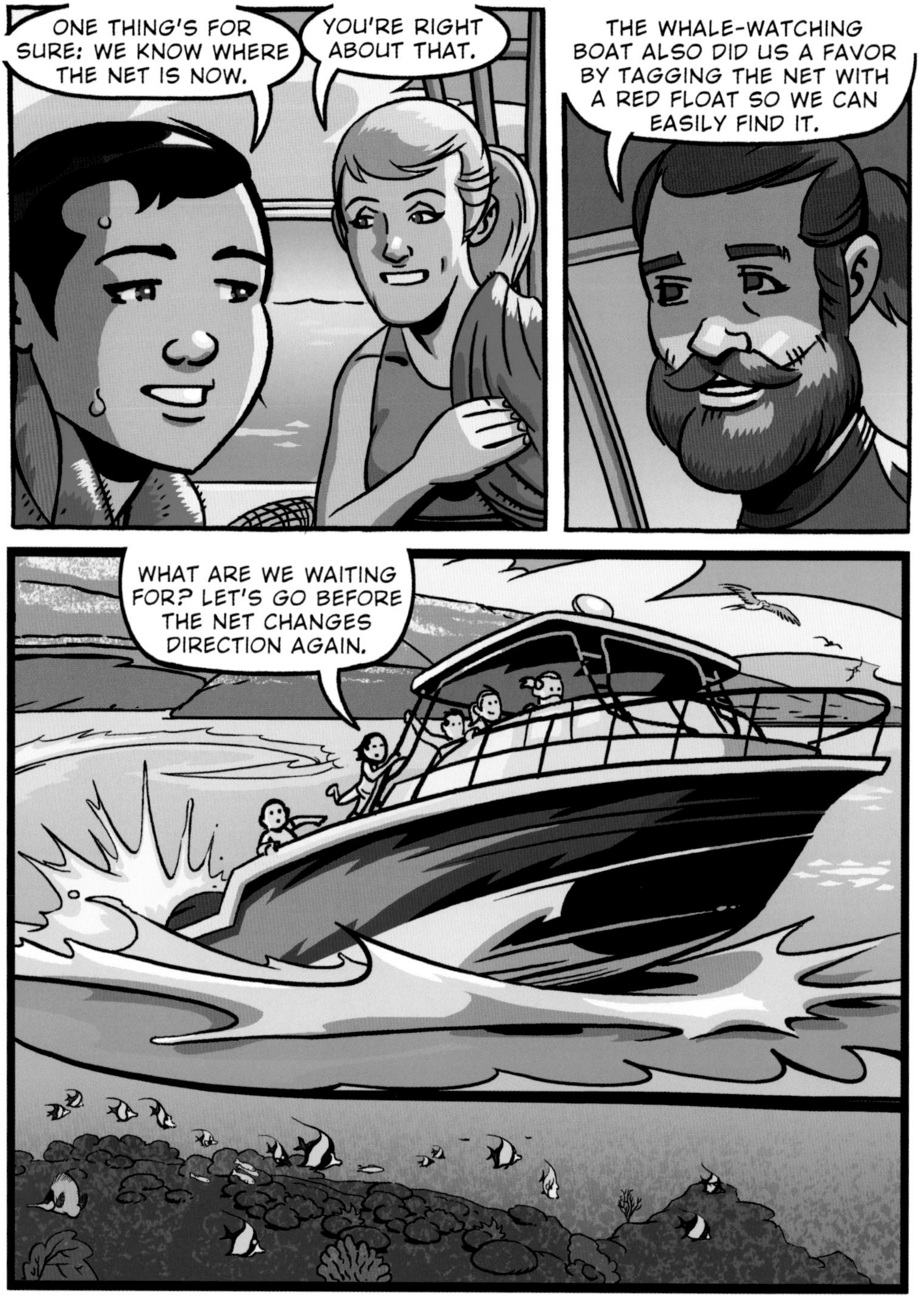
ONE THING'S FOR SURE: WE KNOW WHERE THE NET IS NOW.
YOU'RE RIGHT ABOUT THAT.
THE WHALE-WATCHING BOAT ALSO DID US A FAVOR BY TAGGING THE NET WITH A RED FLOAT SO WE CAN EASILY FIND IT.
WHAT ARE WE WAITING FOR? LET'S GO BEFORE THE NET CHANGES DIRECTION AGAIN.

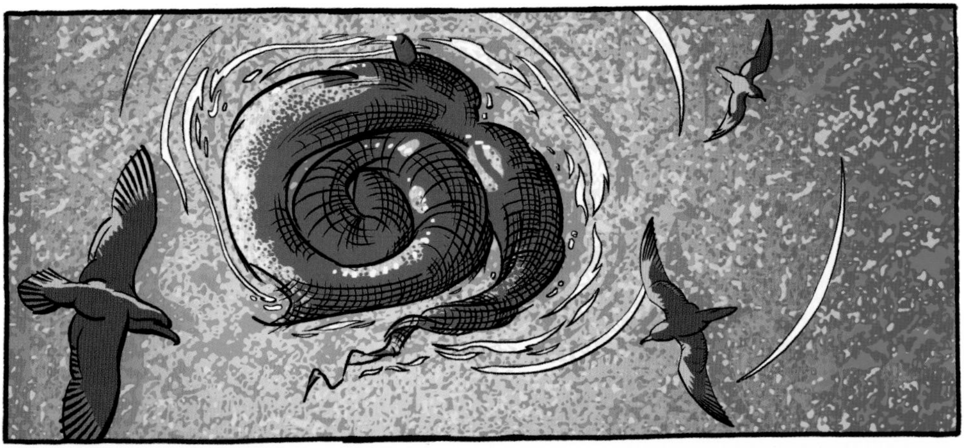

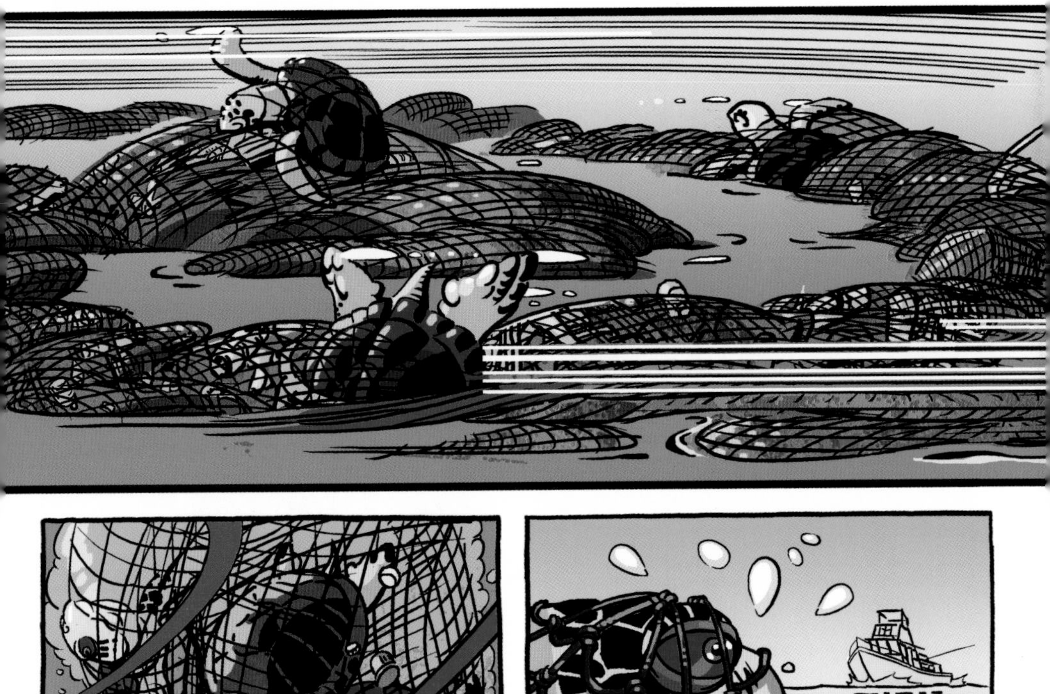

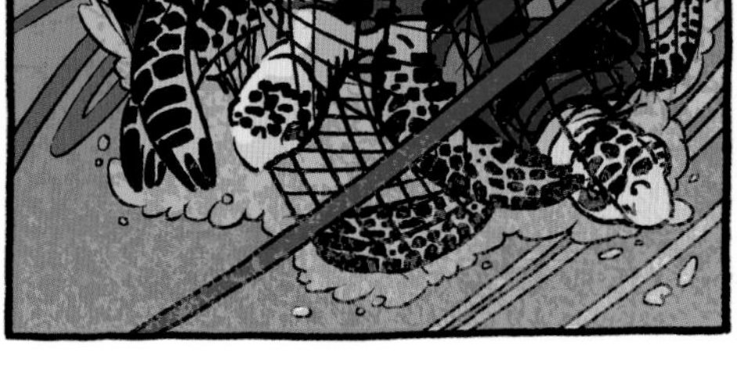

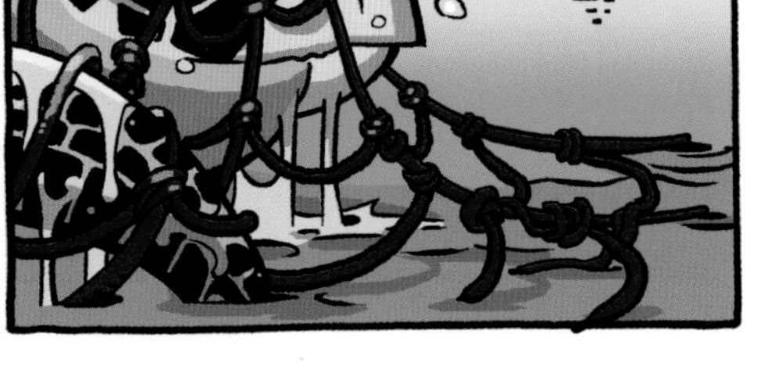

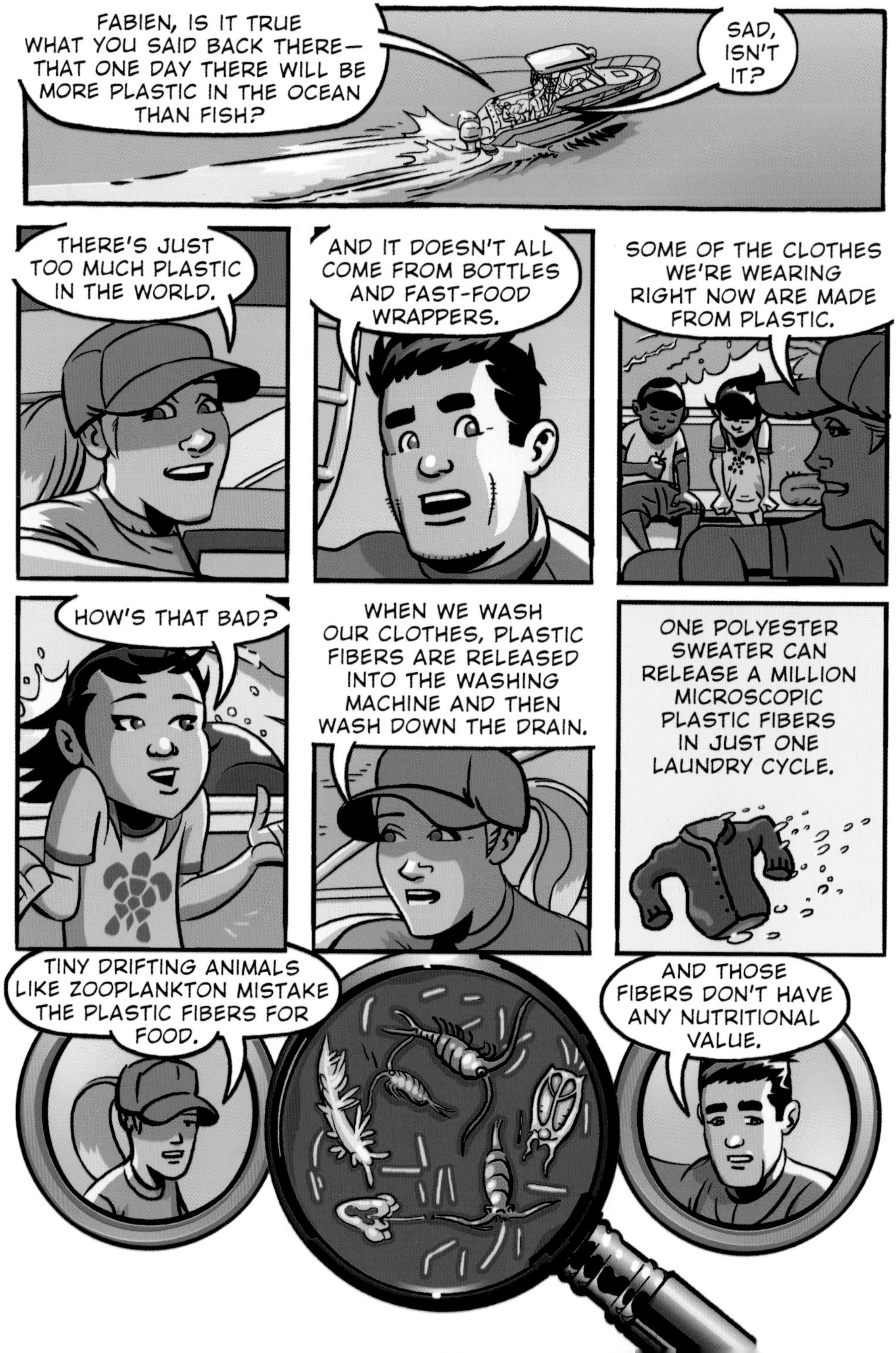
FABIEN, IS IT TRUE WHAT YOU SAID BACK THERE—THAT ONE DAY THERE WILL BE MORE PLASTIC IN THE OCEAN THAN FISH?
SAD, ISN'T IT?
THERE'S JUST TOO MUCH PLASTIC IN THE WORLD.
AND IT DOESN'T ALL COME FROM BOTTLES AND FAST-FOOD WRAPPERS.
SOME OF THE CLOTHES WE'RE WEARING RIGHT NOW ARE MADE FROM PLASTIC.
HOW'S THAT BAD?
WHEN WE WASH OUR CLOTHES, PLASTIC FIBERS ARE RELEASED INTO THE WASHING MACHINE AND THEN WASH DOWN THE DRAIN.
ONE POLYESTER SWEATER CAN RELEASE A MILLION MICROSCOPIC PLASTIC FIBERS IN JUST ONE LAUNDRY CYCLE.
TINY DRIFTING ANIMALS LIKE ZOOPLANKTON MISTAKE THE PLASTIC FIBERS FOR FOOD.
AND THOSE FIBERS DON'T HAVE ANY NUTRITIONAL VALUE.

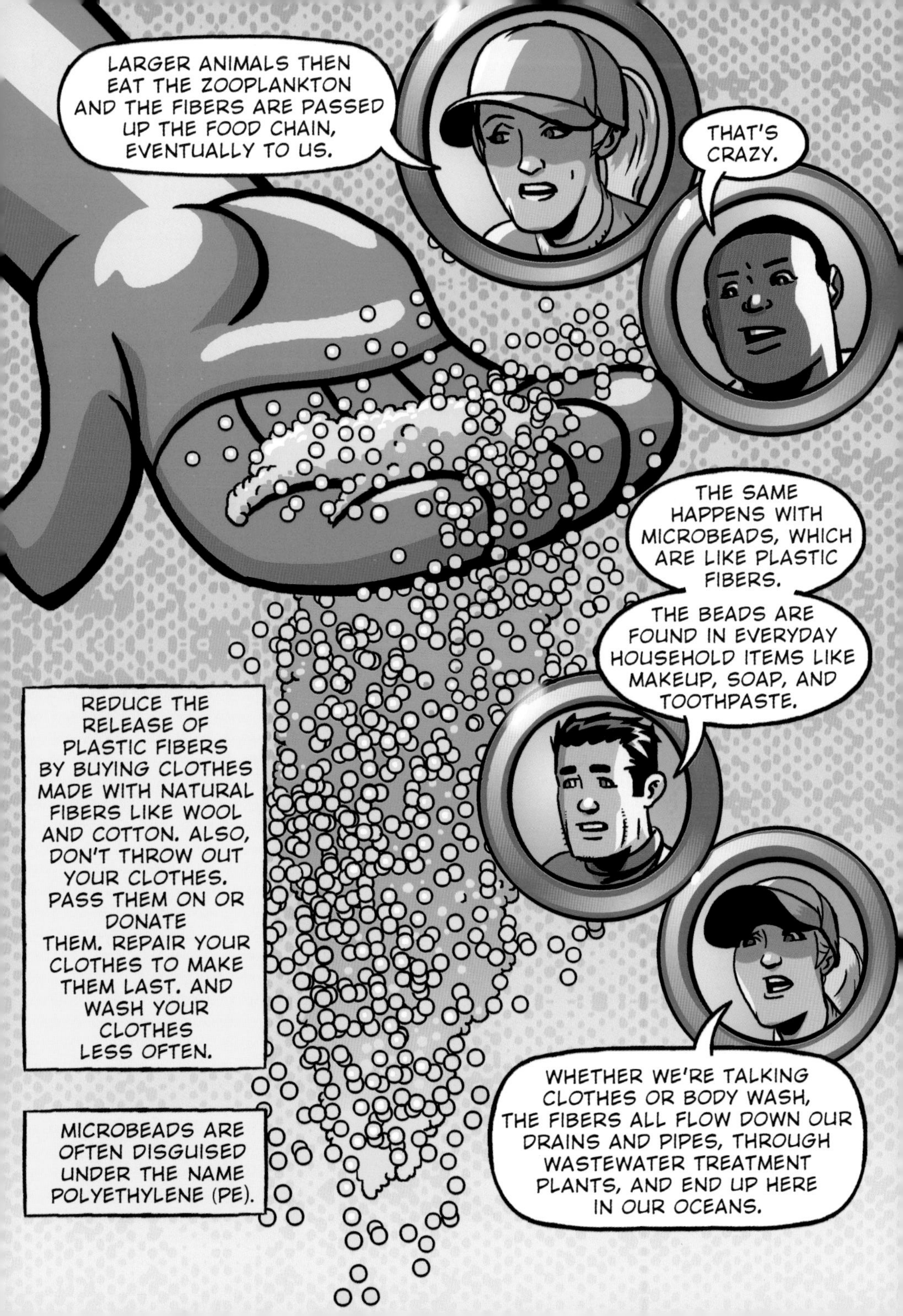

LARGER ANIMALS THEN EAT THE ZOOPLANKTON AND THE FIBERS ARE PASSED UP THE FOOD CHAIN, EVENTUALLY TO US.
THAT'S CRAZY.
THE SAME HAPPENS WITH MICROBEADS, WHICH ARE LIKE PLASTIC FIBERS.
THE BEADS ARE FOUND IN EVERYDAY HOUSEHOLD ITEMS LIKE MAKEUP, SOAP, AND TOOTHPASTE.
REDUCE THE RELEASE OF PLASTIC FIBERS BY BUYING CLOTHES MADE WITH NATURAL FIBERS LIKE WOOL AND COTTON. ALSO, DON'T THROW OUT YOUR CLOTHES. PASS THEM ON OR DONATE THEM. REPAIR YOUR CLOTHES TO MAKE THEM LAST. AND WASH YOUR CLOTHES LESS OFTEN.
WHETHER WE'RE TALKING CLOTHES OR BODY WASH, THE FIBERS ALL FLOW DOWN OUR DRAINS AND PIPES, THROUGH WASTEWATER TREATMENT PLANTS, AND END UP HERE IN OUR OCEANS.
MICROBEADS ARE OFTEN DISGUISED UNDER THE NAME POLYETHYLENE (PE).

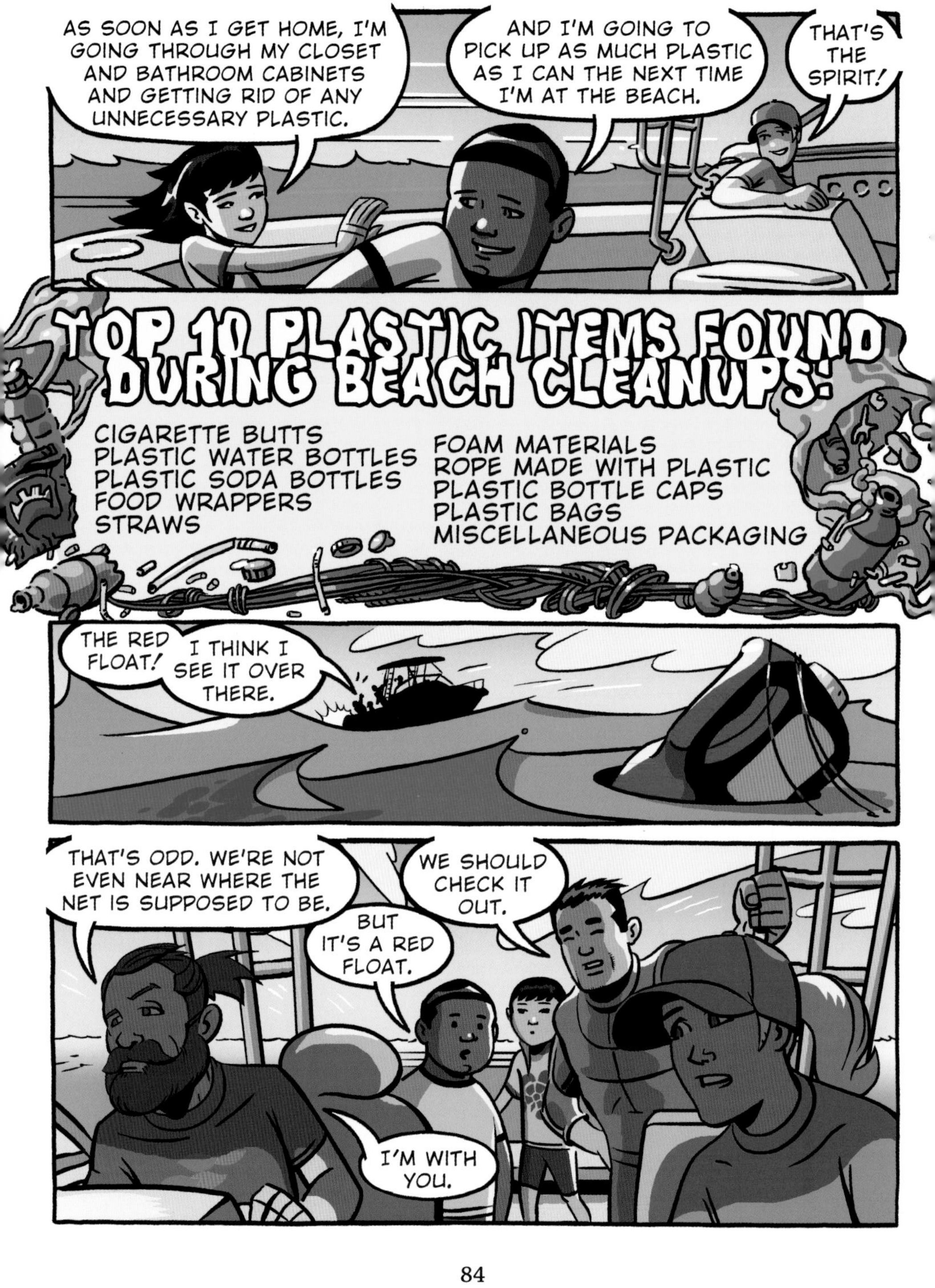
AS SOON AS I GET HOME, I'M GOING THROUGH MY CLOSET AND BATHROOM CABINETS AND GETTING RID OF ANY UNNECESSARY PLASTIC.
AND I'M GOING TO PICK UP AS MUCH PLASTIC AS I CAN THE NEXT TIME I'M AT THE BEACH.
THAT'S THE SPIRIT!
TOP 10 PLASTIC ITEMS FOUND DURING BEACH CLEANUPS:
CIGARETTE BUTTS
PLASTIC WATER BOTTLES
PLASTIC SODA BOTTLES
FOOD WRAPPERS
STRAWS
FOAM MATERIALS
ROPE MADE WITH PLASTIC
PLASTIC BOTTLE CAPS
PLASTIC BAGS
MISCELLANEOUS PACKAGING
THE RED FLOAT!
I THINK I SEE IT OVER THERE.
THAT'S ODD. WE'RE NOT EVEN NEAR WHERE THE NET IS SUPPOSED TO BE.
BUT IT'S A RED FLOAT.
WE SHOULD CHECK IT OUT.
I'M WITH YOU.

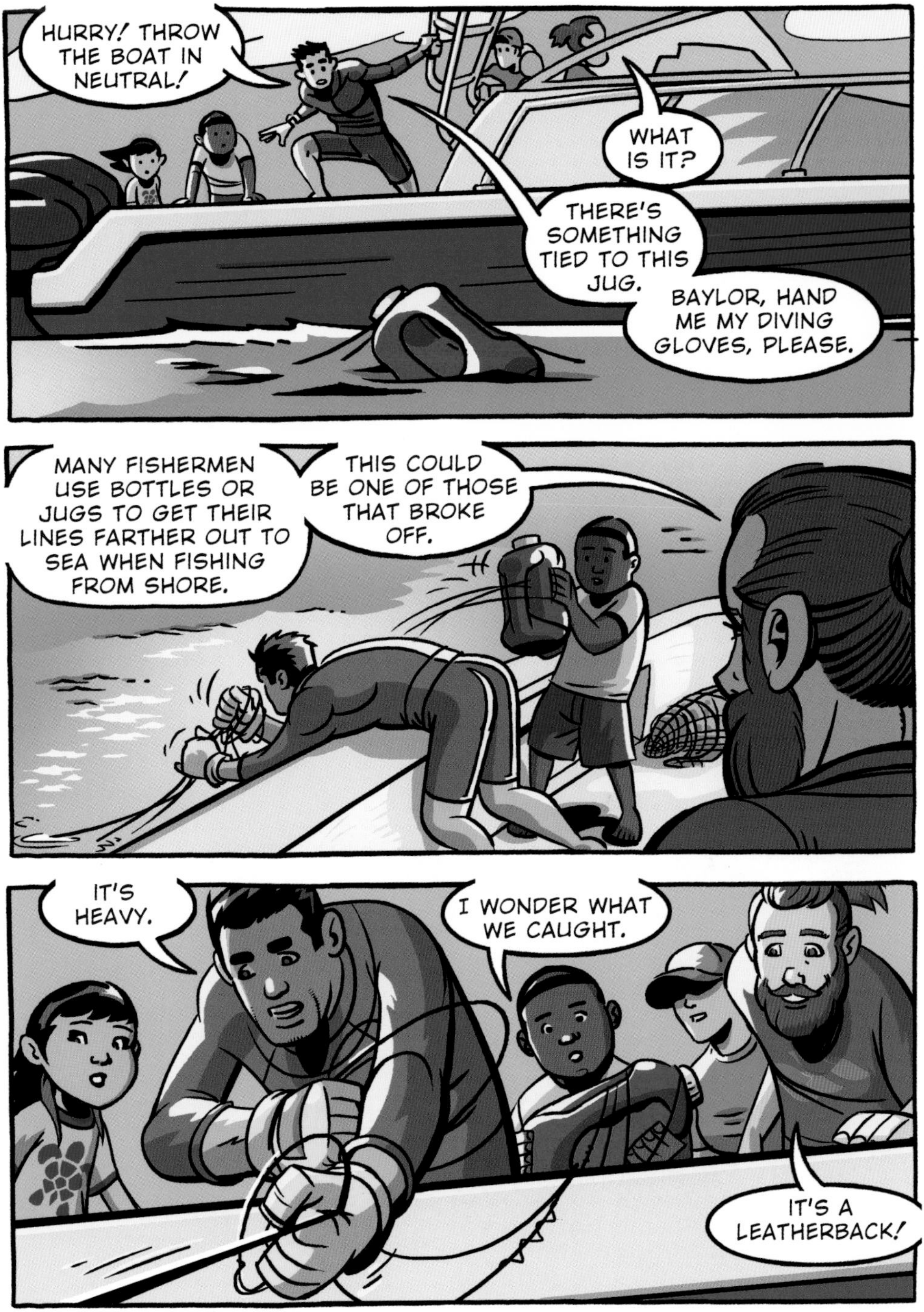
HURRY! THROW THE BOAT IN NEUTRAL!
WHAT IS IT?
THERE'S SOMETHING TIED TO THIS JUG.
BAYLOR, HAND ME MY DIVING GLOVES, PLEASE.
MANY FISHERMEN USE BOTTLES OR JUGS TO GET THEIR LINES FARTHER OUT TO SEA WHEN FISHING FROM SHORE.
THIS COULD BE ONE OF THOSE THAT BROKE OFF.
IT'S HEAVY.
I WONDER WHAT WE CAUGHT.
IT'S A LEATHERBACK!

Leatherback Sea Turtle

(*Dermochelys coriacea*)
Size: Up to 7 feet long and 2,000 pounds
Fact: The largest sea turtle, they have a unique
    shell that is not hard and bony, but
    rubbery and flexible.
Diet: Almost exclusively jellyfish

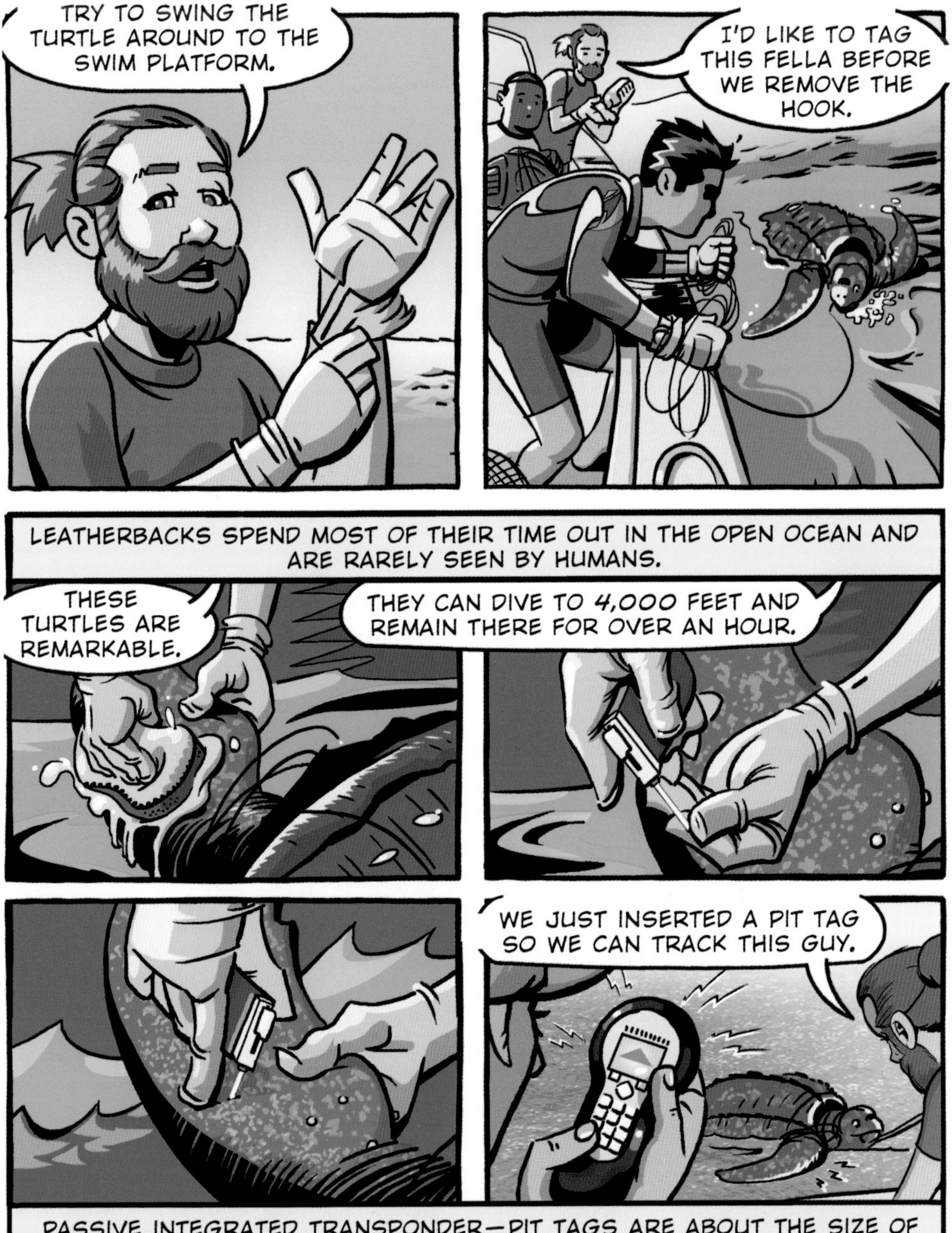
TRY TO SWING THE TURTLE AROUND TO THE SWIM PLATFORM.
I'D LIKE TO TAG THIS FELLA BEFORE WE REMOVE THE HOOK.
LEATHERBACKS SPEND MOST OF THEIR TIME OUT IN THE OPEN OCEAN AND ARE RARELY SEEN BY HUMANS.
THESE TURTLES ARE REMARKABLE.
THEY CAN DIVE TO 4,000 FEET AND REMAIN THERE FOR OVER AN HOUR.
WE JUST INSERTED A PIT TAG SO WE CAN TRACK THIS GUY.
PASSIVE INTEGRATED TRANSPONDER—PIT TAGS ARE ABOUT THE SIZE OF A GRAIN OF RICE AND CONTAIN A COMPUTER CHIP. WHEN A SCANNER IS PASSED OVER THE SITE WHERE THE TAG WAS INJECTED, THE RADIO FREQUENCY DETECTS THE TAG. THE BENEFIT OF USING PIT TAGS FOR MARKING TURTLES IS THAT THE TAG IS NEARLY PERMANENT.

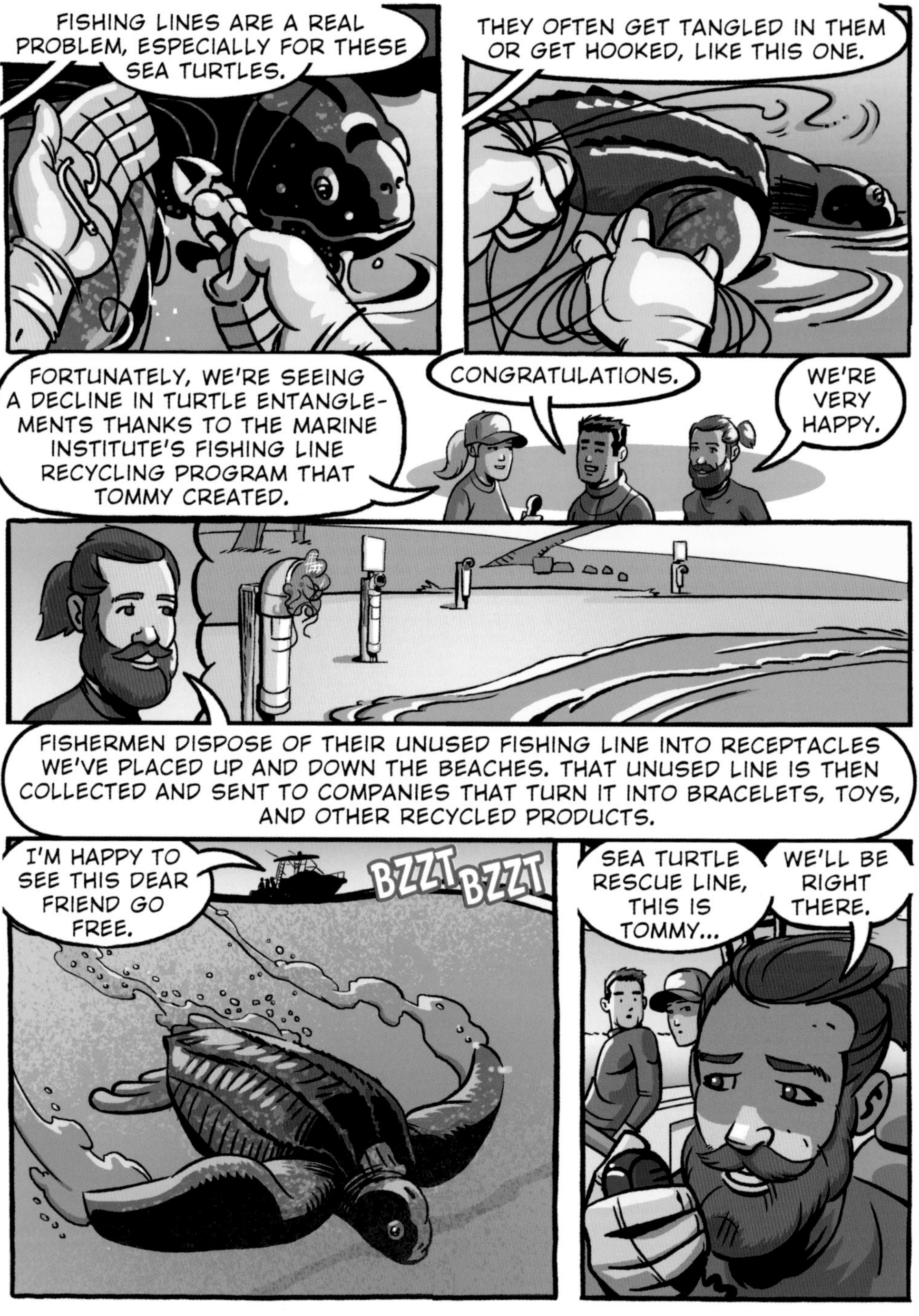
FISHING LINES ARE A REAL PROBLEM, ESPECIALLY FOR THESE SEA TURTLES.
THEY OFTEN GET TANGLED IN THEM OR GET HOOKED, LIKE THIS ONE.
FORTUNATELY, WE'RE SEEING A DECLINE IN TURTLE ENTANGLEMENTS THANKS TO THE MARINE INSTITUTE'S FISHING LINE RECYCLING PROGRAM THAT TOMMY CREATED.
CONGRATULATIONS.
WE'RE VERY HAPPY.
FISHERMEN DISPOSE OF THEIR UNUSED FISHING LINE INTO RECEPTACLES WE'VE PLACED UP AND DOWN THE BEACHES. THAT UNUSED LINE IS THEN COLLECTED AND SENT TO COMPANIES THAT TURN IT INTO BRACELETS, TOYS, AND OTHER RECYCLED PRODUCTS.
I'M HAPPY TO SEE THIS DEAR FRIEND GO FREE.
BZZT BZZT
SEA TURTLE RESCUE LINE, THIS IS TOMMY...
WE'LL BE RIGHT THERE.

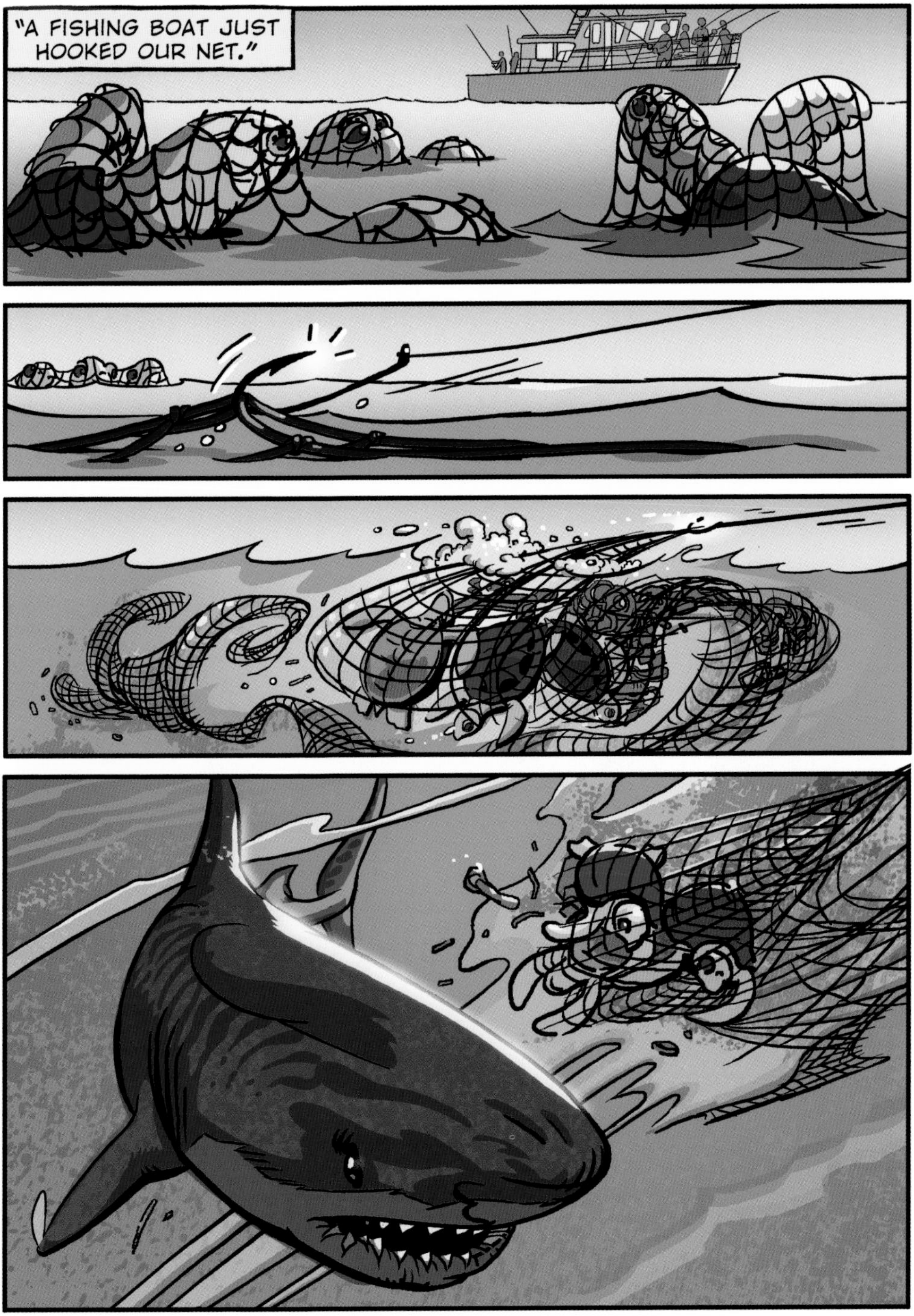
"A FISHING BOAT JUST HOOKED OUR NET."

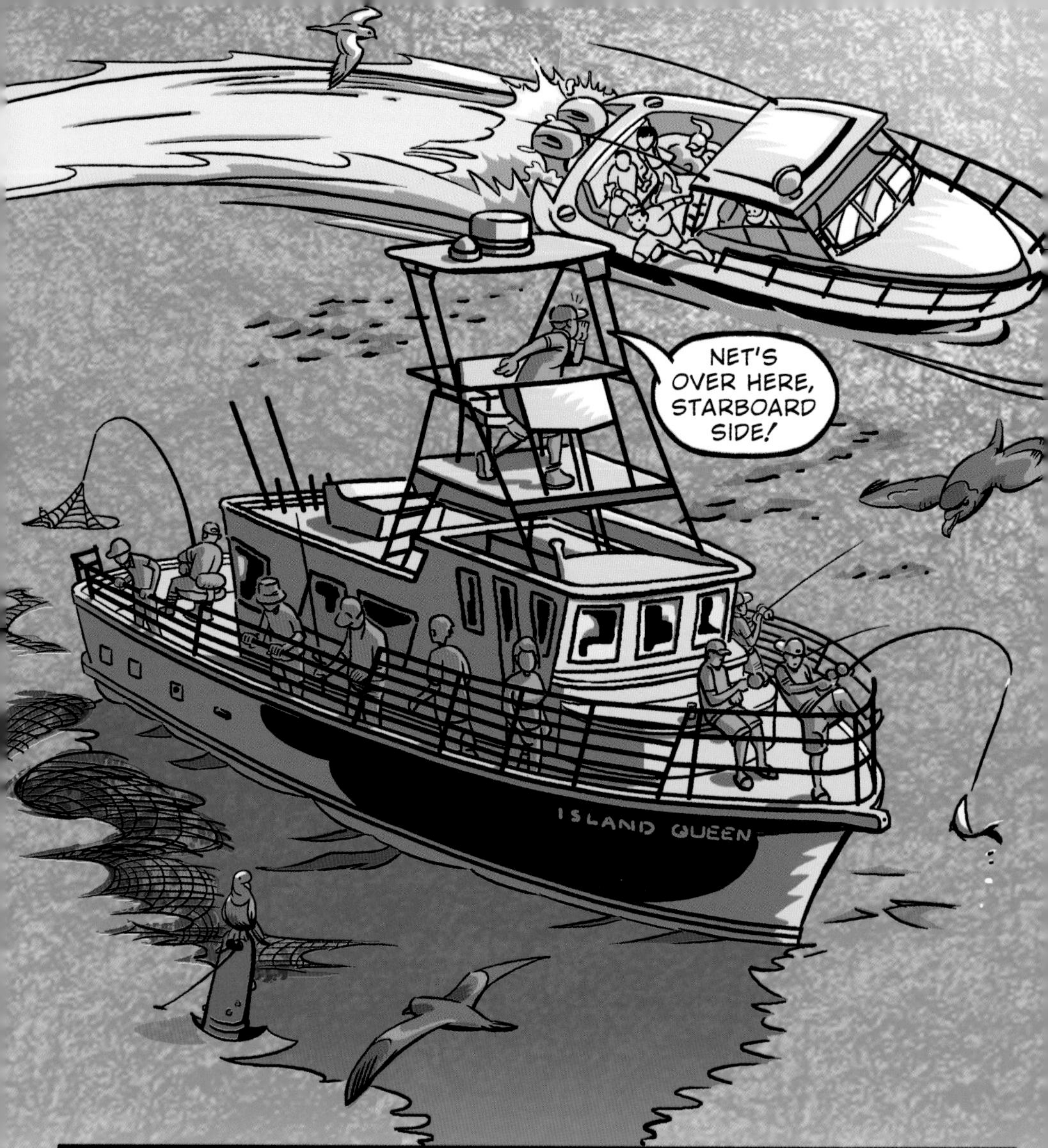
ISLAND QUEEN
NET'S OVER HERE, STARBOARD SIDE!

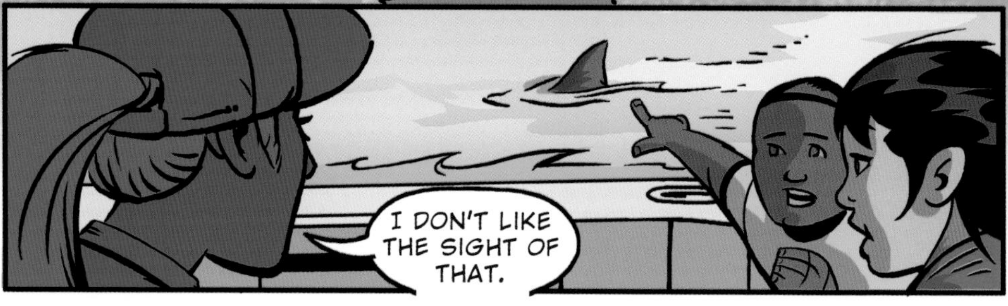
I DON'T LIKE THE SIGHT OF THAT.

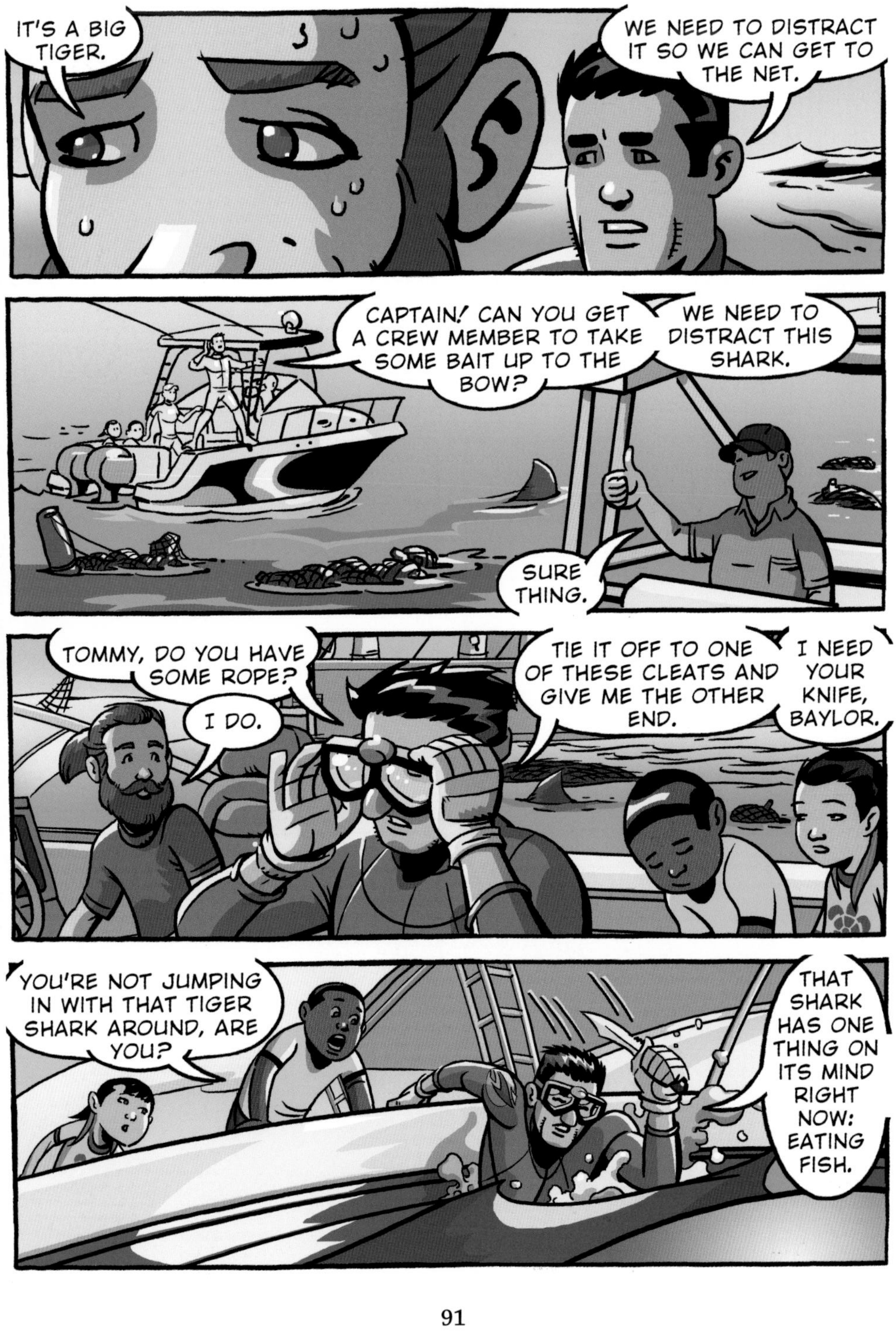
IT'S A BIG TIGER.
WE NEED TO DISTRACT IT SO WE CAN GET TO THE NET.
CAPTAIN! CAN YOU GET A CREW MEMBER TO TAKE SOME BAIT UP TO THE BOW?
WE NEED TO DISTRACT THIS SHARK.
SURE THING.
TOMMY, DO YOU HAVE SOME ROPE?
I DO.
TIE IT OFF TO ONE OF THESE CLEATS AND GIVE ME THE OTHER END.
I NEED YOUR KNIFE, BAYLOR.
YOU'RE NOT JUMPING IN WITH THAT TIGER SHARK AROUND, ARE YOU?
THAT SHARK HAS ONE THING ON ITS MIND RIGHT NOW: EATING FISH.

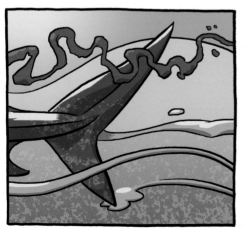

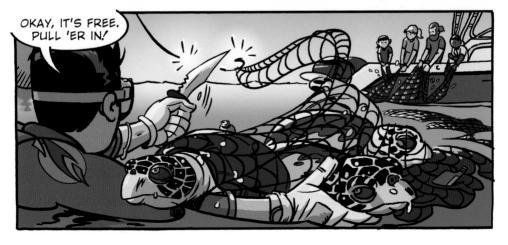

OKAY, IT'S FREE. PULL 'ER IN!

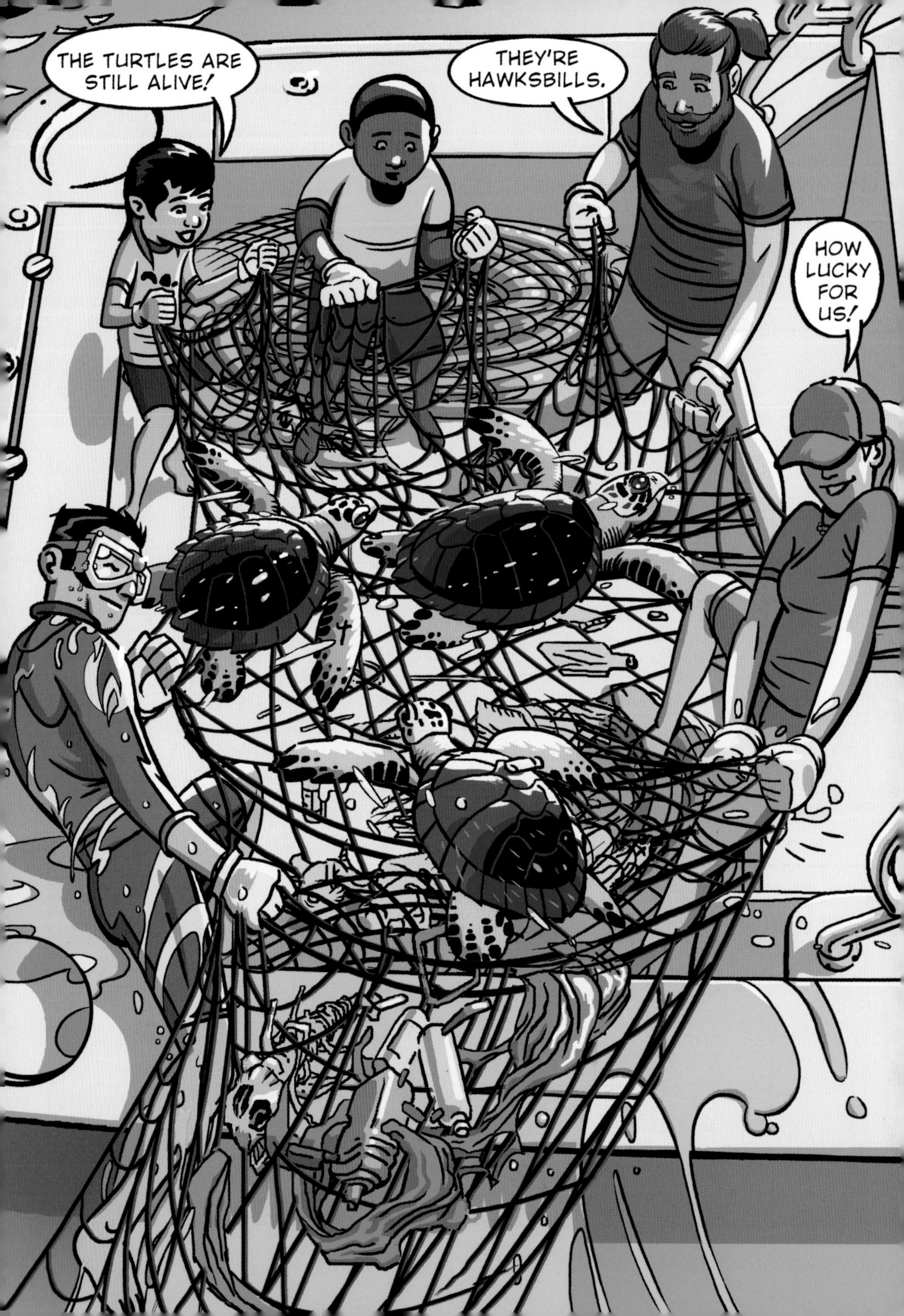
THE TURTLES ARE STILL ALIVE!
THEY'RE HAWKSBILLS.
HOW LUCKY FOR US!

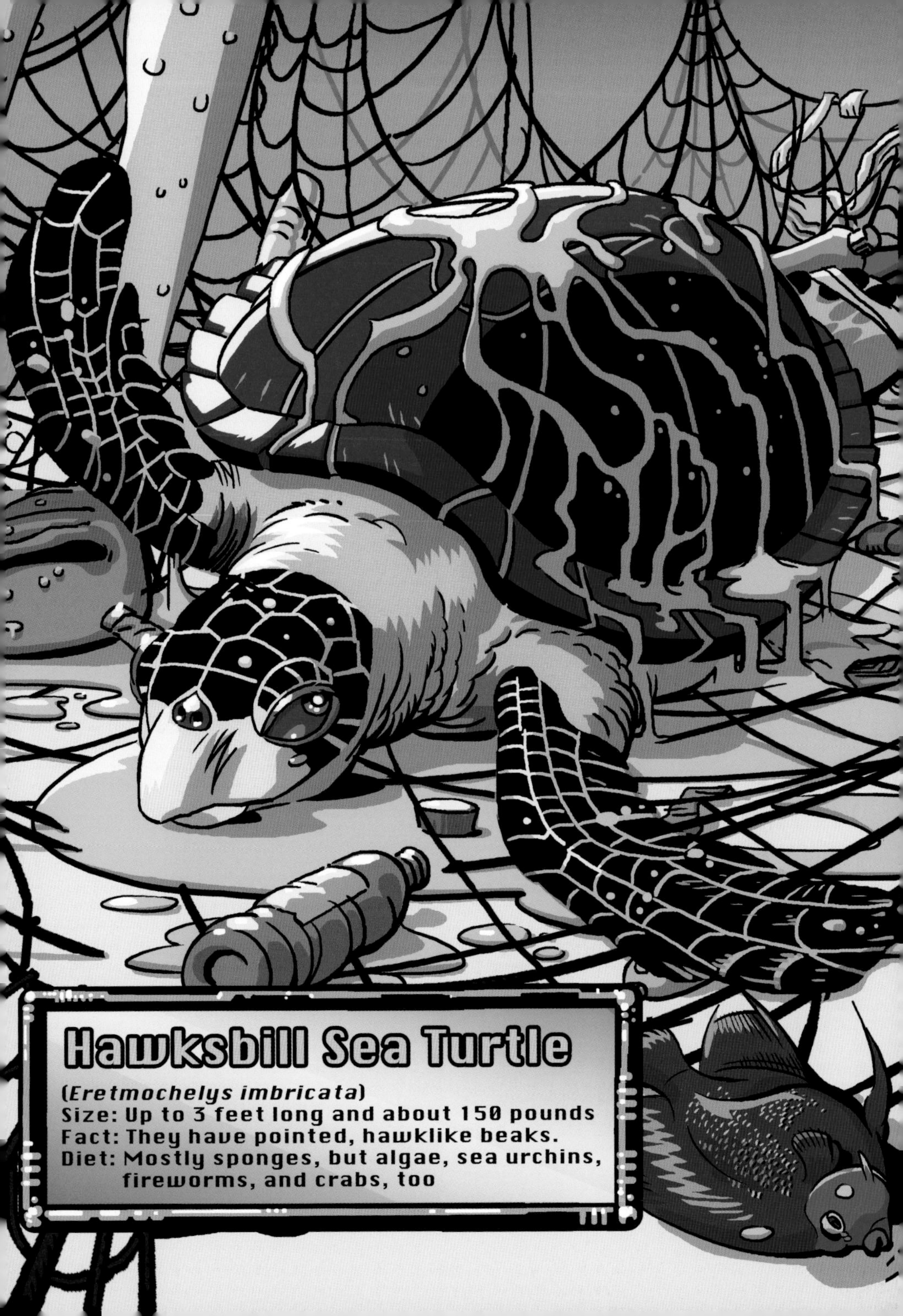

Hawksbill Sea Turtle

(*Eretmochelys imbricata*)
Size: Up to 3 feet long and about 150 pounds
Fact: They have pointed, hawklike beaks.
Diet: Mostly sponges, but algae, sea urchins, fireworms, and crabs, too

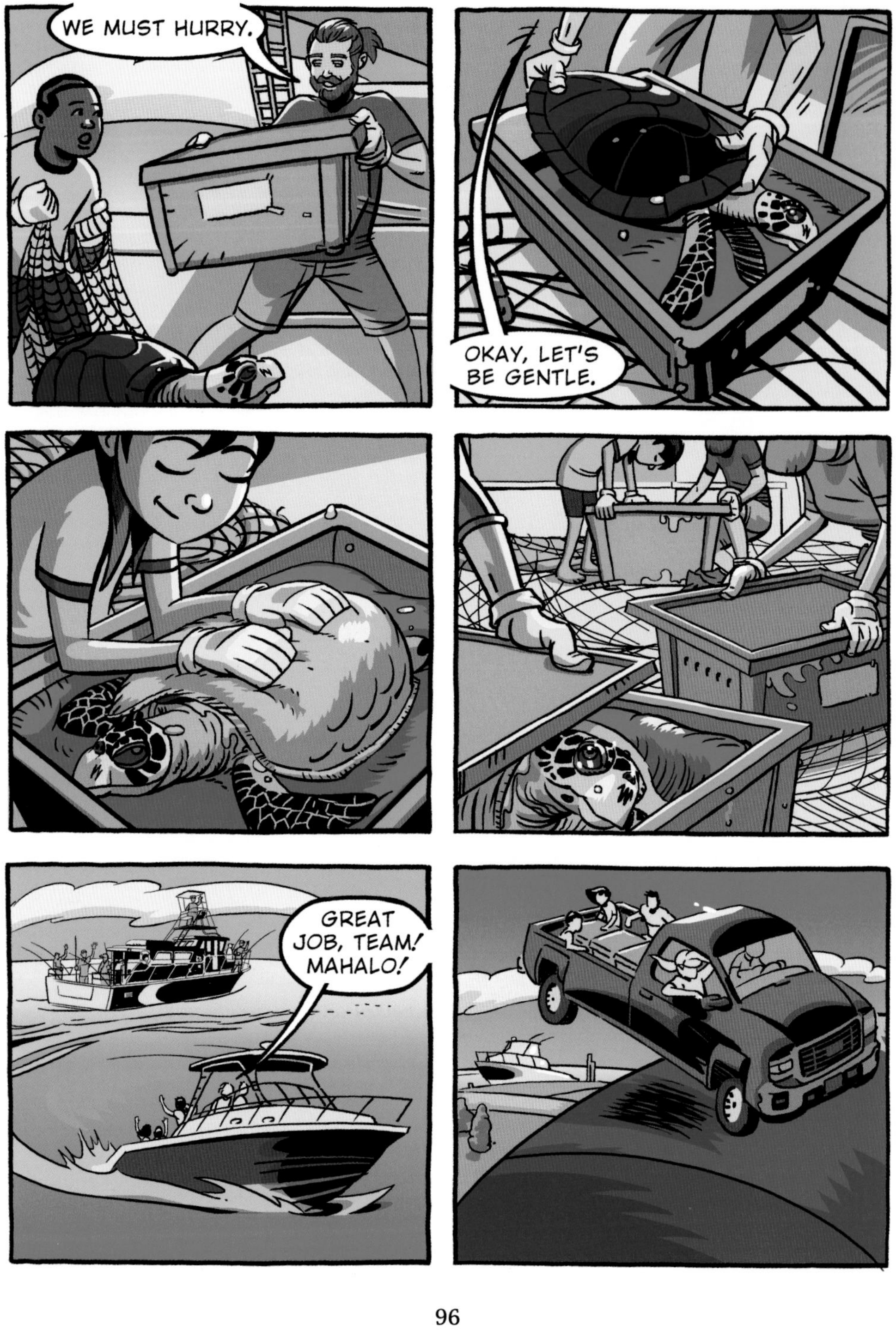
WE MUST HURRY.
OKAY, LET'S BE GENTLE.
GREAT JOB, TEAM! MAHALO!

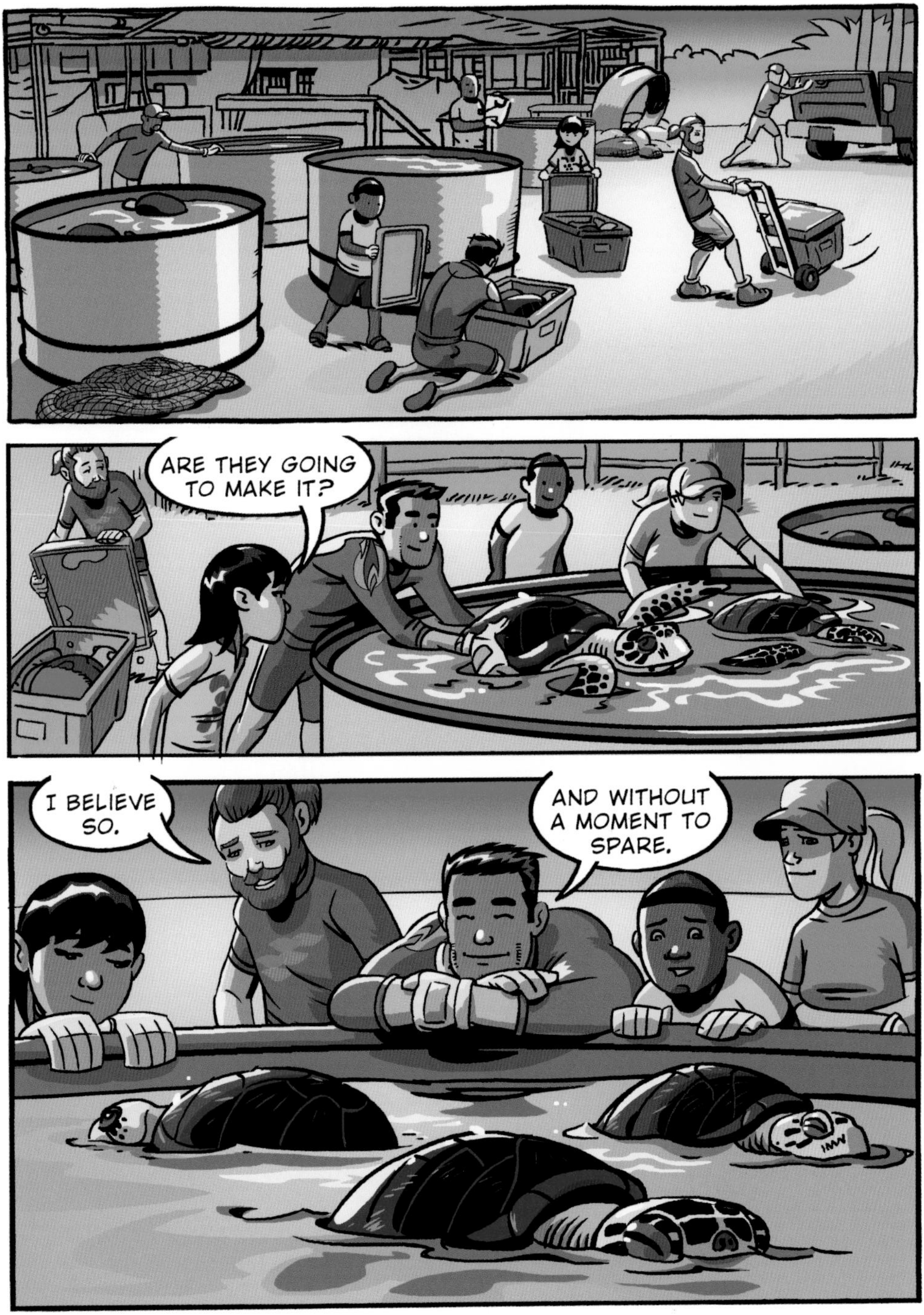
ARE THEY GOING TO MAKE IT?
I BELIEVE SO.
AND WITHOUT A MOMENT TO SPARE.

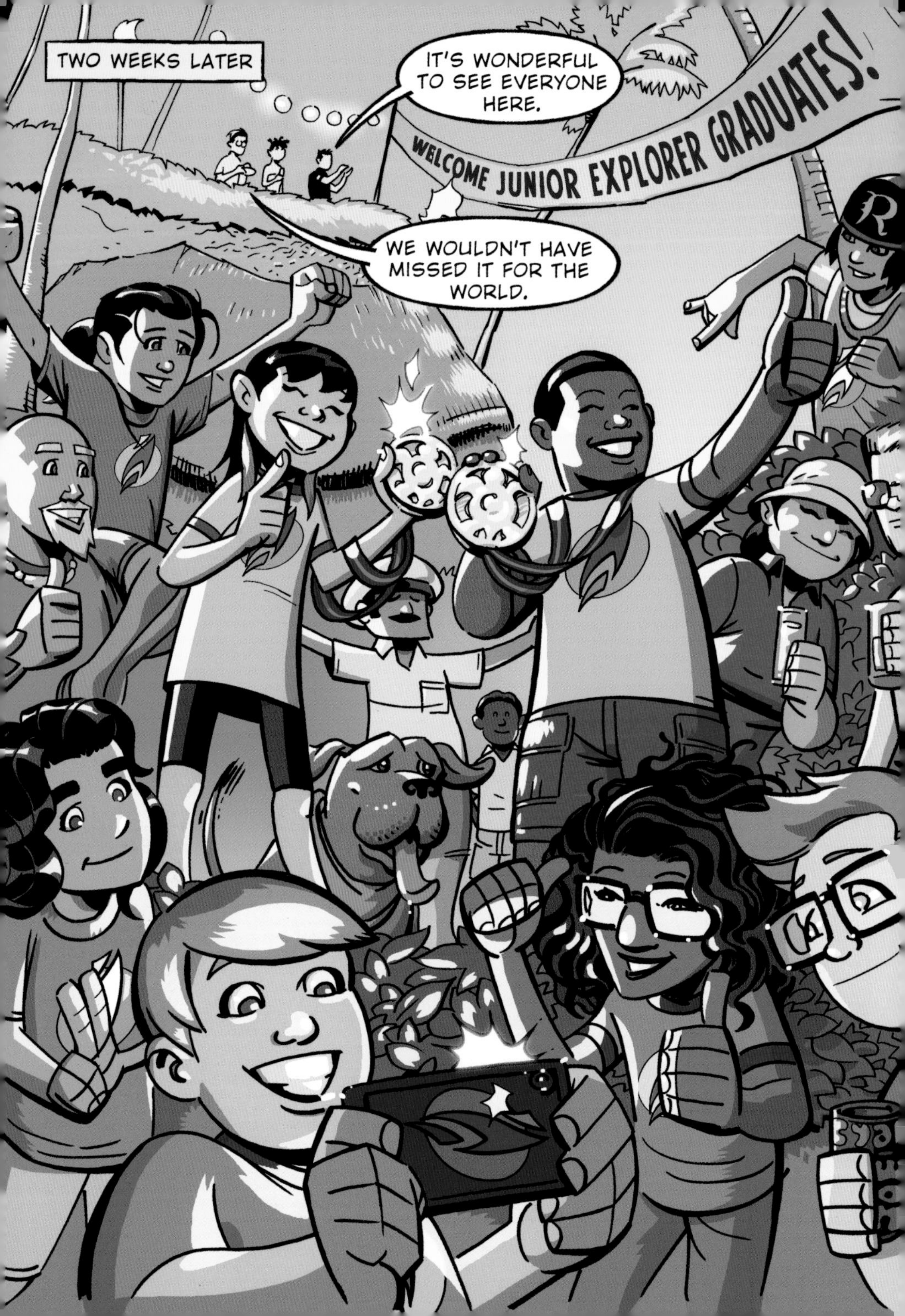
TWO WEEKS LATER
IT'S WONDERFUL TO SEE EVERYONE HERE.
WELCOME JUNIOR EXPLORER GRADUATES!
WE WOULDN'T HAVE MISSED IT FOR THE WORLD.

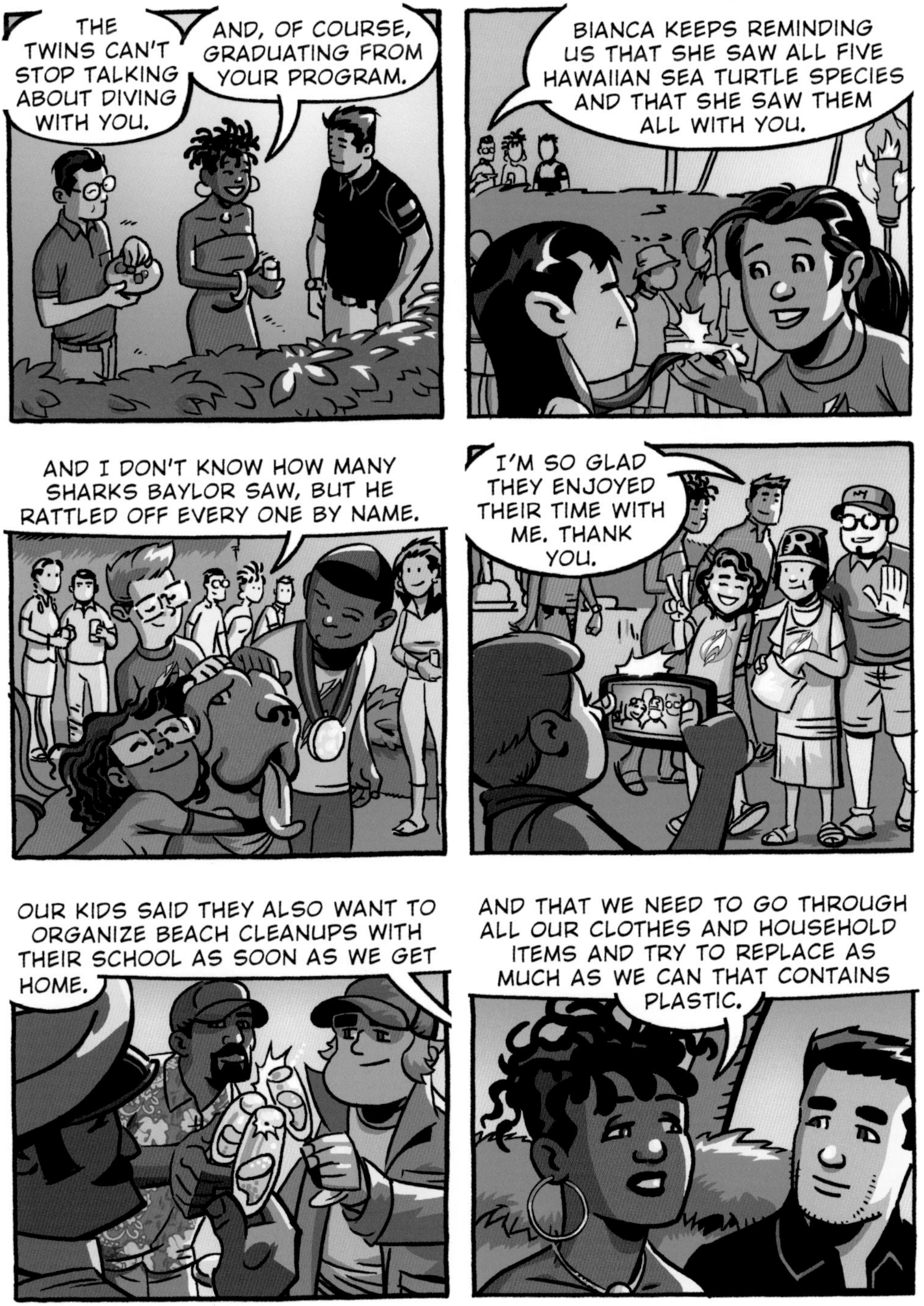
THE TWINS CAN'T STOP TALKING ABOUT DIVING WITH YOU.
AND, OF COURSE, GRADUATING FROM YOUR PROGRAM.
BIANCA KEEPS REMINDING US THAT SHE SAW ALL FIVE HAWAIIAN SEA TURTLE SPECIES AND THAT SHE SAW THEM ALL WITH YOU.
AND I DON'T KNOW HOW MANY SHARKS BAYLOR SAW, BUT HE RATTLED OFF EVERY ONE BY NAME.
I'M SO GLAD THEY ENJOYED THEIR TIME WITH ME. THANK YOU.
OUR KIDS SAID THEY ALSO WANT TO ORGANIZE BEACH CLEANUPS WITH THEIR SCHOOL AS SOON AS WE GET HOME.
AND THAT WE NEED TO GO THROUGH ALL OUR CLOTHES AND HOUSEHOLD ITEMS AND TRY TO REPLACE AS MUCH AS WE CAN THAT CONTAINS PLASTIC.

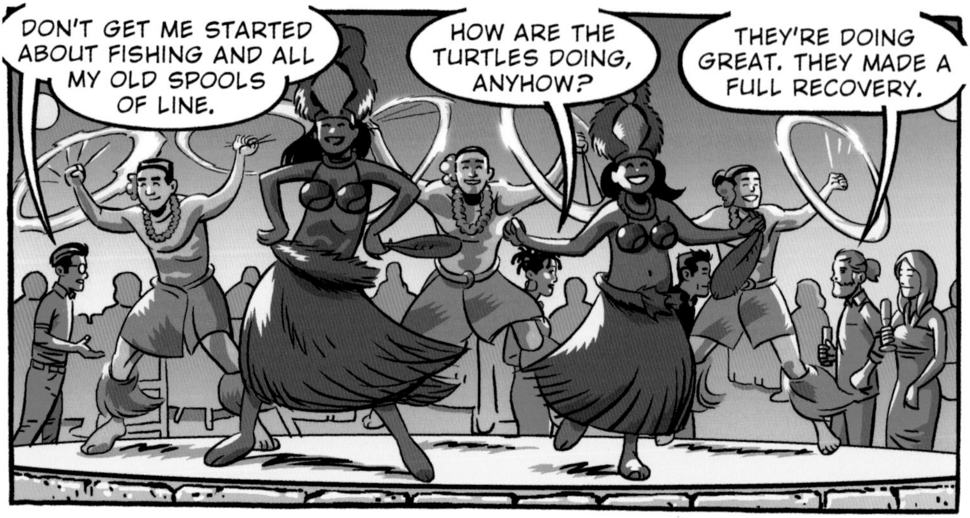
DON'T GET ME STARTED ABOUT FISHING AND ALL MY OLD SPOOLS OF LINE.
HOW ARE THE TURTLES DOING, ANYHOW?
THEY'RE DOING GREAT. THEY MADE A FULL RECOVERY.

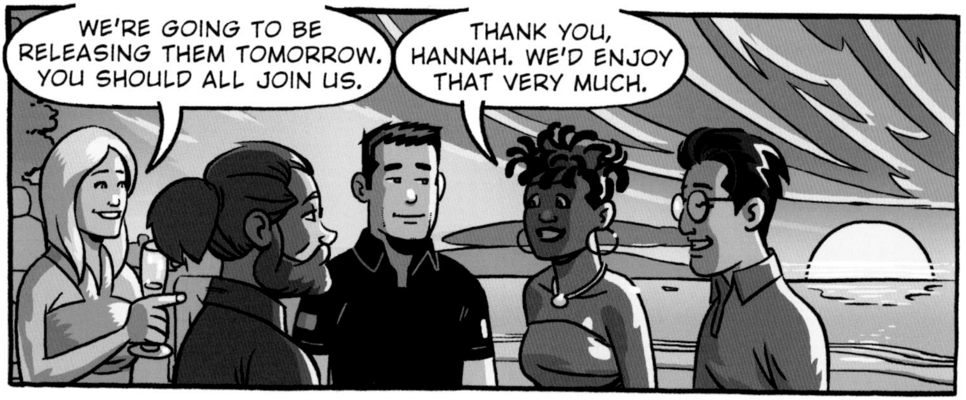
WE'RE GOING TO BE RELEASING THEM TOMORROW. YOU SHOULD ALL JOIN US.
THANK YOU, HANNAH. WE'D ENJOY THAT VERY MUCH.

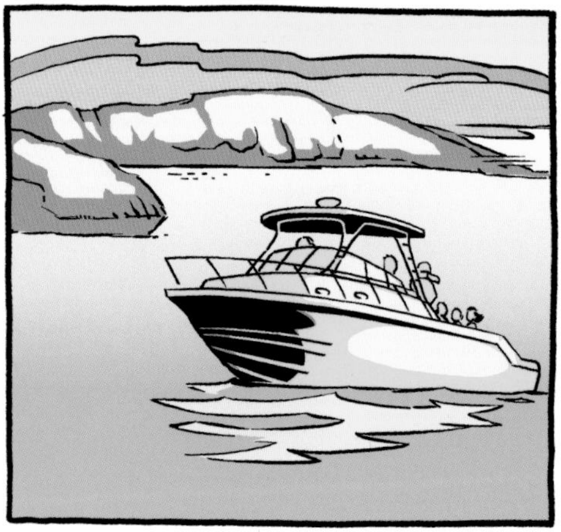

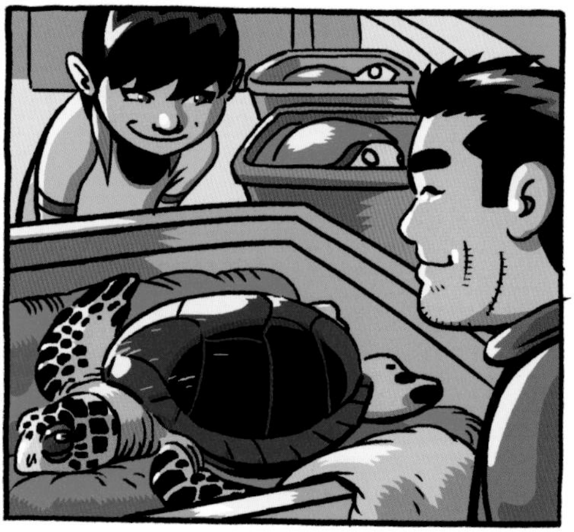

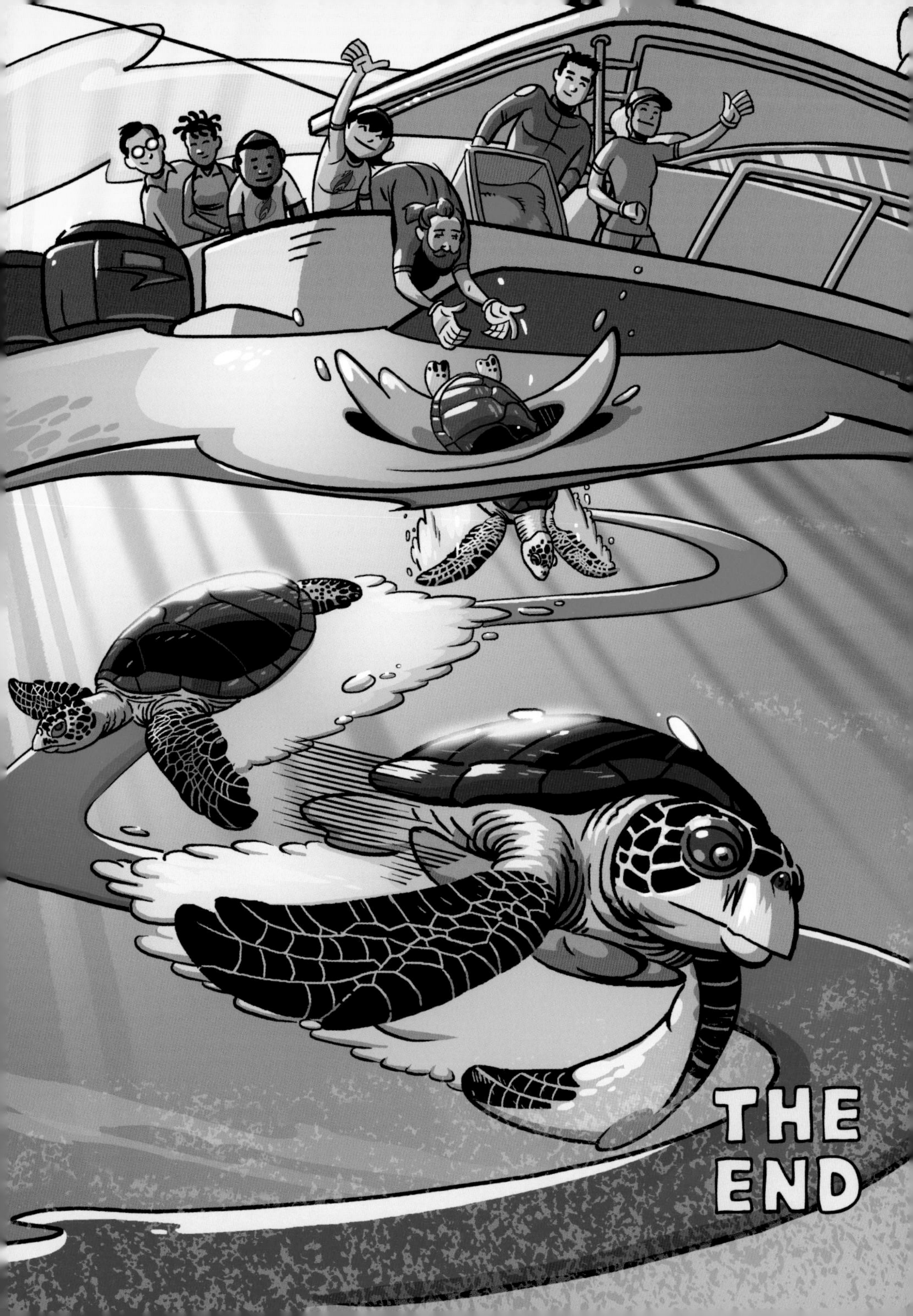
THE END

The authors would like to personally thank:

Karen Wojtyla, Nicole Fiorica, Tom Daly, and the entire editorial/
publishing team at Margaret K. McElderry Books and Simon &
Schuster Children's Publishing. Nicole Frail for her copyediting
assistance. David Tanguay, Michael Angelo Arbon and Sonya
Pelletier for their coloring assistance. Crissa Hiranaga and
the fabulous staff at Four Seasons Resort Maui. The extreme
generosity of Evan Pascual and the Maui Ocean Center, Tommy
Cutt and the Maui Ocean Center Marine Institute, Hannah
Bernard and the Hawai`i Wildlife Fund, Paul Zemitzsch and
Explore Green.

This story could not have been assembled without everyone's
participation and support. Mahalo.

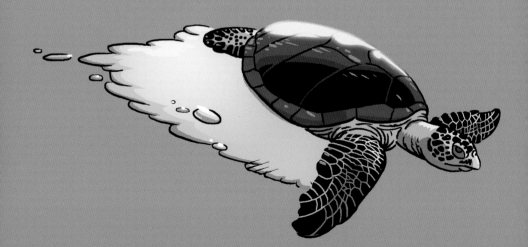

FABIEN COUSTEAU is the grandson of famed sea explorer Jacques Cousteau and a third-generation ocean explorer and filmmaker. He has worked with National Geographic, Discovery, PBS, and CBS to produce ocean exploration documentaries, and continues to produce environmentally oriented content for schools, books, magazines, and newspapers. Learn more about his work at fabiencousteauolc.org.

JAMES O. FRAIOLI is a published author of twenty-five books and an award-winning filmmaker. He has traveled the globe alongside experienced guides, naturalists, and scientists, and has spent considerable time exploring and writing about the outdoors. He has served on the board of directors for the Seattle Aquarium and works with many environmental organizations. Learn more about his work at vesperentertainment.com.

JOE ST.PIERRE has sold over two million comic books illustrating and writing for Marvel, DC, and Valiant Comics, among others. Joe also works in the fields of intellectual property design, commercial illustration, and storyboards for animation and video games. Joe's publishing company, Astronaut Ink, highlights his creator-owned properties Bold Blood, Megahurtz®, and the sold-out New Zodiax. See his work at astronautink.com and popartproperties.com.